GW00786328

Joanna

ANNE E THOMPSON

The Cobweb Press

The right of Anne E Thompson to be identified as the author of this work has been asserted in accordance with sections 77 and 78 of the Copyright Designs and Patents Act 1988.

Published by The Cobweb Press
www.thecobwebpress.com
thecobwebpress@gmail.com

A CIP catalogue record for this book is available from the British Library

ISBN 978-0-9954632-2-6

Cover design and typeset by Geoff Fisher
Geoff.fisher@yahoo.co.uk

Printed and bound in Great Britain by CPI Group (UK) CR0 4YY

For David

Chapter One

My Story

I first saw them on the bus. They got on after me, the mother helping the toddler up the big step, holding the baby on her hip while she juggled change, paid the driver. I wondered why she hadn't got her money ready, been prepared so we didn't all have to wait. I watched as she swung her way to a seat, leaning against the post for support, heaving the toddler onto the chair by his shoulder.

Then they sat, a happy family unit, the boy chattering in his high pitched voice, the mother barely listening, watching the town speed past the window, smiling every so often so he knew he had her attention. Knew he was loved. Cared for. They had everything I didn't have but I didn't hate them. That would have involved feelings and I tended to not be bothered by those. No, I just watched, knew that those children had all the things, all the mothering, that had passed me by. Knew they were happy. Decided to change things a little. Even up the score, make society a little fairer, more equal.

Following them was easy. The mother made a great deal about collecting up their bags, warning the boy that theirs was the next stop. She grasped the baby in one hand, bus pole in the other and stood, swaying as we lurched from side to side. She let the boy press the bell button, his chubby fingers reaching up. Almost too high for him. Old ladies in the adjoining seats smiled. Such a cosy scene, a little family returning from a trip to the town. They waited until the bus had swung into the stop, was stationary, before they made

1

their way to the door. I was already standing, waiting behind them. The mother glanced behind and I twisted my mouth into a smile, showed my teeth to the boy who hid his face in his mother's jeans, pressing against her as if scared. That was rude. Nothing to be frightened of. Not yet.

The family jumped from the bus and I stepped down. As the bus left I turned away, walked the opposite direction from the family. In case someone was watching, noticing, would remember later. Not that that was a possibility but it didn't do to take chances. I strode to the corner, turned it, then made as if I had forgotten something. Searched pockets, glanced at watch, then turned and hurried back. The family was still in sight, further down the road but not too far. She had spent time unfolding the buggy, securing the baby, arranging her shopping. All the time in the world.

I walked behind, gazing into shop windows, keeping a distance between us. They left the main street and began to walk along a road lined with houses, smart semi-detached homes with neat square gardens. Some had extended; built ugly extra bedrooms that loomed above the house, changing the face, destroying the symmetry. There were some smaller houses stuffed by greedy builders into empty plots, a short terrace in red brick. It was just after this the family stopped.

The mother scrabbled in her bag, retrieved her key. The boy had skipped down the path, was standing by the door. The mother began to follow but I was already turning away. I would remember the house, could come back later, when it was dark. I would only do it if it was easy, if there was no risk. If she was foolish enough to leave the back door unlocked. No point in going to any effort, it wasn't as if they meant anything to me. There would be easier options if it didn't work out. But I thought it probably would. There was something casual about her, about the way she looked so relaxed, unfussy. I thought locking the back door would be low on her priorities until she went to bed herself. People were so complacent, assumed the world was made up of clones of themselves. Which was convenient, often worked to my advantage. As I walked back, towards the bus stop, I realised I was smiling.

***

Other People

She realised she was pregnant on Tuesday. She should have known before, of course she should, but she hadn't thought it was possible. No one ever thinks they will be the 'one percent' who gets unlucky, that is just some mathematical myth printed on the packets of birth control paraphernalia.

She stared at the blue line of the pregnancy test and threw it into the small shiny bin with the other four. They sat there, accusing her of stupidity for not believing the obvious. She snapped down the round lid on top of them, hiding them from view. She wished she could hide the truth as easily.

She washed her hands, letting them stay under the running warm water for longer than was necessary, her mind blank. Then she went to her bed, lay there staring at the ceiling, hands on her stomach. Inside, a life fluttered, swam, fought to survive. As yet unfelt but now very real. Now she knew, she felt very pregnant. The world was different. She was different. Could she do this? Could she allow the sorrows of the past to continue? Could she protect her baby from the things that had happened? Her baby. There, she had said it. It was hers. Perhaps the hormones were already starting to build, to gang up on her, to warp her mind so that everything rational was put aside and only the baby mattered. Protecting the baby. But could she? Could she protect this new life? Did she even have the right to try?

She rolled onto her side, eyes shut, mind whirling. She needed to move, it was her turn to cook dinner. Josh would be home in an hour and then she would have to tell him, to share her secret, which would make it even more real. What should she do? Josh, she thought, would be excited. Once the shock had passed, the unexpectedness of it all, he would be pleased. He had wanted children, been disappointed when she told him she would never have any, that wasn't part of her life plan. He loved her enough to marry her anyway, harbouring the thought she might change her mind, caring enough to take the risk that she might not. It was too soon, too early in their life together but it was what he wanted. She knew that. Which made it harder, more difficult to know what to do. Josh didn't understand, not really. She had never told him the truth, the life she had built was too precious, too precarious.

She glanced at the clock. Seven o'clock. She would move in a minute, the bed was comfortable, like a cocoon. She decided she would tell Josh later, after she had spoken to Margaret. Margaret would know what to do. Perhaps it was time to grow up a bit she decided, to face a few things that she had buried long ago, to learn a few more facts. It was so much easier to hide though, to pretend that she was normal, that her life was the same as everyone else's, that she was the same. To ignore those nagging doubts, those fears.

She pulled herself to a sitting position, pressing her hands on the soft mattress, snagging the duvet with her slipper. She would cook sausages for supper. Her default meal, they were easy.

She wandered into the kitchen and pulled open the freezer, pulling out meat and vegetables, setting the temperature of the oven, clattering tins onto the work surface, filling saucepans with water. Her mind was in the past, remembering.

***

My Story

I thought about it some more while I sat on the bus. I had never conducted a project before, there had never been any need. I expect you will find that strange, having been fed a diet of steady lies by novelists and wannabe celebrity killers. The truth is, if people don't mean anything to you, if you have no emotional response to them one way or the other, then to harm them is unnecessary. All the stuff you read, about it being addictive, the need to kill more often to get the same high, the desire to show how clever you are, that's just authors being creative. I'm telling you this because I want you to understand. I had no *need* to kill. Whatever lies you might be fed by other people, you can trust me on this. I had no addiction, no weakness beyond my control. Everything I did was rational, intelligent, a clear choice. I have always been in control.

I was not a violent person, I would like you to understand this. I did not enjoy inflicting pain. The only time I ever hurt people or animals was part of an experiment, a project of scientific interest to see what would happen. That is what this latest venture would be, an experiment. I wanted to know if it was possible and what, if any, the repercussions might be.

It was obviously important that it was done properly, there must be no risk to me. The plan was already vaguely in mind, had been swimming there for years, locked away until the impulse took me. I had what I needed, it was the specifics that needed attention. I planned to simply walk away, but what if I was stopped? I couldn't rely on everyone staying safely out of the way until I had finished, I needed a reason for being there, an excuse in case I was confronted. The bus swung around the corner and I grasped the hand rail, steadied myself.

I have always been highly intelligent; I could have been a professor of chemistry by now if I hadn't been forced into leaving university before I was ready. The world had wasted my talents, my natural brilliance, my flair for both creativity and attention to detail. I could probably have found a cure for cancer, been a world-class researcher, helped to solve some of the many problems that greedy man has created. I was stopped though, thwarted before I could graduate, kept from fulfilling my true potential by those jealous of my skills and abilities. Not that the world deserved my work. My brain is too good for them, too special. Perhaps it was better this way, my intelligence reserved for the one who truly appreciated it. That was me, in case you're not keeping up.

But I digress. I had the means, now to devise the method. What if I was stopped, asked why I was approaching the house? I needed an excuse, a reason to be there. I stared at the white heads in front of me, gossiping women, like sheep. My eyes stared out of the window and I focussed my thoughts, searched for a solution.

My first thought was to carry leaflets, those annoying fliers that advertise goods you would never want which are regularly pushed through your letterbox. If I carried those, I could claim, if stopped, that I was merely a delivery person, doing my job, had every reason for being there.

However, that was flawed. I needed to be at the back of the house, actually inside the house. What if someone discovered me there? What reason could I give for actually being inside? I would have to have been invited. That's it, a party. I could have been invited to a party, one of those ridiculous surprise ones, when everyone waits quietly until the person arrives, then leaps out with shouts and hoots and everyone pretends it is a fantastic idea, aren't we wonderful. Yes, that would be a good excuse. I have been invited to such an event, told to go straight round to the back door and let myself in. However, 'I must have got the address muddled, this isn't where the party is, is it? Gosh I am so embarrassed. This is Garden Walk? I am looking for Garden Close. I am so terribly sorry, how embarrassing, no, I don't need a taxi, my car is parked just round the corner. So very sorry, bye.'

I smiled at my reflection in the grimy window. I could easily do that, look convincingly embarrassed. It was one of my skills, being able to display any emotion that was convenient, expected.

Yes, that would do. The sort of thing people believe. People are so gullible. They would even end up reassuring me, letting me know it didn't matter, I wasn't to worry.

The bus turned off the High Street and began to climb the hill, smoke billowing from the back and gears grumbling. I was sitting near the back, over the engine, where it was warm. Might as well be comfy while I planned.

I just need to look the part and that should be easy, a bottle of wine and some party clothes. Something that showed a lot of flesh, then if it was a man who discovered me, he wouldn't even notice my face, he might even invite me to stay for a drink. I might be remembered but it wouldn't matter. Nothing would be happening for days, maybe even months. No one would link the two events, I would be a long forgotten eccentric stranger by the time anything interesting happened.

The bus arrived at my stop and I jumped off. There was an old lady there too, lowering her tired bones slowly from the step. I held out my hand, helped her, smiled in a friendly manner. She smiled back, thanked me. I could see in her eyes she was grateful for the help, thought me a kind young person. What an idiot. If she was too stiff to get on and off the bus, she should stay at home. I began to walk towards my house, still thinking about my plan.

The delay in results worried me slightly, I can't deny that. It was tempting to want results immediately, to see my handiwork at once. But there were dangers in that, the risks were greater. I had no need to be an actual witness, remember, there were no feelings involved here. This was simply an experiment, done for interest and amusement. I would be patient. I would wait days, weeks, months, until finally it would appear as a headline in a local paper. It might even make the television local news, but I doubted it. I doubted anyone would be clever enough to even do an autopsy. It would probably slip under the radar as a tragic accident, a terrible event that sometimes just happens. Yes, I could be patient. I could sit back, continue my life and wait until the end of theirs was announced.

I was near home now, which was good because it looked as if it might rain. I didn't want to get wet, that would be annoying. It was annoying that I was walking anyway, catching the bus like some council estate kid. That was Ma's fault. Most things were her fault. She had a perfectly decent car, nothing grand but functional and nicely plain so people wouldn't notice it, should it be where it wasn't allowed. However, she was selfish with it, had decided to restrict its use for her own pleasure. She even locked away the keys, denying me the opportunity to share it even should an emergency arise. Ma was like that, had blighted my whole childhood with her cruelty and selfishness. It was surprising I had turned out so well actually, it would be easy to be one of those miserable failures who blames their stupidity on their abusive family or poverty. That wasn't my style though, as you'll see. I had risen over all the setbacks in life, was on my way to achieving great things.

Chapter Two

My Story

I walked to the house where I lived. Lodged really, it certainly did not engender those cosy feelings that the word 'home' brings to mind. It was a squat little house, a modern brick built bungalow. It had a large kitchen, for cooking and eating, with a utility room to one side, a small lounge that I tried to avoid and three bedrooms – one for me, one for Ma and one for the prawn.

I closed the gate behind me and slotted my key into the door. I opened it quietly, heard it click shut behind me and crept to the kitchen. Ma was in there, checking a casserole in the oven. The steam billowed up when she opened the door and I stood still, watching her solid back as she pulled the shelf forwards with her fat, gloved hand, checked the liquid bubbling in the dish.

I inched my way forwards, poised for a second then shouted, "Boo."

Ma turned, frowning. "I wish you wouldn't do that," she scowled, then smiled and asked if I would like a cup of tea.

She hadn't been actually holding the casserole, hadn't dropped it and sprayed boiling stock all over her legs. A missed opportunity.

"That would be lovely," I smiled and stooped to kiss her brown cheek. "How was your day?"

I threw myself into the big pine chair by the window, the one with a cushion, and arms to rest on. Her chair, but I knew she wouldn't say anything, would think I had sat there without thinking. I watched her ample bottom as she moved to the kettle, carried it to the sink and filled it from the tap. She hadn't emptied it first, just topped up the old water that was already there. I hated that, stale water has a metallic taste, it was lazy, sloppy. I wouldn't be drinking the tea. She was talking about her day, telling me that the prawn had made something at her school, as if I was interested. I stopped listening and gazed out of the window.

The garden was small and messy. It always looked worse in the winter, the earth all brown and boring, the remains of dead plants lying limply where they had fallen, old leaves decaying on the pathway. Mind you, it wasn't much better in the summer, when weeds fought for space with the few plants that actually survived. Ma was not a gardener.

I realised she had stopped speaking and turned.

"That sounds lovely," I lied with a smile, "Glad you had fun. My day was just awful–"

I then entertained her with stories from work, most of them true, mimicking my work colleagues, re-enacting some of the scenes. The prawn heard my voice and crept into the kitchen, clambering onto the chair opposite me and was watching, smiling at the playacting, whilst not really understanding. She wasn't much higher than the table when she sat on the low chair, and she rested her chin on the surface, next to the cutlery, straggly hair framing her little face. I ignored her, directed all my attention at Ma, who was also smiling, nodding along with the story.

She poured the boiling water into a big china teapot. It was her favourite one and had big red flowers painted on a white background. I think it was a Christmas gift from someone, it would be a shame if it got broken. I watched her pour two cups, then reach for the milk jug. I didn't want milk. Actually, I didn't want tea – not tea made with water boiled and re-boiled goodness knows how many times. I waited until she passed it to me, then stood.

"Sorry Ma, don't have time for tea. I need to check some things in my room. What time is dinner?" I leant to kiss her cheek again,

I knew she liked that, took it to be a sign of genuine affection. As I walked from the kitchen, I knew they were watching me. My audience, my minions. They were lucky to have me really, to have a bit of entertainment in their dull lives. It was a shame they couldn't be party to my next feat of entertainment, to see something really spectacular. But I couldn't share that. The prawn might keep quiet but Ma never would. She had never been quite as compliant as I would have liked. Something in her eyes told me that, let me know that sometimes she was not as fooled as she liked to pretend. But that didn't matter. As long as we both kept up the pretence, as long as we both played our parts, then coexisting was okay and a lot easier than running my own house. A lot cheaper too.

I walked along the dim hallway to my room, my shoes tapping on the lino. It was grey and worn in places but Ma was too mean to replace it. Sometimes it felt more like living in an institution than a house.

I felt in my pocket for my key and opened the door to my bedroom. I always kept it locked, much to Ma's annoyance. Nosey bitch. She made all kinds of fuss when I first fitted the lock, told me she wasn't having it in her house, what did I need a lock for, what did I intend to do that couldn't be seen by the family? Family. That was a fine one. The whole thing was completely hypocritical anyway. Ma had her own locks and bolts.

She had a large cupboard in her room which was always kept securely locked. Not with a normal lock either, I had tried to pick it and it defeated even me. She kept the key on a chain around her neck and I believe she wore it all the time, even when she was having a bath. I had checked around for it several times but I never found it, she was careful. I had no idea what she kept in there, though I do know the car keys were in there. Like I said, she was mean, didn't like to share her possessions. The cupboard was an insult to my integrity really. I would never spy on Ma or go through her things. She could've just asked me to not go into that cupboard and I wouldn't have done. I am a great respecter of privacy, never even went into her bedroom.

Anyway, I ignored her protests and had the lock on my door fitted. I often left the door wide open (when I was in there of course) so she could see that nothing was amiss. I would sprawl on my bed, reading, and she would come in, stand and chat while her eyes darted into every corner, looking for something she could berate me for. She never saw anything though. I was careful. Sometimes the prawn would come in too, ask me to play with her or read her a story. Sometimes I did. If Ma was listening. It was good to appear loving. I never entirely trusted her to not throw me out but she would never do anything to hurt the prawn and the prawn adored me.

I locked the door behind me and moved the dressing-gown that hung on the hook so that it blocked the keyhole. I did not want to be observed. Sometimes I removed the key and lay on my bed, on full view should someone decide to sneak up and check on me. All they would see was someone relaxing with a book. It was good to always appear innocent, even though they had no right to check – that was an invasion of privacy.

I sat on the bed and reached for the insulated bag. It was in the corner, below my pillow and covered in balls of dust. Ma's housekeeping left a lot to be desired. She had asked once why I kept the bag there. I told her in all sincerity that I was often thirsty at night, I liked to keep a bottle of water to hand but I disliked drinking water that had been heated to room temperature.

It was a habit I had formed during my curtailed spell at university, and the bag had rested beneath my bed for many years now. There was nothing inside that I would allow anywhere near my lips.

I blew off the dust and pulled open the zipper. It was months since

I had checked inside. I hoped nothing had changed. On top was a plastic water bottle, which I placed on the bed next to me. Below it, barely fitting into the cramped square bag, was a plastic container, the sort that might keep cakes or biscuits fresh. This one did not contain biscuits. I eased it slowly from the bag, my fingers squeezed against the sides. Inside, visible through the transparent sides, was a large mass of white. It resembled a collapsed snowball, the type that you try to make when the weather is too cold and although it forms a vague lump, ice crystals fall off and it disintegrates easily. Except this wasn't completely white, it had a slightly yellow tinge – perhaps like snow that has been peed on by the annoying dog from next door. But heavily diluted, not bright yellow.

It was beautiful. My treasure. I had smuggled it in tiny lots from the labs at uni. Not enough for anyone to notice that it was disappearing, was being used up faster than the chemistry class were using it. Tiny packets securely lodged into my white lab coat, nestling below the safety glasses, disposable lighter and hairband that are the standard items for a student's pockets. Molybdenum hexacarbonyl, or $Mo(CO)_6$ as it was usually written.

I had been worried it might evaporate, not knowing how long I might be storing it for. So, although the container had promised to be airtight, I also used the strongest glue that I could to secure the lid in place. It had worked, my treasure still sat there, shiny when the light caught a crystal. But I wasn't completely sure how I would now remove the lid.

I tucked my hair behind my ear, rested the container on my pillow and stared at it. Probably the best thing would be to use a tin opener, the old fashioned kind that had a fierce hook for ripping through metal – the sort you find on penknives, used by scouts around the world. I would need to wear gloves – I wasn't going to mess about with a carcinogenic substance that my skin would readily absorb. I would also need a mask, even breathing it in could be fatal. When I was actually there, in The House, I would just have to hold my breath and hope for the best. A mask would spoil my party-going image.

I tried to work out what else I would need. Obviously a new container to store the remains of my treasure and some more glue to reseal the new lid. A smaller container for transportation on the night, something that would fit into my pocket or an evening bag.

I turned now to my water bottle. It too was securely sealed, safely storing the dichloromethane. I held it up to the light, feeling the weight in my hand. It had been the easiest organic solvent for me to smuggle out of the lab undetected. It was also the one with the most pleasant smell, being slightly sweet, it shouted 'chemical' less strongly than my other choices. There was also a certain symmetry in using it. Until fairly recently, when its links to breast cancer had been broadcast, it had been used to decaffeinate tea and coffee. When added to coffee beans it removed the caffeine. It was amusing that those health freaks who refused to pollute their bodies with caffeine had been ingesting a different toxin instead. Now it could be used in food once again, this time as a means to add something rather than remove it.

I lowered my hand, frowning. I would need to choose carefully. If I added my treasure to anything acidic, it might explode, which would rather give the game away. However, left on its own it might evaporate or be noticed as too granular. I had no idea what it tasted of, that was not a test that could be safely carried out and there was a lack of willing volunteers for obvious reasons. The rats forced to ingest it, who had died in horrible diarrhoea-splattered agony, didn't mention a taste.

No, I should assume there was a taste. It should be placed somewhere that one might be expecting a strong taste, somewhere that you might think, "Ugh, that's off," take a second mouthful to be sure, then throw the offending substance away. Thus helping me to dispose of evidence. That was the beauty of my treasure, a mere half a teaspoon would do the trick, a measly five grams.

I rubbed my nose, lost in thought. I could hear Ma and the prawn laughing in the kitchen but I ignored them. They wouldn't bother me and I had plenty of time until dinner. I rested the bottle of liquid back on the bed. It was by far the best solvent to use. I was beginning to realise that I would have to dissolve my treasure, it was the best way to both transport it and administer it. I needed a small bottle to place it into, something most people had. I sighed. This would be so much easier if I had some knowledge of the kitchen, knew what I was likely to find. Did they drink wine? Use vanilla essence? Anything with a strong smell and taste that might have gone off, but would be tasted before they realised. Nothing that would be cooked or my treasure would evaporate. Any small container I could empty and refill.

I began to place my treasures back into the bag. I might have to make this up as I went along. Which would add to the excitement, but also to the risk. That didn't bother me overly. But it also added to the likelihood of failure and I did not like to fail. I was a succeeder, one of those lucky people who is usually on the winning side.

I pulled the zipper on the bag shut and lowered it back to its place below the bed, reaching to push it into the far corner. Then I flung myself back on the bed, head on pillow, shoes kicked onto the floor. This plan needed more thought.

***

Other People

She was only seven when she lost her mother. No, she corrected herself, not lost. That sounded like she was negligent, had left her out in the rain or something and it wasn't her fault, Margaret had spent many years convincing her of that. No, she was only seven when her mother had been taken from her. That was better, more accurate. She could remember her face quite clearly, and a few events, not everything, but snatches of memory. She remembered walking with her mother, skipping to keep up with her quick footsteps. She remembered being bathed and dried with a rough white towel that was frayed along one edge. She recalled rough kisses, lips pressed hard against her forehead, hugs that were a bit too tight, that pushed all the air from her. She remembered her mother's neat hands and short nails and the way she would hook her hair behind an ear when it fell across her face. How, when she spoke, everyone listened.

Her best memories were the stories of course. No one could tell a story like her mother. Not that she did very often, but when she had time, when she spun a magical web of make-believe. When she whisked people away to other worlds, everyone was captured. Perhaps her mother should have been an actress, used that ability to enchant, to mesmerise, on the stage. Though that was probably too out of character, too mundane.

Then THAT day had arrived, the day which changed everything.

She had been in her room, playing with her dolls, lost in a fantasy world. Most of her early memories were in that world, creating her own reality. She had been disturbed by a blue light, flashing through the curtain, pulling her away from her game, insisting she pay attention. She climbed onto the bed and peered through the window, her nose pressing against the cold pane, watching the car. The knock on the door had been louder than necessary, making her jump. Then quiet voices, too quiet to hear, so she crept from her bed and opened her door, just a crack, just enough to hear. Something warned her not to go into the hall, not to become part of the conversation, those urgent voices, quiet at first then raised, shouting, angry. Margaret crying. A man speaking deeply, calmly.

She didn't know of course that she would never see her mother again. That often happened in life, you never knew when something was the last time. The last time you ate that particular food, the last time you wore that sweater, the last time you saw someone alive.

Her memories immediately afterwards were a muddle, more an impression of being swamped by adult emotions than of actual events. She did remember the policewoman who often visited – to help them, Margaret said. Sometimes when she played her games or read her book the woman would be there, watching. Her eyes were strange and she never smiled. Never touched her.

They moved house soon after that. Margaret told her later, when she was older, that they couldn't have stayed, not if they wanted to have a normal life. She said people thought bad news was contagious, and people never forget, never let you forget. So they left. New house, new school, new friends. She had adapted. That's what children did. Everyone was told her mother had died, but no details, just that one blank fact. They looked at her a bit strangely at first, perhaps the teachers had been a little more kind, her friends a little shyer. Then they forgot, she became a normal person, had a normal life. She grew up with the same ease and struggles as any other girl, her past locked away and never discussed. She always wondered though, wondered how it had affected her. Now she wondered how it would affect the baby. Her baby. This unwanted life inside of her.

She walked to where the phone sat on the little table in the corner of the room. She dialled Margaret's number and stood there, leaning against the wall, listening to the ring-tone purr in her ear. She would ask if she was free at the weekend. Perhaps Saturday afternoon, when Josh would be playing football. Yes, she thought, she would go to see Margaret, let her know the news. Ask her what she should do.

***

My Story

Three days later, I was ready. I had bought the tin opener and replacement container. I waited until I was home from work, had smiled and chatted in a pleasant manner and eaten my dinner, then I locked myself into my room. Wearing gloves, shower cap and a mask I cut a jagged edge around the top of my treasure box. Using a plastic teaspoon, I added some to a tiny wine bottle I had bought; the sort old ladies buy when they want a drink but feel a whole bottle would be wasted. The rest I placed in the new container. I was careful, made sure there were no grains left in the opened box, that I didn't spill any. I performed this operation on a square of plastic sheeting, bought for the purpose from a hardware shop. I applied a thin line of strong glue to the top of the new container and snapped the lid into place. I did not intend to use the rest for a while, possibly years. I then poured the dichloromethane into the wine bottle, only half full, I didn't want to waste any.

When I had finished, checked all lids were firmly tightened, I put the old box in the middle of the plastic sheet. It sat there looking damaged, savaged by the tin opener. The jagged edge was like a wound. I added the protective mask and gloves to the plastic sheet then rolled the whole lot up. I removed the shower cap I had worn to restrain my hair and added it to the bundle. I stuffed it all into a disposable carrier bag and tied the handles. There was a skip round the corner, next to the children's play area. I would dispose of everything there. Tomorrow was rubbish collection day, I had made use of those skips before, knew the bin men's rota. I placed my things back into the black insulated bag and pushed it under my bed. Then I heaved myself to my feet, stretched my back – that had been a lot of uncomfortable sitting – and went to find my coat. I locked my door, took my rubbish bag and left. I don't think Ma even registered that I was leaving the house.

It was a cold night, clear and frosty with a nice round moon shining feebly through the yellow tinge of the street lights. I like nights like this, they feel fresh, exciting somehow. I walked quickly, keeping to the shadows. A man passed on the opposite side of the road. His dog turned as they passed, watching my progress but I don't think the man noticed me at all.

I arrived at the area where the skips were left. They were in a corner of the carpark, each one clearly marked with a large sign showing which kinds of rubbish and recyclables they hoped would be deposited. Usually I would ignore this, but this particular load I wanted to be rid of, didn't want any nosey refuse person noticing it was in the wrong place. I placed it into 'General Refuse' and walked away, keen to leave the area, to be away from the strong overhead light. The rest of the area was in shadow and I paused a while, surveying the scene. Next to the carpark was a large playing field, the ground hard tonight. The grass was uneven, snarled up by many football boots, spectator's wellies and the occasional dog turd. To one side was a children's play area, the swings and slides keeping sentry duty, waiting for teenaged lovers to arrive and hide amongst them. I turned away and walked home.

The next evening, I stowed my treasure bottle in my pocket and sneaked out of the house. I told Ma that I had a headache and wanted to sleep after dinner. She barely even responded, which was typical of her. We always ate ridiculously early, Ma thinking it was good for the prawn. The weather was still dry, which was good, I wouldn't have been doing this in the rain. Beneath my coat I was dressed for fun. I wore a tiny black dress, which showed a nice lot of boob and a fair amount of leg. Both were exceptionally good, would distract any red-blooded male. Beneath lacy gloves my hands were enclosed in thin plastic gloves, bought from the medical section of the chemist, designed to allow movement and feeling whilst protecting hands from germs and blood. They would help to ensure I left no traces of *me* in The House. I had also restrained my hair under a tight net and wore a wig. Long brown strands tickled my face and I wished I had thought to tie it back for the journey. My face was plastered with make-up, the glitter eye-shadow felt heavy on my lids and the bright lipstick was greasy. It felt almost like I had smeared lard across my lips. I didn't usually bother with make-up, being noticed was rarely a good thing. I carried a large bottle of vodka and a party popper. My shoes were high and strappy, and this was something of a problem.

I didn't want to take the bus, decided it was too public and I might be remembered, resembling so closely a hooker. Ma's car was of course out of bounds. It was too far to walk. That left the bike.

It was an old bike, goodness knows where Ma had got it from. It was large and heavy, with big wheels, an uncomfortable saddle, and a basket on the front. I slipped to the shed, removed it from the cobwebs and spades that surrounded it and wheeled it round to the front. As the wheels turned, the pedals moved too, the old chain whirring. It sounded very loud in the silent garden. The basket was helpful for carrying the wine and I added my small treasure bottle too, didn't want it to slip out my pocket, to smash on the road.

I hitched my skirt up so it barely covered my bum but left my legs free for pedalling, wondered if wearing joggers would've been a good idea. I could have left them in the hedge with the bike when I arrived. But it was too late now, I sat on the saddle and left. I pulled the edges of my long coat over my knees with one hand. I worried they might reach far enough to get caught in the back wheel, plus I didn't really want to be seen cycling in an obviously tiny skirt. That might be remembered. The shoes were a pain. They were too high, I was basically only able to push down on the pedal with my toes and I had a way to go. I wobbled my way to the corner, turned onto the main street (that was more difficult than you might think with just one hand to steer) and began to build up some speed. The wig was secure but the hair pins dug into my scalp.

It was cold, my coat wasn't really thick enough, but after a few minutes I was sweating. Physical exercise is a rare treat for my body. A few cars passed me, a whoosh of air and lights. I kept my head low, let my hair fall over my face. My feet were raw with cold, slightly numb. My toes were unhappy, one got cramp, which was pretty uncomfortable. How can you get cramp in just one toe? No chance to stretch it out, so I just kept going, forced the pain to the back of my mind, let it make me angry, more determined to succeed. It was all very uncomfortable and I felt the hot pit of rage start to burn inside of me. No one would even appreciate this, would even know the lengths I had gone to, the trouble I had taken. I turned the rage into energy for pedalling and directed it towards that smug family. They deserved this, causing me so much trouble.

I had checked the address on a map, found a route that mainly took me along main roads. Although I would be passed by more people, I figured I was less likely to be remembered. Mrs Mopp walking her dog would remember a random cyclist in her road, Mr. Bus Driver would pass so many he wouldn't even notice. I arrived at my destination and dismounted, my feet going into spasm when they touched the ground. I moved into the shadow of a large hedge and spent a few minutes stretching out my feet, getting the cramp to go. Then I wheeled the bike further away, removed my bottles from the basket, threw the bike into a hedge made of big fir bushes, the soft branches overgrown and pliable. It hid the bike almost completely, only the edge of the tyres could be seen where they rested on the path. Satisfied, I tottered back up the road, towards The House.

There were lights on in nearly every window. That was mainly good, meant they were home, allowed me to look inside. I stood at the end of the driveway for the briefest second, scanned the street for spectators, then wobbled my way towards the side path. The path went down the side of the house, it was overgrown and I hoped I wouldn't snag my tights. Hoped more that there wouldn't be security lights. As I went, I fluffed my hair, tried to look like a party-goer. I took care to walk silently but not to creep, not to appear as if I was being stealthy. Nothing as suspicious as someone trying to not be seen. The passage remained dark, if they had outside lights they hadn't bothered to switch them on yet. After all, what trouble was there likely to be before seven in the evening? When I got to the back, I turned away from the tiny lawn strewn with toys, looked at the house.

There were two facing windows. One I guessed to be part of a through-room. Light filtered through from a distant space but there was no light actually lit at the back. The other window, next to a glass door, was black.

I approached the lit window, peered through. A blue flicker from a television flashed in the far corner. I could see the backs of armchairs; long legs stretched out from one, the other had shoes next to it where they had been dropped, before the occupant had curled up into their chair. No sign of the kids, they must be upstairs, maybe in bed already.

I moved across to the other window, went closer. No sign of life. I was right, it was the kitchen window. I could make out pots of herbs standing on the sill, still in their plastic pots from the supermarket, a couple of them wilting. There was a table, an array of units and a tall fridge, much too big for the size of kitchen. No dog bowls, no sign of cats, not even a goldfish.

I slid across to the door. It was one of those plastic ones that people buy when they replace their windows with double glazing. There were small red wellies strewn on the ground where they had been kicked off before going inside. I placed my hand on the door handle, it felt odd under my gloves, gradually lowered it. Slowly, slowly, pushing it down, holding my breath. When it was fully depressed I pushed, gently at first, just to see what would happen. There was a slight hiss as the seal was released; the door began to move inwards. It was open.

I stepped inside, closed it behind me, didn't want a draught to be noticed. For a moment I simply stood. I let my eyes adjust to the darkness. I began to see more clearly, was sure there was nothing I might trip over, clatter loudly and alert the targets. I could hear the television through the thin wall, smell the remains of their tea, something fishy. The kitchen was warm, felt greasy.

I moved to the fridge, eased it open. The light inside seemed very bright but there was no reason for it to be seen from the lounge. I glanced inside. There was dried cheese, pots of yogurt, bowls of food covered in saucers, an open carton of juice. And there, in the door, was my prize: a screw top bottle of wine. It was half full, resting in the door well next to odd cartons of milk. I lifted it out, careful to be silent, swung the door shut, moved to the sink.

I was about to open it, pour it away, add my treasure, when I heard a noise. The targets were talking, muffled but audible. One wanted tea, was offering it to the other one. There were sounds of feet, a door opening, footsteps coming towards the kitchen. A light switched on in the hall. The rattle of the kitchen door handle. I was already out the door, pulling it shut behind me. I still held the wine, clenched awkwardly against my other bottles. I was clutching them as tightly as I could in my gloved hands, fearful they might slip or clink together. I moved away from the window just as the garden flooded with light, the target had switched on the kitchen light.

I was confident I couldn't be seen, the garden would appear black against the bare window pane. I watched for a moment, saw the man go to the sink, gaze at his reflection in the black window, smooth down his hair. I was angry, hated him, wanted to smash something.

I stood there the whole time he made the tea. I watched his complacent form move around the kitchen, gathering what he needed, making tea. Some slopped out of the cup when he added sugar. He didn't wipe it up, left it there, knowing his wife would do it. He turned to leave, paused, and as an afterthought, turned, walked towards me and locked the kitchen door. Then he left, back to his chair and television, taking his cup but leaving the lights on. I was furious. I also knew that I should leave. I had the wine, I could return tomorrow, replace it in the fridge, hope they hadn't noticed its absence. Even if they did, if later tonight they searched for it, when they saw it there tomorrow or the next day, it would just be one of those things, one of those moments of madness that we all have. One of those, 'that's strange, I'm sure I looked right there yesterday, how could I have missed it?' moments.

I made my way back to the bike. So angry, frustration brimming out of me. Looking for something to kick, knowing that even if there was a cat it would be useless in these stupid shoes. Everything about the evening was a mess, annoying, beyond my control. I put the bottles back in the basket, cycled towards home, my mood making my legs faster, travelling at speed along the frosty roads. I turned off the main roads, began to walk past houses, pushing the great hulk of a bike. I had moved my treasure bottle back to my pocket, could feel it hard against my leg as I walked. I wanted revenge, for the evening to not be wasted.

As I approached the house I was cautious. Most windows were dark, only the one at the front was lit, the light creeping around the edge of heavy curtains. I slipped into the back, hurried to the kitchen door, eased my way inside. As I stood in the dark kitchen, waiting for my eyes to adjust, I heard a shout. Someone was calling.

"Margaret, can you look at this?"

I waited for the footsteps to pass the door, to enter the room at the front. Then I allowed myself to move.

Chapter Three

My Story

I woke to rain. The hard determined rain that plans to stay all day. It was still there when I returned from work, a nasty wet rain that soaked you as you walked and clung to your hair. I banged the door when I got home, went straight to my room, peeled off my wet clothes, left them in a heap on the floor. Pulled on warm clothes and sat hunched on the bed.

The prawn appeared in the doorway, her eyes hopeful, looking for entertainment, to be noticed. I turned my head, looked at her. She saw my expression, read my eyes, retreated quickly towards the kitchen.

So, what was I to do now? Last night I had thoroughly rinsed the wine bottle, allowed it to dry, added my dissolved treasure. It was less full than before, but I didn't think they would notice. If they did, they would either assume the other had sneaked a quick mouthful or that it must've evaporated during storage. I was ready to go. But for the weather, the nasty, spiteful weather. You surely don't think I could have cycled in that storm? I would arrive dripping, for one thing. If discovered, no one would believe I was a lost party guest. More like an escapee from the Loony Bin. Plus, my feet still hurt from the night before, I had two blisters and my head ached from that wretched wig. No, I wasn't going to be doing that again in a hurry.

On the other hand, it was unfinished business. That family owed me now, it needed to be done. It wasn't my fault it had all gone wrong. A few minutes earlier and I would have finished, been out of there before he even thought about tea. That was Ma's fault, her insistence that we always eat together, pretended we were a happy family. It had delayed me.

No, it needed to be done, tonight, or I wouldn't rest, wouldn't be able to properly relax. But you can forget the party clothes and the cycling. That had always been a flawed plan. No, tonight would have to be a taxi. Not to The House, obviously. I wasn't stupid. But the road behind was near enough and there was an alleyway connecting the two streets, if I was lucky no one would see me.

It would be nice to make it slightly more personal now, to perhaps use a knife. But that wasn't my style. I was a great believer in style. And it would be nice to use my treasure, now I had decided to, gone to so much effort.

Ma was calling, letting me know dinner was ready. I ignored her, waited for her to come to my room and tell me. Or send the prawn, her personal messenger. I didn't want dinner, would've liked to eat alone, in my room. But Ma's rules were absolutes. Like I said, we co-existed but I knew where I stood in the relationship. Knew I had no rights.

The prawn appeared back in the doorway, hovering uncertainly. I glared at her.

"Ma said dinner's ready," she whispered before running off, back to the safety of the kitchen.

I waited as long as I could, before I went to join them. I smiled as I entered.

"Hey, this looks lovely," I lied. "How was your day Ma? It's filthy out there, don't think the rain has stopped for a minute all day. You have no idea how grumpy everyone was at work, so many nasty customers. People are so rude when they're wet, changes their whole personality. And so many coughs and colds, it'll be a miracle if I haven't caught some awful germ. We completely sold out of cough syrup this afternoon."

26

I saw the prawn visibly relax, relieved I had decided to be nice. Ma was mostly ignoring me, spooning heaps of lumpy potato onto plates, passing them to us, pouring water from a big china jug that had a chip on one side. I would eat, appear pleasant and relaxed, then disappear with a book I needed to read. They wouldn't disturb me. I lifted a fork full of potato, tried to ignore the lumps. There would be plenty of time.

***

Other People

Margaret finished the call and stood for a moment. Not thinking, just letting the news sink in, find the right place in her mind so she could assimilate it, recognise the facts. Thinking could come later, deciding what was right and wrong, the best course of action. For now, she just needed to absorb what she had been told.

She went into the kitchen, filled the kettle, made tea. Isn't that what everyone does when they need space, time to get used to an idea? She filled the teapot, the white one with the pretty red flowers – the one that was really a Christmas teapot, but who has a teapot for just one season? – and carried it on a tray into her sitting room. The sun flooded the room with warmth and light, making it safe, peaceful. Margaret put her tray on the tiny wooden table that Tom had made and sat back in her chair. Now she could think.

Her mind went first to Joanna. It usually did. But not the Joanna of today, the Joanna tinged with sorrow and frustration borne from knowledge, but instead the Joanna from the past. Joanna the child.

Joanna was twelve when Margaret first saw her. She remembered her standing awkwardly near the door, as if she might bolt out if she didn't like what she heard, wary. She reminded Margaret of a deer caught drinking in the clearing of a wood, head up, ears alert, pausing while it decided whether or not to run.

The girl was tiny, "a little scrap of a thing," Margaret's mother would have said. Skinny arms and legs, dressed entirely in black, her long hair hanging limply either side of her protruding ears. She wore a wide studded belt that was too big, the holes not allowing her to wear it round her waist, so instead it hung from her hips, looking as though at any minute it might slip down, tying her legs so couldn't escape. She had a button nose and a mouth that might be pretty when she wasn't scowling, but what Margaret had noticed most was her eyes. Blank pools of blue that stared at her as if she were a sofa in a shop waiting to be purchased. An intense, never-ending stare, assessing her, forceful. A complete lack of emotion. There was no feeling behind those eyes. One was tempted to wonder if there was a soul.

Margaret had turned away from the girl to listen to the man who had brought her there. He was little more than a boy himself really, not many years out of university, eager to prove himself in his chosen profession. Margaret had met him a few weeks earlier, a surprise visit that had left her bemused and changed her life forever.

When Margaret had married Tom she had known there would never be any children of their own. He had been completely honest with her right from the start, knowing it was important for her to walk away if that was something she couldn't cope with. Tom was like that, a huge man with a huge personality, someone who made you feel secure just by being present. Margaret was sure that she would cope, that being with the man was more important than producing children. She had married him when she was barely twenty and had never regretted it.

After a few years they began to think about children, not their own, that could never happen, but to raise some who needed love, a safe place. They were visited by social services, answered millions of questions, had their home inspected, their income and personalities scrutinised. Eventually they passed whatever test these people used to assess the suitability for parenting and were given children to care for. They never adopted, preferring initially to provide short term foster care and then finding that it suited them. They were often given children to care for who had been damaged, sometimes abused by the adults who should have been nurturing them, sometimes abandoned. They found they were rather good at it. Together, Margaret and Tom offered stability and safety, firm boundaries and a sense of humour. It was often difficult, sometimes they questioned themselves, wondered if they were managing to help a child, but on the whole they knew that they were. They were able to offer a place for the child to recuperate, to start to put themselves together until a permanent home could be found for them. They began to wonder about adopting, taking in a child permanently, accepting them as part of their family.

Then Tom died. It was as blunt as that. One day he was there, telling Margaret that the cat had been sick but he didn't have time to clean it up before he went to work, he was very sorry, he loved her loads and would make it up to her. The next he was lying on a slab, his poor battered face hidden by the undertaker's make-up, his broken body dressed in his best suit. The car had been towed away to the scrap yard. Margaret sometimes felt like she had been too. The vital part of her that made her alive was missing, muted, while her body went about the daily routines and looked normal.

She thought that without Tom, her days as a foster mother were over. For several years they had been. She forced her empty body into various jobs, continued to meet with friends and gradually she healed, the life in her had grown again. Then, with no warning, this young man had contacted her. She was still on their books, you see, the social services never destroyed her records; she was still deemed a possibility. Her record showed that she had coped with some of the roughest, most broken children who needed care. It was a gift. The young man was hesitant at first, he knew she had lost Tom, wasn't sure how she would feel about returning to her role, if she would feel that she could do it again without his support. But they were unsure what to do with their latest case. He was relatively new to his job, full of ideals and enthusiasm. He didn't want to assign a child to institutional care, not if there was an alternative. He was hoping that Margaret was the alternative.

They had done their checks of course, assessed whether or not she would cope on her own, was still suitable. Margaret found that while she awaited their decision she began to feel more sure. When the man-boy first visited, her inclination was to refuse, to explain that fostering was something she did with Tom, that part of her life had finished. But while she was waiting, answering their questions, having her life peered at, she found she was rather keen to be accepted. Perhaps this child would help to fill some of the gaps that Tom had left, maybe being needed, having a clear role in life, would lend it purpose again, give her an incentive to live rather than mark time. She began to hope they would find her suitable.

They were vague about the girl. It seemed she had a sister, Lisa. The two girls were always housed together, but now the wisdom of this was being questioned. Lisa was a quiet, nervous child. Initially it was thought she might be implicated in some disturbances, now they wondered if she was simply a convenient scapegoat, someone who Joanna could blame. Margaret knew the pair had been in several different homes, though none had "been right for them". This usually meant a child was difficult, possibly cruel or wild, refusing to obey rules, upsetting the other residents. She had seen that before, her and Tom had never cared for 'easy' children.

When she sat down and read Joanna's file, it was full of things which were almost recorded. She gleaned as much from what was

30

not said, as from the actual written words. Lots of fights with other children, fires where the cause had never been verified, smashed windows which the girl denied breaking. Margaret guessed Joanna was intelligent, possessing that cunning ability to avoid blame which some children seem to be born with. She wasn't worried, knew that she could cope with anything a child might throw at her. She was happy now to be welcoming Joanna into her home.

Then Joanna smiled. She turned the full force of her personality on Margaret, stepped forwards to shake her hand and told her how kind it was for Margaret to have her to stay. It was unnerving, to see someone so young be so in control of their actions, to flip from nervous to confident as though it was controlled by a switch. She introduced herself, asked where her room would be.

Margaret showed her where she would be sleeping, left her to unpack her few possessions while she went to make some tea. She had felt strangely unsettled.

***

My Story

I dressed appropriately. Hairnet, wig and plastic gloves, this time under leather gloves, hooded jacket. I had some of those 'slipper socks', the sort made of wool with small plastic blobs on the bottom, to ensure you don't slip on smooth flooring. I wore them under my walking boots. They were bulky, made the boots too tight but it meant I could slip the boots off at the door, leave their clunky noise and wet prints outside.

I had no excuse this time for if I was seen, found in the house. I decided it was unlikely, given the layout of the house. If the problem arose, I would sort it out at the time. I slipped my knife into my pocket, just in case. My make-up was more tasteful than

31

before but also careful. I might need to talk my way out of a situation, there might be a male involved, I wanted to look my best. Just a bit of liner around the big eyes, something to extend the lashes a bit, a smear of colour on the lips, a touch of pink to highlight the cheek bones. Then I raised the hood, let my face disappear into shadow.

I hurried to the main road, struggling to keep the umbrella the right way round. I had phoned ahead for a taxi, given the address of the chip shop on the London Road. It nestled with other shops under an overhang caused by the walkway for the flats above. There was a tiny supermarket (the kind where you always check the use by dates on anything before you buy it), a hairdressers with old fashioned photographs decaying in the window, and a newsagent. The shops were shut, of course, but a few people were waiting in the chip shop, leaning damply against the steamed up windows. I stood outside, hidden inside my big hood, ready to pounce when the taxi eventually swung into the kerb, avoiding the splatter as he ploughed through a puddle.

I opened the door and slid onto the seat. Someone had been ignoring the 'no smoking' sign, and stale smoke wafted towards me. I gave the address of a house near the alleyway and we moved back into the traffic before I'd finished trying to plug in my seatbelt. I gave up, the driver obviously wasn't bothered and I was only doing it because I didn't want him to tell me to, to create a scene he might remember. Unfortunately, he was chatty.

"Where's a nice girl like you off to on a night like this then?" He glanced up into the rear-view mirror, assessing my appearance.

"Babysitting," I mumbled, looking away, watching the wet streets whiz passed.

"Oh yeah? That for family or friends? Easy money I always think," he said, pulling out to overtake a bus.

I steadied myself on the door handle, made myself smile.

"Yeah, I can watch telly all night while they pay me."

I glanced at the meter, counted the correct money into my hand. As soon as we stopped I reached over the worn seat cover that divided us and passed him the money. He checked it, saw there was no tip, barely acknowledged my "Bye" as I climbed out. He was moving away almost before the door shut behind me.

I watched him leave, waited until his red lights had disappeared round the curve in the road, then began to walk. I kept my head down, trying to shield myself from the driving rain, feeling the bottle bump against me as the bag slung across my shoulder swung with each step. I made it along the road and down the alley without seeing anyone.

When I left the alleyway I turned left, kept near the low fences and hedges at the end of gardens, made my way up to The House. People were huddled inside their homes, hiding from the weather. I could see them through the open curtains, very few people had shut them yet, it was still early. There they were, living out their little lives, never considering that anyone might be watching. Some of them had fitted gas fires, the ones with flames which made their rooms look cosy and warm, even though the draughts they caused were often more powerful than the heat given out. Most were watching telly, lost in mindless entertainment that flickered and buzzed, filling their whole consciousness.

I soon reached The House, registered that lights were on: two downstairs and one upstairs. I glided down the side passage, paused in the back garden. As before, the kitchen was in darkness. I wasn't going to waste any time tonight. I bent, fiddling with my laces, loosening them so I could slip my feet from the boots. Then I tested the door handle, holding my breath, hoping it was unlocked. It was. The door hissed open, I kicked off my boots behind me, stepped inside, closed the door, stuffing my leather gloves into my pockets. I could hear the telly in the room next door as my eyes adjusted to the gloom of the kitchen. There was a noise from upstairs too, a child chanting a nursery rhyme while they tapped the beat, perhaps banging a toy against the wall.

I was quick, moved smoothly to the fridge, registering the smell of fried onions, the heap of dirty pans in the sink, the ease of walking across the sticky floor in socks compared to tottering in high heels. The fridge door clunked open, spilling light across the kitchen. Same food as yesterday, no new wine. That was good, would've spoiled the plan. I moved a bowl of hardening pasta to one side, lodged the bottle behind it. They would wonder why the other one had put it there, such a stupid place, no wonder they had missed it the day before.

I shut the door, moved back to the exit, stood a moment until my eyes had completely adjusted once more to the dark. Then checked the floor. No drips, no marks from sweaty feet that I could see, nothing that shouted to the world that I had visited. The door gave its warning hiss as I opened it, too quiet to warn the occupants. I was outside, slipping my feet back into my boots. Then hurrying up the passage, laces flapping against the leather.

I paused when I was level with the front of the house, checked the road was clear, peeled off the plastic gloves and knelt to retie my laces. I pulled on the leather gloves before I strode up the path. I was smiling. It was so tempting to stay, to watch and see what happened. But it was unlikely anything would happen today, perhaps even this week. I knew the chances were high that the position of the bottle would make them suspicious, that they might just tip it away, though I thought they would at least smell it first. One good breath full might be enough, might carry the poison far enough into their lungs to do harm. If I was lucky, if the treasure had started to evaporate already, was trapped within the air of the bottle.

If I was extremely lucky, if the stars were on my side, then they would pour it into two small glasses, there was just enough. I marched back along the alleyway. It was dark, smelt of dog shit and drunk's piss. I wondered if I would meet anyone, if someone would lurch towards me from the shadows. That might be fun, my knife was ready, resting in my hand hidden inside my pocket. But it was too early, too wet an evening.

I turned away from where the taxi driver had dropped me just a few minutes earlier, walking back towards a more major road. I now had to decide what to do. Hailing a taxi would be almost impossible. I could call one, ask to be collected outside one of the houses or pubs that lined the road but that would mean at least a twenty-minute wait in the cold. I could catch a bus, though that would also mean a wait, they were less frequent at this time.

I joined the main road and began to trudge along it, heading for the bus stop. I passed a pub, its door open, light and warmth wafting into the street. There was music playing, the heavy smell of beer, laughter. I slowed, turned, walked back.

I threaded a route to the bar, watched by every male eye. My hips moved enticingly and I slowly unzipped my coat, let it fall slightly from one shoulder, shook out my blonde wig so they noticed. I was glad I had chosen blonde this time, men noticed blonde. I beamed a smile at the bloke behind the bar, ordered a white wine. Seemed appropriate. Then I turned, leant back against the bar, scanned the room. Who looked lonely, bored, in need of company? Someone with a fat wallet. I saw him, sitting in the corner. He had even placed his wallet and car keys on the table, not wanting them to slip from his pocket while he sat. Stupidly announcing that he could afford real leather and a nice car. The remains of a meal were congealing in front of him, a basket of chips to one side. He took a long sip of beer, looked away as if I wouldn't notice he had been watching.

I walked straight over, a shark making its kill. Catching men is easy, something every female should be taught from birth. There are certain things that I learnt very quickly, life-skills if you like.

Firstly, it doesn't matter too much what you look like, not really, not when it comes to ensnaring men. I happen to be well-endowed with a great figure and a pretty face but it wouldn't matter if I wasn't. I have noticed this. Men notice breasts, eyes and mouths but mostly, more than anything else, they notice the way that you move. All this can be learned. If you walk with a certain swing to your step, leading with your hips, shoulders back, a little wiggle – then men will watch you. They cannot help themselves. Breasts are easy, if you have none, buy some from your local bra shop, the bigger the better. Eyes look best under decent eyebrows, so spend some time shaping and darkening them. Mouths need to be clean – no cold sores or dead skin – and smiling. Trust me, a nice smile goes a long way, so practise in a mirror. If you have big teeth, duck your chin down and smile up at him, staring straight into his eyes. He will stop dead and stare back. Then look away quickly, like you're a bit shy. That makes them feel all protective and manly. When you glance back, he'll smile. Always works.

Next is personality. It really doesn't matter a bit what your own personality is like, what matters is that you appear to like his. Give a man attention and he will notice you. Talk about him, ask him lots of questions, appear interested in his answers, smile at him. He will start to think you are a nice person. You can be as corny as you like, tell him he is strong, "Oh, I'm not strong enough to move that, please can you help?" or clever, "Gosh, I never realised that before". They will lap it up. Let them know that you have a problem, something they can easily solve, make them feel like they are doing you a huge favour, the big strong man. They will leap to protect you.

Someone once said they thought all men appeared somewhere on the autistic spectrum. I'm sure this is true. Use this to your advantage. If you don't particularly like them, or find them unattractive, think they're stupid; it really does not matter. As long as you appear to be interested, they will believe you; they never notice your real feelings. I'm sure every femme fatale that ever lived has known these facts. If you look at them, all those women who have been adored over the years, you will see that actually, they are not so great to look at. They probably have big teeth or thin hair or are a bit too thin or fat. What they had was knowledge of how to talk to men and how to move. They made every man feel like he was special, adored. Men love that, they always like the people who like them, they never look very deeply under the surface.

I now needed to use these skills to secure a ride home, no way was I going to walk in that weather. Chip-basket man had got lucky.

I stood next to the stool opposite, hovered as if uncertain, raised an eyebrow. He nodded, straightened his back, keen that I should join him but trying to look in charge, as if he had chosen me, made the move. I saw his eyes flicker over the bare half-moons of my breasts, which were straining against the tight sweater. I sat, leaning forwards slightly, improving his view, shrugged out of the coat and bundled it with my bag onto the stool between us. As if invited, as if I belonged there, with him. My glass resting on the table next to his.

I smiled, chin down, eyes up, asked, "Can I be very cheeky and steal some of those chips?" I watched his blush, the glow in his eyes as he registered that I had chosen him, that maybe I wasn't as far out of his league as he'd first thought, perhaps he would get lucky tonight after all. He nodded and pushed them towards me. I picked one up, moved it towards my lips, completely aware of the image I was creating.

"I'm Sally," I said, "and this is really very kind of you. I hate being in these places on my own". I looked slightly downcast, lowering my voice, added, "I was meant to be meeting someone, but he obviously thought better of it, decided I wasn't worth braving the weather for."

"Jim," he said, "I'm Jim. Really, I don't mind, be nice to have a bit of company. You live round here then?"

I nodded. He cleared his throat, drained his glass, struggling to appear relaxed, normal, like this happened every time he came to the pub for a lonely supper after work. I noted the plaster dust around his nails, saw the hands enlarged by constant lifting, guessed he was some kind of builder, maybe just a labourer. Something mindless. He stood, clutching the empty glass, needing a bit more courage.

"You want another drink?"

I grinned up at him, looked for a second at my full glass. "Yeah, why not? Might as well make a night of it. Another white wine would be lovely. If you're sure you don't mind?"

I watched him walk away. He was taller than I'd thought. Confident now, pleased with his manliness, his ability to pull a pretty bird. He would be boring, probably attempt a clumsy fumble in the car later, perhaps something more. But that was alright. My lift home was sorted. And I had my knife, if he should get out of hand.

Chapter Four

My Story

I had intended that that would be an end to it. I had every intention of leaving the rest of my treasure sealed up, forever if needs be. Until I saw the newspaper. Until I saw that witch again. Then I knew I needed to act, to prove she wasn't quite as smart as she thought she was.

I had arrived home safe enough. Jim had proved safe if boring. After an inexpert fondle in his car outside the pub, I had suggested he drive me home, back to my flat. I had seen the glow in his eyes, had known he was thinking I was suggesting something else. Idiot.

I had directed him back to the chip shop, told him I lived in one of the flats above. With my husband, who was a jealous brute of a man. That had cooled Jim a bit, made him back away almost instantly. He didn't mind a quick one night stand, wasn't so sure he was up for the hassles of being 'the other man'. That might get complicated. He hardly murmured when I asked him to drop me off. I got out of the car, laughed when he mentioned he might see me in the pub again, skipped into the darkness of the stairwell. I waited until he had driven off, then made my way back to the house. The rain had finally stopped. I went to the back, took a minute to pick the pins out of my wig and pull it from my head, and went inside.

That was it. Job done. All to plan. It would have ended there, truly it would, I'm not some sort of nutter. I actually felt a bit strange about it, about the enormity of what I had done. Then I reasoned that it was in the past, it had happened, nothing I could do to change it. There was no point beating myself up about it, ruining my life wouldn't change anything. If I continued to think about it, I might start to feel bad. I put it out of my mind.

It was three weeks later that I saw the local paper. I had been checking it each week, hoping that something of interest might appear. An obituary perhaps, the announcement of a funeral. People seemed to be quite taken with funerals, since Princess Diana died last August, they had become almost fashionable. I was patient. I would have loved to go back to The House, to peer in again, watch what was happening. But that didn't seem very sensible, and I was no fool. Then finally my patience paid off.

I was checking the paper on my way home from work, trying to hold it steady while the bus swayed around corners and lurched into bus-stops. There it was, right in the middle of the front page. The sad report of two parents dying unexpectedly, the police saying they were investigating, details of the funeral.

I didn't feel pleased, there was no excitement in this, perhaps a tinge of satisfaction but nothing much. I was at the point of throwing the paper under the seat in front. Then I glanced at the rest of the report, saw her photo, was livid. There, in the corner of the report which had continued on page four, there was a statement by the police and *her* photo.

I recognised her at once, would know her anywhere. Turned out she was leading the investigation, was some kind of leading figure at the local nick. This changed everything. Let me explain.

I had met her a few years ago, when I was still allowed to drive Ma's car. Like I said before, Ma was mean, disliked sharing her possessions and put all sorts of rules around them. She was the same with the car. At first, I was allowed to drive it, when she didn't need it. The loan came with a whole list of rules: keep the tank at least half full of fuel, not to be used for anything illegal, no speeding, no parking in restricted zones, no transporting of dodgy stuff, no driving while under the influence, etc., etc., etc. The list covered just about everything that anyone could possibly think of. She even wrote it out, gave me a copy. That's the sort of woman she is, nasty. She told me that if I broke any of her rules, for whatever reason, she would remove the car from my use, I would have to use the bus.

Well, I did my best, tried to follow the two thousand pedantic rules according to Ma, but she was impossible to please. Of course, when I got the speeding ticket, through no fault of my own, I knew she would be unreasonable. That was the thing with Ma, when she made a rule she stuck to it like glue, there was no compromise. I wondered if she was a bit autistic too sometimes. Anyway, I knew she would make good on her threat, she always did. I also knew that sometimes you could challenge a police ticket, could argue it was unfair, get it cancelled. I was nothing if not gifted with arguing, so off I went, straight away, to the police station. I marched in, demanded to see someone in authority. I knew it was important to appear knowledgeable from the outset, half the time these police officers don't even know the law, they just make it up as they go along. If I pointed out they had been wrong, ignorantly giving me a ticket when it was unnecessary, I figured they would let it drop. It would save them the paperwork as much as anything.

I would've been fine if *she* hadn't been there. It didn't even affect her, she should've minded her own business and carried on walking. But she didn't. She heard me stating my case and came out to the desk to see what was happening. She took against me at once, told the plod who was dealing with me to take no notice, to more or less throw me out, I was wasting police time and could be charged unless I left. That was it. There was nothing that I could do, I could see that arguing with her wouldn't change her mind. So I left. The ticket arrived in the post, Ma received it, no more car. There was nothing I could do at the time, but I didn't forget. I knew that one day I would get even with the police witch. I'm good at that, waiting until the time is right, saving up my anger until I know I can win, obliterate the enemy.

Now, here she was again, the cause of all my trouble, gazing out at me from the pages of the newspaper. She had made a statement, said they were treating the deaths as suspicious.

That was all from her but the reporter was enterprising, had done a bit of research after attending the inquest. He found out there had been post-mortems, high levels of copper were found. The verdict at the inquest had been 'unlawful killing'. There was some speculation in the newspaper as to who the killer might be, if there was a motive. They actually used that word, 'killer'. That was wrong for a start, I was not a killer.

You disagree? You would give me that label? Well, you would be wrong. I was no more a killer than the bus driver. Than any driver in fact. If a child runs into the street, is hit by a car, they will probably die. That's a fact. Now, the driver of the car in question does not ask the child to run in front of his car, he doesn't force them to do it. He just happens to have put the fast moving car in the same street as the child. Should the child not run in to the road, they will be safe. You would not suggest that just by putting the car there, the driver is a killer, would you? I was the same. I had not forced anyone to eat my treasure; I hadn't even suggested that they should. I had just put it there.

But I digress. When I saw her, the police witch who had caused me so much trouble, I knew this was my chance to even the score a little. She was hoping, no doubt, to earn herself a promotion, perhaps a little fame and fortune along the way. Well, I would stop her. The public had a right to be protected from her sort, those people in authority who think they can ruin things for other people and it doesn't matter. The little people. I would stop her, prove myself her equal. I folded the paper, put it in my bag. I might need

42

to read it again later. Then I stood, ready to jump off at my stop. I was lost in thought, this required some planning.

***

Other People

Margaret learnt Joanna very quickly. Her time fostering with Tom had given her experience that was invaluable. The first thing she discovered was not to believe everything the girl told her. Joanna's ability to lie was quite astounding. She was very chatty, would stand in the kitchen talking for hours, while Margaret cooked or cleaned. Often what she said was difficult to follow, her answers to questions tended to be long but vague, you were left wondering what she had actually said. Even simple questions, like "Do you eat mashed potato?" would be answered in a long ramble about her third foster mother only ever cooking potatoes from a packet, they were bought frozen and would arrive on the table with cold centres and burnt edges. She seemed to be incapable of giving a simple yes or no.

Sometimes she would even contradict herself within a single sentence. Margaret might ask her if she enjoyed playing hockey and she would reply, "I've never in my whole life played hockey actually, the only time that I ever did it poured with rain the entire time and I was in bed with flu for a week afterwards."

Much of what she said was a complete fabrication. She would tell Margaret story after story about places she had lived, reasons for having moved homes or schools. It was mostly untrue. Margaret rarely bothered to correct her, if the girl wanted to live in a fantasy world there was probably a reason. Perhaps her experiences of real life had been too horrible, it was easier to invent than to accept what had really happened. Margaret thought it was an issue she would tackle later, when she knew the child better. Joanna never mentioned her sister. It was as if she had never existed.

***

My Story

I made plans while lying on my bed. I found this was usually the best place to plan. It was important that the police witch was made to look a fool, like she had tried to make me look when I was trying to make a perfectly legitimate complaint.

I therefore needed to throw her a false scent, make her think she was getting somewhere, narrowing down the suspects. In reality she would be making an almighty fool of herself. I decided there needed to be more projects, more people sampling my treasure. If those people were somehow linked to the two already gone, then the police witch would assume the perpetrator was also linked. A jilted lover, or a crazy family member, or someone. I just needed to discover a few facts about the targets, find out something about their lives. If I was to remain out of the picture, which obviously was the primary concern, then it was imperative that they did not look like random killings. I needed to do a little research.

The means was slightly more of a problem. My treasure was beautiful but also there was a slight randomness to it. I could introduce it into their lives but I couldn't be sure they would necessarily ingest it. I considered changing methods. That would be a shame, the link with the original project wouldn't be so clear plus I liked using my treasure. As I said, it had style. Any nutter could wield a knife or a gun, this showed intelligence and resourcefulness.

No, I would continue as before but I would be fussy about my subjects. I would choose many, keep my options open and only use my treasure on those who were suitable, those who stocked food or drink that were easily substituted. The beauty of the project was the time delay. No one could be sure quite where they had acquired the treasure. It was not at all obvious their homes had been violated; there would be no tightening of security, no warnings to lock their doors or check their larders.

I got some scissors from the kitchen drawer and cut out the photo of the police witch. I would keep it with my treasure, remind me why I was doing the projects. Make her fully responsible. She lay there, looking up at me from the lid of my treasure box, resting in my insulated bag. I scowled at her and closed the zip.

I needed to do some research, which would mean a trip to the library. I could check the papers there and use their computers. I also needed my own phone.

One of the best places to acquire the latest IT equipment is the school bus. Honestly, it is a disgrace how many parents give in to their teenager's demands for the latest models and those teenagers are SO lax with their security. I like to see myself as an educator, teaching people early on in life that some people cannot be trusted, that they need to take better care of their possessions. The next afternoon, I left work early and caught the bus that did the pick up from the local private school. I guessed the pupils would have wealthy parents, the sort to buy them a phone before they really needed one.

I dressed with care that morning. I was lucky, if I wore no make-up and tied back my hair, then with the right clothes I could look very young indeed. I was often asked for ID when buying alcohol and yet I was several years past the legal limit. This now worked to my advantage. Although all the school brats would know that I wasn't one of them, I was a stranger; to any adult I would look like a kid. I wore a white blouse and black skirt under my coat, which I removed when I got on the bus. It was cold but bearable for the sake of anonymity.

I caught the bus at the stop before the school, looking for all the world like a kid who had bunked off early and was now catching the bus home so her mum didn't suspect anything. I sat near the back, where I hoped most of the tide of teenagers would gravitate to when we arrived at the school. I wasn't really sure if kids from private schools did that, but I figured a teenager is a teenager and Daddy having lots of money won't change that.

We drew up outside the school and I looked out of the window at the tangled mass of kids waiting in the cold. The driver was something of a sadistic power freak, he kept the doors tightly shut for about five minutes. The kids outside were cold, pushing against each other, eager to choose their seats, to get home and shed their uniforms, to leave school behind them for another day. He was enjoying the power, I could tell, liked that no one could get on until he chose to open the doors, that everyone had to wait in the cold until he decided to let them on.

Eventually he relented and pushed the button to release the doors. The kids surged forwards, climbing the steps before the doors had even properly opened. I watched them carefully. Well actually, not so much them, I watched their bags carefully.

The kid I chose seemed to have sight problems. He wore very thick lenses but even with those, he held things very close to his face if he wanted to see them. His bag was big and square. I moved quickly, pushing my way up the aisle, against the flow of kids getting on until I was level with him. Then I sort of pushed him sideways, so he half fell into a seat. He looked confused, wasn't entirely sure if it was his own fault for stumbling or if I had caused it. But strangers don't push you like that, do they? So it must have been his own fault.

I was instantly contrite, couldn't apologise enough. "That was so clumsy of me, I am so sorry for not looking where I was going. The bus is very crowded isn't it, is it always like this? Could I sit here, next to you?"

If you talk fast enough, join enough sentences in rapid succession, people don't really listen. They get the gist of what you are saying but they don't have time to process it. If you also end with a question, a request, they will almost always agree. I think it has something to do with not wanting to admit they haven't really followed everything you have said, not wanting to ask you to repeat yourself.

The boy nodded and I slid into the seat next to him. He sat next to me, looking awkward, wishing he had an excuse to move. I wasn't going to give him chance to do that, so I continued my monologue. I'm rather good at those. I told him about going to visit my Mum, what I was buying her for her birthday, the film I wanted to see at the cinema. An endless flow of rubbish that stopped him from turning to a friend, suggesting he might move to a different seat. People are so reluctant to appear rude, even to a weird stranger. It is such a weakness. While talking, I was fumbling in my bag, spreading the contents across the seat between us and on my lap. I search my purse, sighed in dismay and told him I needed some change for the ciggy machine, did he have any?

He started to say no, I could see in his eyes. He didn't want to have to go to the trouble of opening his bag, looking for coins. Lazy git. I couldn't allow that, so I waved a fiver in his face, where even he could see it. I told him I was desperate, if he could give me just one ten pence coin I would have enough and he could keep the fiver, make a tidy profit. Greed won over laziness, it usually does. He started to rummage in his bag.

We exchanged money and that was it, he was happy with his profit, I was happy because his bag was now open and I could see my prize, the black edge of a mobile phone nestling amongst his books. One sharp bend later, my bag was upturned on the floor and I was scrabbling around trying to retrieve everything. I leaned heavily into him, he lost his grip on his bag, only for a second but it only takes a second doesn't it? Then I was up, ringing the stop bell, shouting bye, leaping from the bus before it was fully still. I started to trot away, behind the bus, clutching my bag with his phone inside. I am not sure he even realised at that point it was missing.

Next point of call was Brian's. Brian was my IT man. I had known him since we were kids and we often helped each other out. He could get round any password protection on any machine; the skills of a half-blind school kid were no problem. He lent me a cover too, so it was a bit disguised, for when I used it in public. I promised he could have both the cover and the phone when I had finished with them. It pays to keep useful people sweet.

I went straight to the library. It was busy with teenagers doing homework and chatting, mothers helping little kids to find books they would enjoy. I ignored all that and went upstairs, to what they called their 'work room.' There were computers you could use and heaps of the day's papers, with old copies filed on heavy sticks, hanging in dated order. There was a man up there, he had that vacant look unemployed people get after too many boring days. I ignored him and started to read.

You need to remember, all this is a few years ago now, things were a little different. If I had been working on this project just a few years later, I could've used Facebook and saved myself a lot of time.

You would not believe the stuff people put on Facebook. I hear so much about it living here. Apparently, there are pictures of people's kids, so you can see the schools they attend, photos of their hobbies, with a bit of cross referencing you can easily work out what times during the week their houses will be empty. Finding addresses is also possible with some time and effort, if you compare a few photographs with the images on Google maps, especially if they have given clues of places in their details. Of course, some people are more canny, they set everything on their accounts to the most private settings. But most people don't, most people let the whole world look at their lives. My friends tell me it's great, a brilliant source of information. Some people even post smiling photos of their family while they are actually away on holiday. Why would they do that? They might as well post a big sign that says, "We are in a foreign country, our house will be empty for a few days, do go and party."

But no, this luxury was not available to me. I was still in that world that people have forgotten so quickly, the world before social media was how people lived their lives. I was stuck with newspapers and clunky search engines on public computers. The papers were helpful though. I found out the couple's names and that they had another, older, child, who attended a school.

I looked up the school on the computer but there weren't any details, I just got some blurb from the local authority, nothing helpful. I found the *Times Educational Supplement* and looked for the name of the school.

Well, you will not believe my luck. There was an advert for a new teacher. They wanted someone to teach year one, they listed a whole host of things they wanted the applicant to have, lots of qualities and qualifications. But, most importantly, they included a brief bio of the school and suggested that applicants should visit to have a look round before they applied. That was one invitation I was not going to refuse. This was obviously meant to be.

I went downstairs and found some books and magazines to help me. I found out the normal qualifications that a teacher has, places you could study for them, stuff like that. There were some sample application forms in one magazine, which were really helpful. I started to plan who I would be, the sorts of things I could say while I looked around.

What I wanted were addresses of other pupils, to know where

49

their parents lived. I could do it the hard way, turn up at the school gate and follow some home. But that would take ages, days, possibly weeks. Plus, I was almost certain to be spotted at some point; I couldn't believe that loitering around a school gate is something that wouldn't be noticed. No, I somehow needed to get into the office, I didn't think security would be very tight, they must have a list of names and addresses somewhere.

I looked up the location of the school. I found it on an area map. It wasn't that near, probably the kid had caught a bus or been taken by her dad or a taxi or something. I didn't fancy using taxis or buses, not when I wanted it to look like I was a teacher, surely a teacher would be able to afford her own car? I needed wheels.

I collected the books and leaflets into a heap and returned them to the woman at the front desk. Normally I wouldn't have bothered, but I didn't want her to notice me or pay attention to what I had been looking at. She put them all back on the mountain of stuff she needed to return to the shelves. The map was a good one, so I had slipped that into my bag. When I found the addresses of pupils, I could mark them on the map, decide which ones were worth visiting.

I walked towards the bus stop, making plans. This evening I would be looking for Jim again. I decided he was about to start a steady relationship. I needed to use that car of his.

Chapter Five

My Story

After dinner I dressed for Jim. Lots of flesh but not too obvious, I didn't want to look like a tart. A skimpy top but with a big cardigan draped over it, one that could slip off, show a bit of skin but like I hadn't intended to, like I was modest. Men like tarts for one night stands, I wanted to become a bit more than that, I might need his car a few times.

The wig was a problem. I didn't want to wear it for my school visit, it was too uncomfortable and didn't really suit the image I hoped to create. I would have to explain it away to Jim somehow, perhaps say it itched or something. My own hair was alright, if I washed it and brushed it out a bit, curled the ends. It was nice and long, men like long hair, and it was easy to change your appearance by tying it up or back or curling it, even if you didn't wear a wig. I combed it out and called for a taxi.

When I arrived at the pub it was just as crowded as before. You could hardly hear the music that someone had put on, there were lots of heated conversations in progress. I guessed a whole group of office workers had descended, they were spread around two tables, some standing, the men with their white shirt sleeves rolled up, ties loosened, beers in hand. They were loud. Too many over-confident men fuelled by alcohol and the thought of the weekend.

At first I thought Jim wasn't there, then I spotted him. He was at the bar, tucked around the corner, engrossed in conversation with a skinny chap who needed to visit an orthodontist. I ordered a wine and sidled over, slowly, like I was a bit embarrassed, a bit unsure about meeting him again.

"Jim?" I said, like I wasn't sure if he would remember me. He looked a bit confused for a minute, probably the hair change had thrown him. I watched his colour rise, his almost smile.

I touched my hair, flicking it over my shoulder. "Do it you like it? My ex liked blondes but this is the real me. Is it too plain?"

The other guy was looking between us, wondering who I was, if he would get an introduction. I ignored him, he wasn't part of the plan and I hoped he would leave. I kept my eyes firmly on Jim, holding him with my gaze, absorbing all his attention. He registered the "ex," looked relieved, started to grin, think about possibilities. His friend was looking pissed off now, started to mutter.

"Right, well, nice to chat Jim, better go, see you around I guess." He sidled off, looking for someone less rude, who wouldn't ignore him.

I moved into his space, stood very close to Jim and peered up at him.

"Sorry about the other night," I said, so quietly that he had to bend to hear me. Made him look big, protective. Made him focus his attention even more. I looked round quickly for his friend, said, "Oh, your friend has gone. Sorry, was that my fault? I didn't mean to butt in. I can go away again if you were busy."

He was quick to reassure me. I knew he would be. He said he was pleased to see me, he liked the hair, what did I mean about an 'ex'? I saw a table was free in the corner and I suggested that we took it, if he had time, if he honestly didn't mind me butting in like that. I wouldn't take too much of his time, I had just wanted to say hello, apologise for the other night.

He led the way, weaving between bolshie office workers and bored workmen, over to the table. It was sticky with spilt beer, the varnish thick and tacky. I slid onto a stool which was too low and wobbled slightly. I made as if I was about to fall and he quickly put out a hand, protective. I smiled my thanks. He was hooked.

I explained how my husband had come home drunk once too often, I had taken as much as I could, had told him to leave. Jim nodded, pleased, trying to look sympathetic. I said it was painful to talk about, that my life was boring anyway, how had he been? Had he won that contract he had been bidding for?

I didn't want to say too much, better to let him talk. Lies were best if kept simple, not too much embellishment. Although people never notice contradictions in your story, even if they do they assume it was their own fault, they must have misheard, not understood properly or something. Like I said before, people always assume you are the same as them. They don't tell lies so they assume no one does. It makes for an easy life, but it's still best to keep it simple. So I turned the conversation back to him, tried to stay awake while he droned on about his day, the work he hoped to win, his football team. I smiled a lot, appeared captivated, didn't check the time too obviously.

We ended up back in his car. I explained that my Mum was staying, had come to look after me, so we couldn't go back to the flat. He was completely understanding, asked if I wanted to go back to his place. I looked surprised, asked him if he was sure that was okay, would he be able to drop me back at my flat early, I had work tomorrow. He grinned, knew that meant I would be staying for a bit. I then nestled back into the seat as he drove me there.

His flat was surprisingly not too bad. It was quite clean and although the furniture was cheap, looked like he had bought a job lot from the junk shop or his aunt had died at the right time, it was quite comfortable. It was just one room really, with a sofa bed that I doubted ever got turned back into a sofa, plus a tiny kitchen and a bathroom. He pointed at the doors when we arrived, his equivalent of 'The Grand Tour'. Then he grabbed a heap of old newspapers off the coffee table, threw them onto a pile by the door and offered me a drink. He was a bit nervous, I guessed he didn't often take people there. He was trying to tidy up a bit while he talked, flinging odd clothes into corners, collecting up empty cans and yesterday's mugs. I didn't mind, apart from a bit of dust it didn't smell or anything.

We could hear the telly from the flat next door while he did what he wanted. I considered the possibility that this might turn out to be a good backup, if I decided Ma was not worth the hassle. Except he might want me to share the rent. I would have to be sure any arrangements were completely on my terms.

I waited until it was over, he was smoking his ciggy, looking content. I knelt beside him, wrapped up in his tatty duvet and told him that I was thinking of applying for a job. I pulled the brown cover tight, like I was cold, made myself look worried. I needed to earn a bit more now my ex had gone or I would have to move in with my Mum and Dad, so I had decided to go back to teaching. That surprised him, me being a teacher. I could see him absorbing the information, that he liked the idea he had bedded a posh bird, someone a bit more classy than he usually pulled. I told him about the school, said it looked perfect but I didn't know how I would get there, I couldn't arrive for an interview on the bus.

Of course, he was all understanding, jumped into the trap at once. He told me that him driving me there was no problem, he could easily sort out his work so he would be free, I should go ahead and make the appointment. I thanked him, snuggled back, wondered how long I needed to stay for.

***

I telephoned the school the following Monday. I called from work during my coffee break, squashed into the washroom so no one would hear me. The kid's phone worked great and I had worked out how to add numbers to the directory so I could store them for when I needed them. I hoped no one else would come in, pull the flush before I had finished. Phoning from a loo didn't seem a very teacherly thing to be doing. I was lucky though, I managed the whole call undisturbed. I booked to visit the following day, at ten in the morning. The woman who replied asked a few questions, if I was currently teaching, did I have much experience, stuff like that. Nothing difficult, nothing I couldn't answer. She didn't take any details, just my name, so she had no way of checking anything. I was careful, but I could've said whatever I liked.

I phoned Jim as soon as I had finished the call, checked he could take me then. I told him 9:45, I didn't trust him not to be late and I wanted to appear professional. He said he would pick me up from my flat. Someone came in then, so I thanked him quickly, shoved my phone into my pocket and started washing my hands.

The following day I was outside the chip shop in good time. I wasn't really sure what teachers wore when they were just looking round a school, so I decided to opt for something safe – a smart skirt with low heels and a sweater over a blouse. If I'd owned a suit I would've worn one. I hoped I looked professional enough. I tied back my hair, winding it into a knot at the back of my head and fastening it with a big plastic clip that I'd taken from the hair aisle at work. I wore enough make-up to look old enough to have done a four-year education degree and graduated last summer.

I could tell Jim was impressed when he saw me; his whole manner was different, a bit respectful. That made me smile; it was like he saw me as a different person, not just an easy lay from the pub. I spent lots of time thanking him, saying how kind this was of him, I would've been stuck without him. I didn't want him going cool on me, I made him feel like the big strong man again.

I suggested he drop me off just before we got to the school and

I would meet him round the corner afterwards. I hoped he would wait, I had no idea how long this would take but I told him it would just be half an hour. He had brought a paper to read, he said it was fine. I figured if I was hours he would leave, which would be inconvenient but not the end of the world. Him coming into the school would ruin everything though, so as an afterthought I went back to the car, told him to leave if I was ages and I would get the bus home and meet him in the pub this evening.

I walked up the pathway to the school. They had a security system, you had to stand at the door until someone released the catch from the inside. I'm not sure what it achieved really, unless a madman was daft enough to arrive with his weapon easily visible, I think they would've buzzed him in anyway. I noticed they had security cameras and an alarm though, which would make breaking in during the night more difficult. If I wanted addresses I needed to get them on this visit.

The office was easy to find, it was just inside the first door you came to. I went up to the little window, trying to ignore the smell of feet that wafted up from the nylon carpet. I told the woman there that I was Judy Smith and I had come to look around the school. She checked my name on her paper, smiled and asked me to sit and wait while she went to find Mr Gadsdon. That was the head teacher. She gave me a plastic badge to wear which told everyone that I was a visitor. It wouldn't be difficult to make a copy if I needed to, though I wasn't sure if there was a less secure entrance.

The only place to sit was some low chairs between a bookcase and a fish tank. None of the kids had thought to add bleach or anything to the tank, so it was full of fish swimming mindlessly through plastic weeds. There were a couple of kids looking at the books. I thought they might know some information, so I smiled at them and said hello. They looked a bit worried and continued searching through the books. Kids today are just rude.

Mr Gadsdon appeared from the corridor to my left. He had grey hair that matched his worn suit and he was carrying a pile of papers. He stuck out a hand and I hurried to my feet, returned his handshake with a firm one and smiled into his eyes. Good first impressions count for a lot. He ushered me into his office. I sat on a low plastic sofa while scanning the room. There were no papers of interest that caught my eye. He started to tell me about the school and I asked lots of questions, about the catchment area, the ethos of the school, things I had read about in the school blurb. If he noticed that I was making questions from the information he had written, he didn't react at all.

He then asked me a few questions about myself, which was trickier. I tried to speak quickly, giving lots of information in short bursts that didn't really link. He would get a general impression, but not many actual facts. I explained that I had graduated the previous summer, we had to move due to my father's health, my degree was a good one, I hadn't had time to job-hunt before, I had always loved working with year one, they were my favourite teaching practice age group, I hadn't brought my certificates with me, could I bring them next time, if I was called for interview?

He seemed satisfied and rose to take me on a tour of the school. We headed for the classroom, which was annoying, I thought that addresses would probably be kept in the office. The kids were all working when we arrived. Some were sitting round a table with a teacher, others were writing or drawing pictures. There was lots of stuff stapled to the wall and I asked if I could have a look, see what they had been doing. He looked pleased at that, it obviously showed some teacher skill that he was hoping for. I wandered round the room, looking mainly at the walls but casting quick glances over to the teacher's desk, looking to see if she had anything of interest.

We wandered around the rest of the school, me trying to not

look bored, to think of things to ask him. I mainly talked about him, asked him how long he had been there, if he liked it, where he had worked before. He was a man. Men like to talk about themselves and it used up the time very nicely, he hardly remembered to ask me anything at all.

We came to the end of the tour and I had absolutely nothing to show for my time. I didn't want to go back into his scrubby office again, there was nothing of interest in there. I did try a few flirtatious looks but they seemed to have no effect, so I figured he was either very careful when he was working to appear professional, or else he was gay. There was certainly no response that gave me hope. I knew it was my last chance, so on the way back to his room and the exit, I asked if I could use the washroom.

He looked a bit surprised, perhaps teachers don't use the toilet much, but he showed me the way. He asked if I could find my way to his office, he would wait for me there. Just the words I had hoped to hear.

I waited until I was sure he would be gone, then peered around the door. I could see his back, disappearing down the corridor. When he was out of sight I left the washroom and started to follow him. I wasn't really sure where to go. The office was my best bet but that was occupied. I passed a table of books and I grabbed a few, held them in front of me, as if I had a job that involved them. A few kids passed me but they didn't seem to think it odd that I was there. I stopped one, asked him when the teacher called the register each day. He looked surprised, told me it was every morning. I asked where they were kept. He said they were in a rack outside the office. That had potential, and I hurried back to where I had started. Mr Gadsdon was waiting for me.

I told him I was just looking at the books I was carrying and then put them on the table next to the shelves, as though that was a normal thing to do. I then asked him again about catchment areas, how far did most of the children travel? He was a bit unsure, especially when I started to actually name road names, did any come from as far as the new estate on the North Road? I could tell that he didn't think it was important but neither did he want to appear rude. He leaned through the window in the office, asked the woman who was working there. She didn't know either but she produced a list, said it was the contact sheet that the PA had produced. Not everyone was on there, but I was welcome to look if I wanted to. I think they just wanted to get rid of me and my strange questions now. I had struck gold. I barely even looked at it, just kept strong eye contact on her while I asked if she could tell me how many free school meals they gave, what numbers were classed as special needs, and what percentage had siblings in the school. I told her I was trying to build up an idea of the demographics of the school. All the while I was carefully folding the address list, moving it to behind my bag, extracting a plain piece of white paper that I had brought to write things on, to look professional. While she was still speaking, I laid the plain paper on the table, where she couldn't reach it, thanked her for it, so she would think it was her list I was returning. I shook Mr Gadsdon's hand and thanked him for his time. Then I left, walking slowly, restraining my urge to run quickly down the pathway. I had it. I had a list of names and addresses.

I hurried round the corner to find Jim still waiting. He had the motor on to keep warm and was hidden behind the newspaper. I flung myself into the seat and beamed up at him, waving the list in triumph.

"What's that then? Did you get the job?" he asked.

"No, silly, there has to be interviews first," I said, "But this is my consolation prize. They liked me but they wanted someone with more experience. But they thought I was good and they wanted to help. So they gave me a list of parents who might want private tuition, you know, to pay a teacher to come in the evenings, to give their kids a bit of extra help.

"Can we drive round, have a look and see if they're nice houses? I don't want to take work with them if they're dodgy."

Jim's face clouded and he made a sucking noise with his teeth.

"I don't really have time for that now love, I need to get to work," he said. Then, seeing my pout, my disappointment, he added, "But I could take you later. Perhaps we could have a drive round this evening? Have a quick look?"

I gave him a quick hug, told him he was the best, I would owe him big time. He started smiling and I knew he was thinking about how I could repay him. Let him dream.

He dropped me at the chip shop, I didn't want him knowing where I worked. By the time I got the bus there it was nearly lunch time. The manager was snotty, said that I couldn't keep leaving early and arriving late, if I was ill then I should phone and let them know. Next time I wasn't there on time she would fire me. I listened and said how sorry I was, assured her it wouldn't happen again, told her how I really needed the job and she had been really kind to me. She lapped it up, said I could have one more chance. We had these conversations every few months.

***

Other People

Living with Joanna was always difficult, mainly because Margaret never trusted her. There was something about the girl that she couldn't define but which made her wary. Her affection and obedience were a little too perfect, as if she was playacting, being something she had learned to be. She would hug Margaret, occasionally kiss her cheek, but the older woman knew that it was usually because Joanna wanted something, was rarely, if ever, spontaneous.

She was fun to listen to though. Margaret smiled as she remembered how the girl would bound in from school, hoist herself onto the work surface and sit there, legs swinging, while she told Margaret about her day. She would use different voices for each of the pupils she was describing, a stiff Germanic voice for the teacher. It was funny, Margaret would be laughing by the time she finished. As she remembered those days, Margaret sighed. Her own feelings towards Joanna were far from simple.

There was so much that she loved. The girl had unlimited energy, she would get up early for school, chatter endlessly until it was time to catch the bus. In the evenings she would entertain Margaret with stories. She liked to cook and would spend her evenings creating food, usually devising her own recipes. Margaret was aware that everything was on the girl's own terms, if Joanna didn't feel like talking, she would be silent. If someone invited her to go out after school she would go, even if she had asked to cook dinner that day, the fact that Margaret would be waiting for her was of no consequence. But when she was happy, when she wanted to do something creative or fun, there was no one better.

School was a whole different challenge. Joanna arrived as a gawky twelve-year-old child. Within a year she was behaving like a woman, even if her body still had some maturing to do. Margaret had to set early curfews and watch who she was dating – always much older boys – with as much diligence as she was able to. Joanna was always glibly dismissive, told Margaret that she worried too much, was old-fashioned, didn't understand how teenagers today behaved. It was an impossible task but she tried to keep the girl safe, even when the main danger was herself. She wasn't quite sure what the girl had already encountered, what abuse she might have been subjected to. But if she was honest, the girl just seemed to be naturally promiscuous.

Margaret bought her the regulation uniform, white blouse and a grey skirt which fell to below the knee. She was well aware that all the girls rolled up the waist band while walking to the bus stop, that they all arrived at school wearing mini-skirts. But Joanna had a certain swagger to her walk, a way of moving that made grown men notice her when she was still very young, a child really. The only thing Margaret could think of to keep her young, to protect the girl and warn the men that she was not as old as she acted, was to have braces fitted to her teeth.

Those braces had been the cause of so much anguish. Margaret smiled to herself as she remembered. Joanna's teeth had been fairly straight, there was only really one that was misaligned. However, Margaret decided that it needed to be straightened and she found an orthodontist who was willing to help. The problem was not severe enough to be covered by the National Health Service, but Margaret considered it a small price to pay for a marker that would shout 'child' to anyone who saw Joanna's teeth.

Joanna was not at all worried about the procedure – in fact Margaret couldn't recall ever seeing the girl frightened. Even when she needed vaccinations or fillings, she barely even flinched. She let the dentists take their impressions, fiddle in her mouth with their uncomfortable tools. When she saw what she would be wearing though, she was furious. Two rows of "train tracks", the heavy metallic braces that would be permanently in her mouth for at least a year. Margaret had been delighted. It had been worth the money, the long hours sitting in a stuffy waiting room, the inconvenient appointment times. Joanna was, in effect, branded as immature, a child. If a man chose to ignore that, there was nothing Margaret could do, but he couldn't claim Joanna had fooled him into believing she was older.

***

Jim was waiting in the pub when I arrived. He was holding a pint in his greasy hand, having a laugh with his mates. I soon put a stop to that. He was there to meet me, not socialise with a load of builders. I shook my head when he offered me a drink, told him that I wanted to get going, that I had rushed straight from work to be there early and I didn't think we should waste any more time. He looked a bit surprised but he downed his beer and led the way to his car.

It was a clear evening, cold but bright. Perfect for scouting a few possible targets. I pulled my coat tight as we crossed the car park towards his car, leaning into him, letting him think I was grateful, liked being with him. He stopped for a kiss when we got to the car, pulling me roughly to him, leaning against the driver's door. Like we didn't have something better to do, like we weren't in a rush. I pushed him away, told him he'd have to wait 'til later then skipped round to the passenger door avoiding holes in the tarmac, waiting for him to unlock.

I pulled out my map. I had marked all the possible houses with a cross, and planned a route that took us past most of them. I also wanted to check out the roads nearby, it's not like Jim could sit outside the target house while I went inside, was it? I needed somewhere quiet for him to sit and wait. I was careful for him to not actually see the map, he needed to know approximate areas, that's all. I wasn't stupid, wasn't going to point out actual targets. Just in case he remembered, linked the two when things started to appear in the newspapers. I thought the risk was tiny. He wasn't exactly the Brain of Britain plus he would be completely besotted by then, wouldn't want to believe anything bad about me. But silly to take unnecessary risks.

When we got to the town where most of the possible targets lived we drove along the High Street first. The shops were all in darkness, groups of teenagers huddled under puddles of light from the street lamps. There were a few kids in thin jackets and trendy jeans laughing on the corner, older people hurrying towards restaurants or homes, a woman walking her dog. A few cars meandered along, searching for parking spaces so they could get to their dinner or pub, meet their friends, unwind after a long day at work. One shop was still open, doors shut against the cold, a bored assistant sitting amongst bottles and cans, hoping for a sale, wishing he was at home.

One of the targets was a flat above the newsagents. I peered at it as we passed. The entrance was enclosed though, a front door that probably led to stairs up to the actual flat itself. Not a possibility.

As the shops became fewer, started to merge into garages, offices, light industry, we passed another possible target. This one was a tiny semi, one of six that were crammed between a dry-cleaners and a builder's merchant. They seemed to have a shared back access, a single lane that ran down the side next to the builder's merchant. It had a high brick wall next to it, was dark and narrow. I guessed it would lead to a pathway that would run along the back of all the houses, giving them outside access to their back gardens. It looked perfect. The target house was the third from the end. It was dark, possibly no one was home. The only problem would be where Jim should wait.

There was the town car park, a cramped affair next to the station, where shoppers and commuters squeezed their cars into tiny spaces. The problem with that would be walking along the High Street. I would have to pass lots of shops and I couldn't be sure which ones might have security cameras. If the plod ever realised that my treasure had been administered in the target's homes, then they would scrutinise those cameras, looking for anyone who might be responsible. I didn't intend to be on them, even though the risk was tiny, minuscule given that they wouldn't know for sure when the treasure had been administered. However, if that car park was the only option, it would be a risk worth taking.

I directed Jim to take the next left, to follow the road that backed onto the target house. It was no use at all. Full of larger properties with secure back entrances. No way I could slip over a bush into the road I wanted and too far for me to walk back. Not to mention that Jim would be very obvious, sitting in a parked car. It was not a road that welcomed cars parked on the road, everyone had long driveways, plenty of room to accommodate legitimate visitors. No, it would be the town car park or nothing, I would give it some thought.

I directed Jim towards the next few target homes. We were in residential streets now. A whole range of houses, from the grand ones that stood alone on a large plot, to smaller ones which were styled to copy the bigger houses but they had no garden and were almost within touching distance of their neighbours. Jim drove obediently, but kept trying to chat, to discuss the houses we passed. He also asked which house I was actually looking at, where did my potential tutorial students live? I didn't want to chat, I was concentrating. I told him I had bit of a headache, if he would just shut up for a minute then it would probably go, I would probably feel better later. But if he kept talking it would get worse. I just wanted to sit quietly and look at the houses.

He understood what that meant. He knew that a headache meant he wouldn't get his reward later. He was silent after that, just kept giving me the occasional pat on my knee, like that would make a headache disappear.

I was surprised by the variety of target houses. It became obvious that a whole range of families attended the same school, from the comfortable to the hard-up. Quite a few lived in flats. I really couldn't understand why you would attempt to raise kids in a flat. Way too cramped. I thought it was selfish. None would be suitable. Unless I had a way to get into the front door, which I didn't, even the ones with a public stairway were too difficult. The only possibility was if I was still working on my project in the summer, when a ground floor flat might leave a window open. But that seemed unlikely.

A couple of the larger houses were possibles. They had plenty of gardens planted up with big trees that would cast helpful shadows. They all had side access, some were completely open, no fence or gate at all. That told me there wouldn't be dogs, I could easily wander round the back. There might be security lights, but the whole 'wrong address for a surprise party' excuse would work if they actually chanced to notice them. I suspected that most people would be so engrossed in mindless telly that even if their lights floodlit the whole garden they wouldn't notice.

I was encouraged by two more houses. One was a tiny terraced house. It was quite near to the High Street, still close enough to some industrial units for the land to be cheap. It was a whole estate of red-brick houses, arranged around central parking areas. They had tiny patches of tatty grass at the front and I could see wooden fences at the back that enclosed their square of garden. Jim could easily wait in one of the parking areas in a different square to my target, I could nip round the side and be back in a jiffy. Dogs might be a problem, there didn't seem to be a sensible correlation between the size of dog that people owned and the size of their house. But life was boring without a bit of the unknown.

The other house was similar to my first target. It was a semi-detached house with the same access down the side. It was set in a whole maze of residential roads, Jim could easily wait in an adjoining street while I walked there and back.

Jim was beginning to get antsy, to ask how many more I needed to look at and how was my head? Did I want to stop and buy some aspirin?

I told him my head was better, let's go back to his place. I shuffled round in my seat, drawing up my knees, facing him, looking adoring. I told him how grateful I was, how I couldn't do this without him, he had really saved me. I talked a lot about missing teaching, how good at it I was, I had always loved helping people and I really missed being able to do it. Now here he was, giving me a chance to go back to it, to take on some tutoring in the evening, after my normal work. The extra money would be great, maybe we should use it for a holiday, go away one weekend or something. It was only fair that he shared the money, as he had been such a help. We could go to a hotel, somewhere a bit posh, have a couple of days together, if he wanted, if that sort of thing appealed to him.

I could see he was lapping it all up. He liked the idea that I was dependent on him, all men like that sort of rubbish. He was keen on the holiday too, I could see that glow in his eyes as he considered possibilities, going somewhere different, having a complete change. He would like going somewhere with me too; someone who other men would notice, wonder how he managed to catch me, what he had that made me attracted to him. He wasn't used to being noticed.

Jim was one of those people who get overlooked; I knew that the very first time I saw him, sitting all alone eating his supper. He was used to being lonely, being asked to join things only if he could be useful, the sort of person that people talk to in the pub because he'll buy them a drink. It was nice of me to give him some attention, to offer him something to look forward to. He would enjoy planning a trip away, it would brighten up his boring life for a few weeks. We wouldn't actually go, of course, I would've finished needing him long before then. But he could enjoy the thought of it.

We arrived at his flat and I checked the time, decided it would be worth going in with him. I wanted him to take me out again later in the week, perhaps Friday, when I'd thought a bit more about which house to target first. I needed to keep him happy, make him feel I was worth the effort. I smiled up at him, my shy smile with the big eyes. Then I followed him through his green front door.

Chapter Six

My Story

I was ready by Friday. I had chosen one of the nicer houses, a detached brick building which was styled to look Edwardian or something, a bit poncey, like the owner thought a lot of themselves but actually didn't have that much money. It was on a tiny plot, with other identical houses in a cul-de-sac. The houses all sat on their own plots at strange angles, so they weren't facing each other or straight with the road. There were no fences or hedges. I supposed it was artistic, gave the impression of more land, more green, than there really was. The cul-de-sac was on a turning from another residential road. This had houses that were smaller, less pretentious, had parked their cars on the street outside. Jim could wait there, back a bit so he wouldn't notice where I went.

I had put my dissolved treasure into a small wine bottle. The face of the police witch stared at me when I opened the insulating bag and I sneered at her. She was impotent. I spent Thursday evening preparing, moving stuff around, disposing of the plastic safety sheet, just like before. I was a scientist, we did things properly.

The bottle was in the bottom of my bag, under some ring files I had bought to give a teacherly impression. This was an easy house, a stranger wandering round to the back wouldn't be as unusual as at those houses with more boundaries, fences and gates. I wouldn't be crossing any physical barriers.

I thought a collecting pot would be sufficient cover. I had picked up the tub from the counter at work, a collecting pot for blind people, where customers could throw their loose change. If challenged, I would say I was collecting for charity, had tried the front door but got no answer so had decided to try the back. It was odd but not, I hoped, sufficiently odd for them to overreact and call the police.

Jim picked me up outside the chip shop. He was starting to get a bit narked at never coming to my flat, had hinted a few times that it would be nice to see where I lived. I had told him my ex was being difficult, that the flat was actually in joint names and until we were legally separated he still had the right to go there, drop in unannounced, cause trouble.

I climbed into his car and leaned across to kiss his cheek while he pulled out into the traffic. He told me off, said I shouldn't distract him while he was driving. He liked that, being the responsible adult, having to hold me back a bit, like I was too eager. I pretended to be put out, like I couldn't keep my hands off him, sat gazing at him while he drove, chatting about my day.

I directed him to the road where I wanted him to park. We were lucky, there was a space next to a fence, not overlooked, and it was far enough from the turning to the cul-de-sac, before the road curved away, so he wouldn't see where I went. I gave him a big kiss, full of sloppy promise and picked up my bag. I had told him that I had an appointment, would be chatting to the family to see if they could use my services. It wouldn't take very long I didn't think. I offered to get a taxi home afterwards but Jim insisted on waiting. I knew he wanted to spend time with me but he was also keen now that I shouldn't waste money. He was already planning that weekend away, wanted us to have enough money to go somewhere really special.

I turned once when I was walking away, gave him a little wave, then disappeared round the curve in the road. I had dressed in dark clothes. Tight black top and trousers to keep Jim happy but big coat over the top. I pulled up the hood, disappeared into its shadow. I walked quickly but not enough to attract attention. As I went, I rearranged the bag a bit, pulled the bottle to the top, put on thin plastic gloves, took the collecting pot into my hand. It was one of those plastic tubs, with a loop of material to hold and a slit in the top for people to put their money. It wasn't very heavy, most people are too mean to give money unless the pot is actually rattled in their faces or they know the person collecting. Then the whole world is generous, when it will be noticed. No one wants to look mean, even if they are.

I turned into the cul-de-sac and walked towards the house. There was a narrow path next to the road but it was very open, not shielded by any hedges or fences. I guessed it was all part of the original plan, to have these wide spaces of green. It made me very exposed though, I didn't like it. I considered veering off, walking next to the actual houses themselves. It would mean walking across their bit of land, would look odd if anyone happened to be watching.

I stayed on the pathway until I came to the target house, then walked up their driveway. I could see lights on, lots of them, both upstairs and down. I knew from the address list that there were two kids who lived here, both a bit older than the ones I had seen in connection to my first project. The house looked alive and warm. I could see the blue fuzz from a television in the front room and people moving around in there. There was a light on in the room next to it. As I got nearer I could see it was a dining room. It had been decorated entirely in white, with a bleached wood table down the middle, surrounded by white leather chairs. I caught sight of a fancy silver candle arrangement in the centre but no people. Then I detoured away, across the grass, heading for the back of the house. There was a light on in the kitchen. I stood in the shadow of a bush and watched.

A man was in the kitchen, easily seen through the sliding patio doors. I didn't like the look of him at all. He was the shape of a guinea pig, fat tummy and fleshy bum. The fat continued up his neck to his face, which came to a point at his big nose. He had very black brows over piggy eyes. It was a mean face, a face full of self-importance. The face of a man who wouldn't notice you unless he needed something, who wouldn't think twice about being rude. The sort of man who always challenges the bill in a restaurant, who laughs too loudly and drives too fast. He walked across to the sink and stood at the window, washing his chubby hands while he talked to his peroxide blonde wife. I could see him watching her in the reflection of the window. Kind of funny really, me watching him while he watched her.

She was wearing a coat, bleached yellow-white like her hair. She tottered across the kitchen carrying a dish of something, her handbag slung across her other arm. She started to wipe surfaces, it looked like she was telling him to hurry up. He looked at the watch on his thick wrist, I glimpsed a pasty arm speckled with hairs and the gleam of a gold watch. He dried his hands, stared at his fat face in the reflection of the window and turned to follow her out. They switched off the lights as they went, only the light from the hallway shone through into the now empty kitchen. It had looked as if they were preparing to go out; either that or they'd just arrived home. But shouts to whoever was upstairs let me know they were leaving. I stayed where I was. I heard the front door slam at the front of the house, and the clunk of the car being unlocked. They were talking but I couldn't really hear what they were saying. Then, after what felt like an age, the motor started and I listened to the car driving away, fainter and fainter until it was gone.

I realised I had been holding my breath and I exhaled. Now to business. I moved out of the bush and crossed the tiny patio to the house.

I was pretty sure they would have locked the back door before leaving and when I checked it, I was right. There I was, in the dark back garden, with an empty house apart from a couple of kids and a locked door in front of me. The door and windows were all

71

modern and plastic, I couldn't force my way inside without causing damage and making a noise. I considered trying to blag my way inside. I could knock at the front door, say my car had broken down, would they mind if I used their phone, then hope I had the opportunity to use my treasure. But the risks were too high and the result too uncertain. Probably they would stay with me the whole time, there might even be a babysitter. At the very least they would have seen me, would recognise me again, which would rule out a second visit if I was unsuccessful. No, the sensible thing to do was to call it a night, to know I had been unlucky and to go back to Jim. I sighed and began to walk back to the car.

Jim was hidden behind his paper when I approached. I would tell him that no one had been there, they must've forgotten I was due to go. I would phone them tomorrow, find out what had happened, make another appointment. I would tell him to drive me straight home now. No way was he going to get lucky if I hadn't. I crept up to the window and banged loudly. Jim jumped, went all red, nearly dropped the paper. He grinned when he saw it was me and opened the passenger door.

The evening went from bad to worse soon after that. I let Jim give me a quick cuddle, another one of his attempts at a fondle, always awkward in a car with the gear stick in the way. I yawned and asked him to take me home. Jim was annoyed then, moved quickly back to his own side of the car. He said he'd thought I was going back to his place, he'd hardly seen me that week, he wasn't just a taxi service. I didn't feel like calming him down, I was cross myself. I told him that if he didn't like spending time with me, I would get a taxi in future, or find someone who would be kind enough to give me the odd lift without complaining. He went all moody, stopped talking altogether for a while. He started the engine and pulled away from the curb.

When he did speak again, it made me even crosser. At first, he started by saying how sorry he was, he didn't want to argue with me. I expected that, if you never give an inch in an argument, people always think it must have been their fault, they must have said something bad to make you cross. But then he really annoyed me. He said he was going to visit his Mum over the weekend, he was hoping I would go with him. I told him he couldn't go, I wanted to spend some time with him. We both had Saturday off, I thought we would spend the day together, just the two of us. He had suggested that himself, earlier in the week and I had told him I thought I would be busy. Inside, I was fuming. Jim was mine; I didn't plan to start sharing him with some needy mother. I made out I'd changed my plans so I could be free, like he asked me to.

He said it was her birthday, he had forgotten about it until today when he'd checked his diary. He said he *had* to go, it would be really nice if I went with him. He was frowning, confused by what I had said. He knew I'd refused to spend Saturday with him when he initially invited me, now it sounded like I had planned to all along. He was sort of asking me to go with him but he was cross too, I could tell. There was something a bit stiff about the way he was speaking, the sentences were a bit too polite, too formal.

Well, there was no way that I was going to visit his mother and no way that I would allow him to either. He couldn't split his loyalties like that. I started to shout, saying that I thought he loved me, how could he just use me like this. I told him that I was nothing but a sex object to him, if he really loved me he would want to spend time with me, I should be his priority. Maybe I had made a mistake, perhaps he wasn't ready for this kind of grown-up relationship, I might just call it a day and look for a real man. I watched his face go red, I thought for a minute he might even cry. I explained that I clearly wasn't good enough for him and that if he still didn't love me, after all I had done for him, then it was better to end it now. His hands clenched the steering wheel and he glared at the road ahead. We were driving back through the High Street now. I told him to stop the car.

He swung over into a space between the parked cars, my hand was already on the door handle and I jumped out. I told him I would get a taxi home, he needn't bother himself with me anymore. I marched off, back the way we had come so he couldn't follow unless he turned the car round and that would take time with the flow of traffic. I ducked into the doorway of a darkened shop and sneaked a look back. Jim was standing next to the car. He was scanning the road, looking for me. I guessed he'd have come chasing after me if he'd seen which way I had gone, but I had been too quick for him. I watched him thump the roof of the car, get back in and drive away. I waited. Sure enough, a few minutes later he passed me, driving slowly back along the street, searching for me. He must've turned around at the roundabout at the end. I waited a few more minutes, figured he would give up eventually. When he passed me the second time, heading back towards his flat, I watched until he was out of sight, then began to walk back up the High Street.

I wasn't too worried about Jim. I would give him some time to cool off, to begin to worry that he might have lost me, then I would phone him. I would let him apologise, tell me that he loved me. I would probably decide to forgive him straight away. His car was useful.

Now I was stuck with getting myself home. I knew there was a taxi rank at the end of the street, next to the station and I began to walk that way. My bag was heavy on my shoulder and I wished I had thought to throw some of the stuff out in my temper, to leave it in Jim's car so I didn't have to carry it home. I passed a litter bin and I pulled out the folder and the collecting pot. No point in carrying them if I didn't need them. I could easily replace them both next week. The pot went in easily, fell to the bottom with a clunk. The folder was more effort, it was a bit too wide for the slot at the top. In the end I just stuffed the contents – an educational magazine – into the bin and flung the empty folder into a shop doorway.

I pulled my coat tighter to keep the wind out, held onto my bag strap so it didn't slip and hurried towards the taxi rank. It was cold. The wind tugged at my hair, pushing against my coat, freezing my fingers. I stopped again and pulled the plastic gloves from my bag. They were thin, too thin to protect me much against the chill but they were better than nothing. I walked on, leaning forwards, feeling the wind push me back, slowing my steps.

I passed a wine shop, bottles glinting in reflected light from the street. There was a bakers, the shelves bare, wiped clean ready for the next day. Next I passed a shoe shop, dim shapes balanced on empty boxes, the prices too small to be seen in the dim light. Then a carpet shop, rolls of flooring like great bear carcasses hanging ready to be skinned. Finally I came to the restaurant and that is when my luck changed, that is when the evening became a success.

It was a Chinese restaurant, the type that serves take-away food as well as having tables for people who want to eat there. Some of the tables were next to the window and I peered in. I saw them immediately, they were right there, sitting in the window, waiting for me. It was Mr. Guinea Pig and Mrs Peroxide. I kept walking, kept my head low, just another pedestrian hurrying home. When I was well passed, out of their field of vision I crossed the road and walked back. I stood, shielded by a bus stop and checked out the possibilities.

They were sitting at a table for four, opposite another couple. They looked equally intellectually challenged, the kind of people who get on in life by bullying, being rude, demanding their rights and giving nothing in return. The type who are supremely proud of themselves. The type who the world wouldn't miss. Really, I would be doing the world a favour to remove them, it would almost be seen as charity.

The women sat opposite each other, their identical heads bowed close so they could hear each other above the noise of the restaurant. I wondered if they shared the same bottle of peroxide, or maybe the same hairdresser. The other woman was smaller than my target and slightly older. Her scraggy arms stuck out from her too tight dress and I wondered if she had ever considered sleeves would be a good idea at her age. Both favoured pastel pink lipstick. I supposed it blended well with the hair even if it clashed with the slightly orange tan.

The man opposite Mr. Guinea Pig was also older and smaller. He was bald and thought that a white sweatshirt looked good over grey work trousers. He sat right next to the window and I could see his whole profile, from his pointed nose, past the fat belly and down to his scuffed brown shoes. I wondered at the wisdom of placing them in such a public spot, perhaps the restaurant owner had hoped the women would take the window seat.

The restaurant itself was busy. I could see waiters scurrying around taking orders, some carrying platters of food. There was an area next to the door where people could wait for take-out orders, a few chairs in the corner around a low round table scattered with magazines. I could make out a bar just beyond that, glasses and bottles shining in the candle light.

I didn't need long to plan, this would be exciting and I would make it up as I went. I had a lot of wasted adrenaline to use up. I knew it would be better to wait until they had finished their meal and were waiting for the bill. The timing would be tight though, if I got it wrong they would pay and leave too quickly. It added to the excitement.

It was too cold to be comfortable but I was a patient person. I went back to the shop I had seen that was still open and bought some cans of drink and some snacks. No alcohol, I didn't want anyone to notice my breath. I settled back at the bus stop, nestling into the shadow where I wouldn't be seen, as far out of the wind as I could manage. Hidden inside my hood. It was a long wait. I saw their food arrive. I watched their plates being emptied. The women hardly ate anything, the overweight men happy to eat their share. They all drank beer. When I predicted they had nearly finished, I made my move. The dessert menu would arrive after their plates had been cleared but my guess was that they weren't pudding people. The restaurant was still busy, nothing was going to happen very quickly. I hoped.

I crossed the road and pushed open the door. The warm spices rushed to meet me and I kept my head low as a waiter hurried over. I spoke quietly, so he could just hear me, had to lean in close. I muttered something about a take-away, asked where the toilets were. He frowned, not sure if I wanted to order food or had come to collect some previously ordered. But the toilet request he understood. He waved his hand towards a staircase and went back to the kitchen to find out which dishes were ready for serving. He could sort out my food order later. It had been a long evening, he was tired, just wanted to finish these last orders and move people out.

I climbed the stairs, my shoes echoing on the wooden slats, my plastic gloves skimming the handrail. At the top I pushed open the door marked with the picture of a woman. There were two cubicles and no other people. The facilities were reasonably clean but not especially inviting. I guessed that if you ate here often you would try and wait until you were home rather than relieve yourself here. That was fine with me. I peeled off my coat and dumped it in the corner with my bag. Peering in the mirror I saw my hair was somewhat windswept, so I did my best to comb it through with my fingers, to make it a little less like a bird's nest. Not being noticed was important so I didn't hurry this; I spent as long as I needed to tease out the knots, to smooth it back into place so it would fall over my face when I leant forwards. The sink was now full of stray hairs, so I swept them up and flushed them down the toilet. Then I washed my hands, still wearing my plastic gloves, so it felt strange, sort of artificial. My skin was back to room temperature now, which would help me to move smoothly, to not make mistakes. I pulled my sweater straight and wished I had worn my black blouse. Never mind, if I was quick, said the right things, they wouldn't even look at me.

I carried my treasure bottle and walked back downstairs. My targets were still waiting for their bill to arrive. I hovered for the briefest moment, absorbing the positions of everyone in the room. Six tables still eating, one waiting to be cleared, two waiting to pay. Three people waiting for take-away food. Four waiters ferrying food and drink, answering the phone, disappearing into the kitchen. No one was manning the bar. This was meant to be.

I glided past the bar, barely even pausing as I picked up four shot glasses, my fingers plunged into their depths, clasping them tightly in one hand, my treasure bottle in the other. I had shed my plastic gloves, they were too obvious and might have been slippery against the smooth glass. I advanced on the target table, head bent forwards, hair like curtains across my face. I muttered something indiscernible, something about "complimentary drink" and "bill just arriving". My voice was deep, foreign sounding. I never once looked up. I simply plonked the glasses on the table, poured four shots from my treasure bottle, moved away again. If you don't look at other people, they usually don't look at you. They watch what your hands are doing but don't give your face more than a quick glance. Especially in a restaurant, especially if you are a mere waitress and they are superior beings.

I hurried back to the stairs. Being stopped by a waiter was more likely, a risk I was hoping to avoid. I would pretend that I knew the targets, they were old friends, I was just sharing a quick drink with

78

them. But it was a conversation I didn't want to have and one I managed to avoid by being focussed, not pausing for a second. If you walk with purpose, look like you belong there and are busy, people rarely stop you.

Back in the Ladies' I grabbed my coat and bag, swung them over my shoulders as I descended the stairs, was straightening the sleeves as I re-entered the restaurant, pulling up my hood. I didn't stop. I pulled my coat closed, kept my bag close, headed for the door. A waiter started towards me, trying to be helpful, to take my food order. But I was gone, out the door and up the street. Let him think I had taken ill in the toilet or got bored with waiting to be served. Let him think whatever he liked really. I was out and free.

I couldn't resist going back though. I know you'll think I was daft, taking unnecessary risks. But really, I just had to see what would happen. When I was clear of the restaurant and sure no one was following, I crossed the road again and wandered back to the bus stop. They were still sitting there, looking bemused, like they weren't quite sure what to do. Their shots sat in front of them, untouched but not removed. They stared at them for a bit longer, then Mrs Peroxide lifted hers, took a sniff. That was alright, like I told you earlier, dichloromethane smells sweet, it was why I had chosen it in the first place. She raised her eyebrows, in a "not sure what it is but it smells okay" sort of way. They were clearly bemused but not especially suspicious, after all, this was a Chinese restaurant, foreign people do weird things all the time. They hadn't seen enough of me to know if I was Chinese or not. The older man made his decision, he wasn't going to be beaten to it by a woman. If it came to being brave, tasting something a bit different, he would lead the way. Even if it was some super strong Chinese alcohol, he could handle it. If it took his breath away he would warn his wife not to drink it, though seeing her splutter might be kind of funny. He tapped his glass on the table, downed it in one. Before he'd even swallowed, Mr. Guinea Pig had copied, he wasn't one to be left behind. The women giggled, pretended they were a bit scared, then followed suit. But I was already leaving, I had seen enough.

I knew how the scene would finish. The waiters would bring the bill and remove the glasses – straight to the dishwasher I hoped. The group would pay, maybe quibble a bit about the bill, just because they always did. They would certainly check those drinks weren't included, that girl had definitely said something about them being complimentary, that meant free, whatever language you spoke. Then they would take their coats, gather their bags. There would be loud conversation in the street outside but not for too long, it was cold. Someone would suggest going for a nightcap, but half-heartedly, he was beginning to feel a bit rough, hoped they hadn't served him dodgy food in there. The others would refuse but promise to make another date. The women would air kiss, the men would kiss their cheeks, maybe move in a bit too close for a bit too long, they looked the type. Then they would move away, back to their cars. I wondered if they would all make it home before their guts exploded.

***

Other People

The girl was reasonably intelligent. When she decided that she enjoyed science, she began to work, to complete homework and to stop disrupting lessons. There were often problems in her classes, but the teachers couldn't usually be sure that Joanna had caused them, she was clever at not being caught.

The other pupils would lose personal items but no one ever had enough evidence to accuse Joanna, she had been seen lurking around the lockers but not actually breaking in, and the stolen items were never discovered in her possession. When Margaret did once find a stash of jewellery hidden under the girl's bed, Joanna was relaxed, glib even. She said she was keeping it safe for a friend who was going away on a Scout camp and who hadn't wanted to take it. Margaret had phoned the girl's mother, asked if this was true and been told that no, the necklace had been stolen from her locker the previous week. When confronted, Joanna changed her story, as if that was a completely natural thing, as if Margaret herself must have misheard or made a mistake. She told her that she had found the jewellery but hadn't had chance yet to return it. Margaret was sure she was lying, sure she had stolen it, but what could she do? She had no proof. She returned the necklace and told Joanna she didn't believe her but she felt impotent to do more. Joanna often made her feel like that. She made her question her own actions, nothing was ever straightforward.

Even bullying, the victimisation of a weaker pupil, tended to be carried out by those close to Joanna, never by the girl herself. Joanna always had a small group of close friends. They followed her around, ready to do whatever she told them to. They were never the strong personalities, the girls from stable homes with good brains. Joanna seemed to gravitate towards the weaker children, those who were easily manipulated, those who felt honoured that Joanna had deigned to choose them as her friend. There were five girls who Joanna accepted into her 'inner circle'. They would visit the house, with their long tangled hair and their socks at different heights. As they matured, the socks changed for tights (usually with snags and ladders in), and the hair was fussed over for many hours, first with heated curling tongs, later with straighteners. They always looked the same to Margaret though, a group of girls who adored Joanna, felt lucky to be included by her and were happy to do her bidding. Margaret suspected that they were a little afraid of her.

Joanna looked for excitement and thrills in life, often devising activities for her friends that bordered on dangerous. Soon after she joined Margaret, she was discovered playing 'chicken' with her friends. This involved lying in the road, waiting for a car to arrive. The first person to stand up and run away was the 'chicken', the person who remained lying there the longest, watching the car get closer, was the winner. Margaret discovered the game when walking home one day. She was walking back from the local shops, her plastic bags heavy in her hands, wondering what to cook for dinner, when she had seen the girls. She wondered why they were all lying in the road, a line of girls, stretched out on the hard tarmac, a couple of them shuffling, all raising their heads to watch for cars. It was a quiet road in a residential area, so the traffic was light, not fast, but cars passed every few minutes. If the driver failed to notice the bodies lying on the road, they would certainly be run over. The girls were a distance from her, too far for her to shout, too far to reach them if she ran, even if she dropped her shopping. She watched in horror as a car approached, saw a couple of the girls quickly stand and sprint to the kerb, the others lie there for slightly longer, poised ready to move but still in the path of the approaching vehicle. Then the rest of the girls stood, rushed to safety as the car got nearer and nearer. Only Joanna remained, lying still, not moving, refusing to stand even though the car would definitely have gone over her if she stayed there. At last, when Margaret was sure it was too late, the other girls started to wave their arms and rush towards the car, pointing at the prone Joanna, making the driver stop. The driver, a man, slammed on the brakes and hurried from his car, assuming at first that someone had been taken ill. When he saw the girl stand up, heard her ridicule her friends for cowardice, run away with them laughing, he was angry, shouted abuse after their retreating backs. Margaret stood there, unnoticed. She decided to not acknowledge that she knew the girls, watched the driver storm back to his car and accelerate away. Later, at home, she told Joanna what she had seen. She asked her why they would play such a game, told her it was dangerous, she mustn't play it again. Joanna had turned that blank stare towards her, said, "Okay," in the light dismissive voice she used when she wanted Margaret to stop talking. There was no argument, no discussion. Margaret was never sure whether the girl had even listened.

Any kind of discipline was seen as a challenge by Joanna. Margaret found that her rules needed to be absolute, with no compromise at all. If she was at all flexible, Joanna would find a loophole big enough to hang them both with. She tried to make as few rules as possible but those rules she did make, she expected Joanna to obey. She also learned that rules were only obeyed if there was a penalty for disobedience and she must only threaten things she was determined to carry out. Empty threats were no use. The only way to modify Joanna's behaviour at all was if it was in Joanna's own interest to do so. Margaret thought of their struggles over the washing machine and smiled a grim smile.

Margaret had owned an expensive washing machine. When Joanna was fourteen, Margaret decided she was old enough to start washing her own laundry. It would be good for her to take responsibility for something, to show she could be slightly independent. When she explained this, the girl had flashed her that dead look, the one that made you feel cold inside. Margaret knew she didn't want to do her own washing, that was a normal response, no teenager enjoys doing chores. She also knew that the actions which accompanied that response would probably not be normal.

At first, Joanna feigned ignorance. Every time she needed to wash clothes, she would ask Margaret to help her, to repeat the instructions about how much detergent to use, which number to set the program. She was hoping the woman would decide it was as much bother to help Joanna as to simply do the washing herself and she would forget her plan. But Margaret did not, she was fully aware she was being manipulated, that it was important to not back down. She had written out a list of simple instructions and glued them to the laundry wall. If Joanna asked for help, she told her to follow what was written.

Most teenagers would at this point have admitted defeat and done their own washing. Not Joanna. She stuffed the machine so full that the door would hardly close, leaving a slither of towel protruding through the door seal. When the machine staggered through its cycle the floor was flooded due to the leaking seal. When it came to spin the weight was too great and the machine ground to a halt, black smoke rising from the back.

Margaret was as determined as the girl, she would not allow antisocial behaviour to win. She was not particularly calm when she told the girl that the launderette was in the town centre and she could pay to have her clothes washed out of her weekly allowance. She then bought a new washing machine and a lock for the utility room door. She informed Joanna that she had a choice. She could smell due to dirty clothes, or she could use the launderette in town, or she could apologise. If she said she was sorry and used the machine correctly in the future, then Margaret would allow her to use it. If the machine broke within four years (which was the life expectancy that Margaret designated to the machine,) then Joanna would never use it again. The girl chose to apologise. The machine lasted for four years.

That was how Margaret managed to modify Joanna's behaviour. Always making it in her own interests to obey, always having immovable punishments if she chose not to. It was an uncomfortable way to live but it worked. Or at least, Margaret thought it had worked. Until that terrible day when she discovered what was really happening.

Chapter Seven

My Story

I arrived at Jim's flat early the next morning. I wasn't too sure what time he'd planned to go to his mother's, so I made sure I was there before he would have left.

When I'd got home the previous evening Ma had made a fuss about me being late, not letting her know that I wouldn't be there for dinner. She'd served mine onto a plate, in case I arrived, and then shoved it in the fridge when her and the prawn had finished eating. That was good, I was starving. Cold and hungry. Being a scientist, an expert, doing these projects, was tough work. It was a shame I'd never get any credit for it.

After dinner I played with the prawn. She had all her dolls out, spread across her bedroom floor in a tangle of naked legs and matted hair. I helped her sort them out, squeeze their silly plastic arms into the tight clothes, fasten the Velcro, and sat them up. Then I made up a story, moving them around, giving them all voices and personalities. The prawn sat on her bed, watching, giggling, absorbed. Ma looked round the door at one point, nosey cow. She stood there smiling, watching us play. Then the prawn decided she wanted to join in, to hold some of the dolls. That was boring, so I left. I spent the rest of the evening on my bed, reading.

I had caught a bus to Jim's. As I stood on his doorstep, waiting for him to come down the stairs and open the door, I fluffed up my hair a bit and undid my coat. I stood there, tight sweater clinging to me, coat slightly off one shoulder, face framed by hair that I'd washed that morning. I knew he would smile when he saw me.

He did smile, though he tried to squash it pretty quick. He looked uncertain, like he wasn't sure if I'd come to fight some more, to put the boot in. His eyes were tired, as if he'd hardly slept all night. I moved closer, in case he decided to shut the door.

"Have you got any coffee?" I said.

He grinned then, opened the door wider, let me into the tiny square hallway while he shut the door. I didn't wait to go upstairs, I turned, moved into him, lifted my face for the kiss that smelt of stale alcohol and morning breath. I grimaced.

"Oh, yeah, sorry. It's early, haven't had time to shave or anything. Why don't you wait in the lounge while I shower?"

I thought 'lounge' was pushing it a bit for one room with a sofa bed and a table but I let it pass. I walked ahead of him up the stairs, moving my hips in a 'come and get it' swing. His bed was a mess, a tangle of duvet and newspapers and empty glasses. It occurred to me that he might not have slept last night. It smelt of old socks and I could see his clothes from yesterday on the floor where he had peeled them off, next to an empty whiskey bottle. I waited until I heard the shower running, then went to join him. I would make him forget all about visiting his boring mother.

We both slept afterwards. He had an alarm clock but I'd taken care to switch that off while he was scrubbing his teeth. I woke to a headache and a heaviness that worried me. I felt as if my bones had turned to paper, no energy at all and I ached all over. I edged myself up, leaning back against the wall for support, watching the room swim. The coffee table, television, cheap print in a plastic frame, all moved fuzzily before my eyes, rotating in a bizarre dance that made my stomach churn. I was ill and it scared me shitless.

Jim woke when I moved. "Hello Gorgeous, are you ready for seconds already? Oh, you look a bit rough. You alright?" He put out a hand, the size of a dinner plate, felt my forehead. "Hey, you're burning up baby. Are you ill?"

I started to say yes, to move from the bed to the toilet but I didn't make it. Somewhere on his tiny landing the spinning floor rose up to meet me, slamming into my knees, smashing into my cheek. Ma's dinner gushed out of me, all over his faded grey carpet.

I thought he might shout, might kick me out the door, tell me I was a revolting bitch and to take my stinking vomit somewhere else. But he didn't. He must think I'm *really* good in bed. I felt him pick me up, as easily as if I were a rag doll. He carried me into the bathroom, moved the stained plastic curtain to one side and sat me in the bath. I held on to the cold plastic sides for support. He pulled off my vest, checked the temperature of the shower on his hand, then hosed me down. He handled me like I was made of glass, something fragile and precious.

When I was clean he dried me, rubbing me on the same damp towel I'd used earlier. My stomach churned again, so he sat me on the toilet, wound the towel around my shoulders, left the room to give me some privacy. I sat there, shivering enough to almost fall off, waiting for the violent flow to end, the explosion in my stomach to pass. Jim came back, carried me back to the bed. All the time he was talking, telling me it didn't matter, he would look after me, I would feel better soon. He dressed me in an old white vest from his cheap pine drawers, a clean pair of his faded boxers. You could've fitted two of me inside. He left me with an old bowl in case I was sick again. I could hear him, on the landing, working away with a bucket of water and a disinfectant spray, cleaning up my mess.

I lay back on the pillow, the pain in my head like a rock of fire, hard, solid, pressing against the inside of my skull. I cannot begin to tell you how worried I was. I was going over everything I had done yesterday evening, over and over; trying to work out if I had had any physical contact with my treasure. I was sure that I hadn't. I hadn't been wearing gloves when I poured the shots, that would've been too obvious. But I had been careful. I had unscrewed the bottle, then held the end while I poured. Not a drip had spilt, I was sure. Then when I resealed it I had only touched the outside edge of the lid, no contact with the wet rim at all. Could I have inhaled some? It was unlikely but possible. I had been speaking, telling them the drinks were complimentary. I hadn't been able to hold my breath, not the whole time. But I had known the risk, I had kept my face away from where I thought any fumes would float. If I had inhaled any it would be miniscule. And it was a cold night, there was no reason for too much of my treasure to have evaporated, not that quickly.

That morning, before I had come, I had rinsed out the bottle. I might have wanted to use it again and I wanted it clean. It was the hygienic thing to do. I had washed it thoroughly under the bathroom tap, then left it under my bed with the lid off to dry. I thought I had been careful but perhaps a tiny splatter had touched me, been absorbed. I decided that must be it. Which wouldn't be fatal, I was sure I would recover soon enough, my body was just reacting to a chemical it hated. I relaxed a bit after that, the pain was intense but it wasn't scary anymore.

Jim was back in the room, fussing. He wanted to call a doctor, get me checked out. That was not going to happen. I was not going to be submitting any samples for analysis, just in case. I told him I was fine, must've eaten a dodgy curry last night after he had dumped me. That made him change the subject, reassuring me again, saying he didn't quite know what had happened last night, he'd never meant to make me angry, he was glad I was back. I let him talk. The pain in my head was terrible, I wanted him to leave but I was worried he might throw me out, get rid of me and my mess. And I wanted to stay you see. Even if I made it back to Ma's, managed to sit in a taxi long enough to get there, I knew she wouldn't listen to me. She never did what I wanted, it was always me who had to fit in with her. She would insist on a doctor, with all his prying investigations. He would start asking questions, checking samples, looking for causes. That mustn't happen. They would hinder me, might even stop the projects altogether. No, it was much better that I stayed with Jim.

So I looked weak, like a dependent patient, tried to be brave. I held his hand, like it was a comfort, snuggled against his side, whispered that I loved him. I felt his smile when I said that, the grin reached right down his back, a ripple of happiness that I could feel while I lay next to him. I knew I was still managing to press the right buttons. I slept.

I woke to the sound of the television. I could see Jim's back, perched on the end of the bed, staring at the tiny screen, the volume turned low. He turned when he felt me move, smiled and came to me, asked if I was feeling any better. I was actually, though I was still very weak. But the pain in my head had subsided to a dull thump and my stomach was calm. I struggled to sit up and he came back, put his arms around me and hoicked me up to a sitting position, fussed about putting pillows behind me, pulling the dirty cover higher. He couldn't resist brushing my breast with his hand as he passed. I didn't react, if that's all it took for him to let me stay it was still a good deal.

The bed was none too clean, looked like the sheets hadn't been washed for a month. If I was going to stay for a bit they needed to be changed. I asked him if he had a spare set of covers, told him I was worried he would catch my germ, I didn't want him getting ill. He went to the cupboard on the landing, came back with his arms full of blue cotton. I climbed out of bed and sat on his chair, the rickety wooden one with arms that was next to the table. I still felt very lightheaded, wasn't sure I would be able to walk very far. My body was clammy, greasy. I needed another shower but thought I might faint if I attempted one.

I leaned back into the hard chair and watched Jim. He pulled off the dirty covers and dumped them in a heap on the floor. They smelt stale, of bodies and spunk and spilt alcohol. No wonder I had been ill. He stretched the sheet across the mattress, stuffed the pillows into fresh cases. Then he turned to the duvet, grinned, told me he hated changing the duvet cover, it always got into a tangle. He was right, it did. He had a weird method of climbing right into the cover with the duvet, standing there like a blue ghost, fumbling around trying to find the corners. When he emerged, shook it out, there were lumps and bumps all along its length. He bent to fasten the poppers. Weird to watch a big man trying to match tiny plastic poppers with great sausage fingers.

He flung it onto the bed, then came across, put his hand under my arm, helped me back into the bed. It smelt much better now, synthetic flowers rather than dust. I lay back and he pulled the cover over me. I wriggled a bit, let him notice the shape of me under the thin clothes he'd dressed me in. I was feeling weak but much better, I didn't need him to be helping me walk and stuff but I liked it, made me feel special. I saw no need to encourage him to stop. Not unless it got irritating.

The telly was still mumbling away in the background and he went to turn it off, said he would make me some toast if I thought I could eat something. It was late, early afternoon already. He told me that it was too late to visit his Mum, he had phoned her, told her he couldn't go. I didn't bother to say I was intending to stop him going anyway. I acted all sorry, said I had planned to go with him, I hadn't wanted to ruin his day. He came over, all attentive, gave me a cuddle, told me that being with me was much better anyway, he really didn't mind. That was what I wanted to hear. I pressed into him, then suggested that the toast he'd mentioned might be a good idea.

He went to the kitchen, then came back and started to pull on his boots. He told me the bread was mouldy, he'd nip to the shop down the road, buy some more. Was there anything else I fancied? I told him lemonade. Ma always gave me flat lemonade when I was ill as a kid, the sweetness helped to settle a dodgy tummy.

I heard his heavy footsteps stomp down the stairs, the slam of the front door when he left. I kicked back the covers. I reckoned I had at least ten minutes, time for a quick snoop.

He had a bookshelf in one corner. It mostly held old books, the kind of thing he was probably given as a kid, adventure stories, war novels. Nothing interesting. There was a stack of papers on the bottom shelf and I had a quick rummage. It was mostly work stuff, old receipts, bills, invoices, an accounts book.

In a drawer in the kitchen were his valuable papers. There was a roll of money, his passport, some old certificates that went right back to when he was a kid at school. Why would you keep your swimming-fifty-lengths certificate? Saddo. It was all muddled up with elastic bands, old shopping lists, a black diary from the previous year. I peeled off a few notes from the cash, went and stuffed it into my bag. There was loads there, he must get paid in cash for his work, he wouldn't miss a few.

I knelt down, lifted the mattress. Nothing there. Under the sofa were some porno magazines. I had a quick flick, might pick up some ideas. There were some letters too. I opened a couple. They were from some girl, probably an ex-girlfriend. Lots of soppy sentences and dirty suggestions. There was a photo of her too. She was plain, fat and spotty. Looked the sort who wouldn't be fussy. The letters were dated a few years ago, goodness knows why he'd hung on to them. Perhaps he'd thought she was the only girl he was ever going to get, was holding on to an old memory. If he hadn't owned a car, been in the right place at the right time, that might have been true.

I heard the door opening below and scooted back to the bed. I was lying still with my eyes shut when Jim looked round to check on me before going into the kitchen. He whistled while he made the toast, happy to have me there, to have some company. The pillows were wonderfully soft and I'd drifted off again by the time he came in, burnt toast in a stack on an old plate. It was chipped but clean, so I sat up, took it from him, had a nibble. At first my stomach reacted badly, started to churn again. So I took it slowly, little nibbles with sips of water, breathing in lots of oxygen. Gradually it settled down, the hunger took over and I managed to eat a few slices.

Jim was talking all the time. He told me he had bought a newspaper when he was at the shop, and began to read it while he talked. He checked the sports results, then turned back to the main story on the front page, before flicking through the rest, going backwards and forwards, relaxed, trying to entertain me. He read out snippets of news, but nothing interested me until the last story. There had been an article about the Chinese restaurant in the High Street, happened last night, we had passed right by it. Did I know the one? It was down the end, quite near the station. Wasn't that a coincidence? Apparently some people had eaten there, got ill really fast and been taken to hospital. Three of them were dead already, the fourth one was in hospital but it wasn't looking good. The police thought it was suspicious and were investigating the restaurant.

I took the paper from him, had a look. It was on the front page, but near the bottom, not deemed important enough for major headlines. There was nothing there that Jim hadn't told me. No pictures or anything and no details about the people. It didn't say why the police were involved, which was what interested me. Why would the local plod be there? Surely it was a matter for health inspectors? If they thought it was dodgy food in the restaurant. Jim was still prattling on, so I folded up the paper and passed it back. It didn't really interest me to be honest. The project was all about muddying the waters for the police bitch, about pitching my brain against hers. Once the project was done, the treasure was administered, I lost interest a bit. It's not like the targets really mattered, not after each stage of the project was complete.

"I wonder what they did, the cooks I mean," he said, rambling on. "Mind you, you have to feel a bit sorry for them, the people who own it. They probably don't deserve that, hard enough owning your own business as it is. Anyone can make a mistake, be given dodgy supplies or have a machine go wrong so things don't cook properly. Always looked clean enough when I went in there, must've eaten food from there a dozen times and never got ill. Even if the health inspectors say it wasn't them, nothing dodgy in their food, they'll never recover from it will they? I mean, who wants to eat in a restaurant where people have been so poisoned that they died? Won't be my first choice in future. I wonder what they did, what caused it." He turned to me then, as the thought occurred to him.

"Hey, are you sure it was a curry you ate and not a Chinese? Do you think it might be connected? Where did you buy it?"

He started to look really worried. "Perhaps I should phone the doctor after all. You might have something really serious."

I did not need this. I did not want him connecting the two things for even a second.

"No, you silly, how could they be linked?" I put down the plate of toast crumbs, made sure the cover was pushed down to my waist, that there was just a hint of flesh on show. I needed to distract him, despite how awful I was feeling. I gave him a full blast of eyes, beckoning him nearer. "I just had a bug I think, one of those twenty-four hour things. Why don't you come here and you'll see how much better I'm feeling."

He came. He forgot all about the news.

I stayed the night. I phoned Ma, told her that I was with a friend and had a stomach bug; I wouldn't be able to make it home. The prawn answered the phone so I gave the message to her, told her to go and tell Ma immediately. It didn't pay to break Ma's rules and I wasn't ready to move out just yet. Jim's house was a nice reserve option but his cooking didn't compare, and his flat wasn't as comfortable as Ma's house.

When I ended the call Jim was watching me. I wasn't sure why at first, then he asked why I had called myself Joanna. It was a stupid mistake on my part, but I had a lot on my mind and I was ill, you have to admit it was an easy mistake to make. I covered it up quick enough. I told him that Joanna was my first name, what Ma had always called me but I hated it, I chose to use my second name, Sally, when I was with friends. It was the name that suited me best, was who I was. He still looked unhappy, started muttering about me being able to trust him, I should tell him things like that, he didn't know anything about me really. This was not a line of thought I wanted his tiny brain exploring. I rolled over so I was facing him, put my hands up to his face and held him there while I looked full into his eyes. I told him that he knew everything important that there was to know about me. Of course I trusted him, I would never hide anything from him. There was nothing to know really, I was just an ordinary girl, I didn't have secrets. The name thing was silly, just a childish dislike of mine. And I loved hearing him call me Sally, made me feel all warm and special.

I had intended to stay for Sunday too, to ensure that his mother never got a visit, or even another phone call. But I was woken early Sunday morning with the sound of Jim vomiting in the toilet. Turns out that I had just had a bug after all!

I pulled on my clothes and was ready to leave by the time he emerged, all greasy faced and yellow. No way I was staying while he was revolting. I told him that I would clear out of his way, let him have some space if he was feeling poorly. He would be more comfortable if he was on his own, without me there disturbing him. He looked a bit surprised, perhaps he thought I would stay and play nursey. Not my style. I spoke very quickly, said I would call him later, find out if he needed anything. I had another appointment tomorrow, could I borrow his car?

He wasn't too ill to put his foot down at that, said he would need it himself for work. Just selfish some people. I didn't let how annoyed I was show, I just blew him a kiss, told him to get himself back to bed and sleep it off. Then I left, trotting down those stairs as fast as I could. I didn't want to catch it again, did I?

***

Other People

Joanna appeared to have no conscience. She would often say she was sorry when caught doing things wrong, often accompanied with a hug or a kiss. But she never meant it. Margaret would see nothing but cunning in her eyes. When she tried to appeal to her, to point out that taking something had caused someone a lot of upset, or that letting her friends bully a child had hurt their feelings, Joanna would turn those blank eyes on her and shrug, as if knowing that made no difference and she was surprised Margaret had thought that it would.

Margaret found her mind intriguing and wondered for a while if she would turn out to be an artist, something where seeing the world differently to other people was seen as a skill, admired. She recalled the year they had gone to Devon on holiday. Margaret's brother had allowed them to stay in his holiday cottage for a week so they had driven down one Friday after school. Joanna had been moody, not wanting to leave her friends for a whole week, to be somewhere unfamiliar, but Margaret had ignored her, thinking the change would be good for them. They didn't have a camera, so she bought the girl a disposable one in the local chemist shop, suggested that Joanna might like to take photographs of the scenery. All week Joanna ignored the camera, left it sitting on the window sill next to the front door, as if Margaret's suggestion was a silly one, below her.

The cottage was tiny, just two rooms downstairs and a couple of bedrooms. There was a log fire in the lounge and Margaret lit a fire even though it was summer.

One day they had gone for a long walk. As they strolled along a lane, overgrown with brambles, with great hedges towering above them, there was a terrible smell. Margaret knew at once that something had died, possibly a deer or a sheep. It was a dog. They found it beside the road, probably where it had fallen after being hit by a car. The smell was overwhelming but Joanna was fascinated. Margaret tried to leave, to continue their walk away from the decomposing corpse but Joanna wanted to see everything. She got a stick and poked at the maggots that were squirming through the eye sockets, pushed at the remains of matted fur that was rotting on its back, ran the stick along the lines of teeth in the exposed jaw bone. Margaret turned away and tried to ignore the grisly scene by looking further away, at the hills and trees above the hedge, her hand across her mouth to try and cut out some of the stench, waiting for Joanna to finish her examination.

The days passed easily. They ate in the local pub and went for walks along the beach. Joanna swam in the sea. She was strong and swam well, always going out to sea much further than Margaret felt comfortable with, always making it back to shore. She enjoyed worrying Margaret. Nothing terrible happened, and with Joanna one could never assume that. The shed did not catch fire, no windows were broken, she did not go out on her own and not come back all night. It was a relatively peaceful week.

When they got home, after the holiday had ended, Joanna handed her the camera and asked if she would develop the pictures. Margaret was surprised, thinking the camera was empty. She took the camera back to the chemists and a few days later, collected the long creamy envelope of photographs. She opened them in the car, wondering what Joanna had seen fit to record, wondering if it would be the little coves where she had swum or the rolling hills they had hiked along. Twenty-four photographs, all from a different angle, all of the dead dog. She must have sneaked back at some point with the camera.

***

At sixteen, Joanna took her O Levels and passed six with reasonable grades. She was fairly intelligent and whilst no one would say she had studied particularly hard, she made some effort in the science subjects. She asked Margaret if she could continue with A Levels. When she was eighteen, her grades were good enough to study chemistry at a decent university. Margaret agreed she could continue to return to her home during the holidays.

It occurred to Margaret that, although Joanna had asked at each stage if she could continue her studies, it had all been rather well managed by her. At each point, when Margaret went to discuss things with the school and with the social services team, she found Joanna had been there ahead of her, explaining her plans, sharing her hopes, persuading everyone it was an excellent way forward. Many children in care chose to leave their foster homes when they were sixteen, certainly most of them were independent at eighteen unless they had been fully adopted by their carers. It seemed Joanna was keen to stay with Margaret and had contrived to make that possible.

That was when Margaret had a heart-breaking realisation,

something which had never been obvious before. She had known for a while that Joanna did not have the same emotional responses as most people, she seemed unable to feel the same feelings that are innate in everyone else. She suspected that, despite her often saying the word, Joanna was incapable of feeling love for anyone. However, for the first time, she also had the dreadful understanding that this resulted in Joanna also being unable to *feel loved*. She had no emotional understanding that Margaret loved her and wanted to care for her. She judged everyone to be like her, how she viewed the world was how she assumed she was also viewed. She only did things that benefitted herself, therefore, if someone was kind to her, it must be because they considered it must ultimately benefit them. She could not comprehend that anyone would do something simply because they liked her, loved her, cared about her. Those were not simple feelings for Joanna, she was completely unable to understand them. Margaret realised what a desperately lonely world Joanna inhabited.

Joanna wanted to continue living with Margaret, probably because it was comfortable and she liked the food and knew it to be safe. But rather than being able to think that Margaret might let her stay due to affection, she needed to provide her with a reason, to manipulate those around her so everyone agreed she could stay, so it would have looked churlish for Margaret to refuse. For the first time, Margaret began to understand a little of why Joanna behaved how she did, that her actions were most akin to a wild animal in a threatening territory, where everyone was looking out for themselves, where trusting someone was foolish. She felt overwhelmed with sadness for the girl.

When Joanna went to university, Margaret felt something of a relief. She also felt guilty for having those feelings but if she was honest with herself, having Joanna in the house every day made it hard to relax. She missed her during term time, missed her humour and fun, but she didn't miss the erratic mood swings, the bad language, the lack of trust that had to exist between them. Joanna surprised her by writing occasionally, letters explaining her studies, describing her room in the halls of residence. Margaret suspected that she wrote so her foster mother wouldn't change her mind, decide that she should move into a flat on her own. Joanna was marking her territory. But whatever the reason behind them, she enjoyed the letters and it was nice to maintain contact.

Of course, nothing went smoothly. In the first term Joanna was fined for drunken behaviour and damage to the common room. She asked Margaret to lend her the money for the fine, explaining it was not her fault, they had muddled her with another student and Joanna had been asleep in bed at the time of the incident. Margaret refused to pay, telling Joanna she could get a job during the weekends to earn money for the fine. She was not about to start trusting Joanna, she knew where that would lead.

In the second term Joanna failed her exams. She had been drinking with friends the entire night before and had gone straight into the exam from a night club. Her results weren't terrible, she had a good brain, but the university would only allow her one retake. If she failed again she would have to leave. She had passed, with a thin margin, but good enough to stay.

In the third term, Joanna wrote to say she was pregnant.

Chapter Eight

My Story

I decided to do the next part of my project on my own. Jim had been ill for ages, the rest of the weekend and through Monday. I sent him a card, figured he would like that. I used some of the money from his flat, bought him a great big one and stuffed a bar of chocolate inside, to show that I cared. It was important to keep him sweet for a bit longer.

While I was in the shop I had a quick look in the newspaper, to see if there were any updates on my project. There weren't. Nothing they were putting in print anyhow. There was certainly nothing linking the targets to the school. Perhaps my red herring was too subtle for the police witch, perhaps I had overestimated her intelligence. That would be a shame, I like a bit of a challenge, a decent competition.

I picked my next target by finding someone who lived on a bus route. It was a woman, I assumed a single mother. No father was listed, just the mum and her kid. I wondered if she resented the kid as much as my mother resented me or if this kid was in a cosy home. Not for long either way.

I decided to skip supper and go a bit earlier. I had got back after work and prepared everything. Then I went into the kitchen, just as Ma was about to serve the food. I told her I had to pop out, a friend had phoned me and asked me to meet her, she was upset about something and I didn't like to refuse. Ma was instantly suspicious. She's like that, she would never help anyone so she assumes the worst in other people too. She told me she hadn't heard the phone ring, who was this friend anyway? I said it was someone from work, I would eat later, she could just put it in the fridge.

I knew she hated that, it was one of her picky rules, that we all eat together. Ma cross is bad news, it makes her even more suspicious and vindictive. I wanted her happy, trusting me, at least until I had finished the projects.

The prawn was there, sitting at the kitchen table with her drawing things. She had spread crayons all over the pine surface, was busy colouring a flower blue. I asked her if she had brought her book bag home from school, said I had time to hear her read before I went out, if she'd like me to. I knew that would stop Ma moaning. She liked me to spend time with the prawn, to appear like I cared.

The prawn slid off her chair, dragging half the crayons with her. I bent to pick them up, told her to be quick. When she skipped back with her book I picked her up, pulled her onto my knee. That surprised both of them, I wasn't a great one for cuddles. I like to surprise people. She got out her book. It was one of those thin ones that are mainly pictures. Someone had covered it in sticky-back plastic and stuck a huge green sticker on the back. The prawn told me that was because it was a Stage Two book. I told her that was brilliant, Stage Two was very clever for her age. In the corner of my eye I was watching Ma gradually let her anger slip away as she stirred boiling water into the gravy mix.

I got the prawn to tell me about the story. I knew that was what you're meant to do, Ma had made me go with her to a talk at the school once. This poncey teacher had talked for ages, telling us lots of boring stuff about how children learn to read and what you should do to help them. As if anyone cared. If a child has a brain, they will learn to read. If they're as thick as pig shit, no amount of talking about stories will change that. But I knew Ma lapped it all up and she had been seriously annoyed with me lately. It was all about power struggles with Ma, letting her think she was in control. So I sat there. I listened to the prawn tell me about her boring book, then listened while she stumbled over the words, pointing at each one with a finger that was soggy from her chewing it all the time. Then I read it to her, except I added voices for all the animal characters and I added a different ending, so Mr. Snail peed in his pants. That got the prawn all giggly, she loved stupid things like that. When she laughed it made Ma smile too. Always worked. People are so predictable.

Well, after all that, I nearly missed my bus. I hope you are noticing how difficult all this was for me, how many obstacles people put in my way. But I didn't miss it, I saw it coming and ran to the stop, my bag bumping against my side, waving my arm frantically in the dark, hoping the driver would see me. He did. He pulled into the stop and waited for me to reach it before swooshing open the doors. Probably fancied me.

I climbed up the front steps, paid and swung my way down the aisle, giving him my best smile, laughing about how I'd nearly missed it. The bus rumbled off, down the main road and round the roundabout. I made sure I was sitting on the left hand side, behind a girl wearing a woolly hat. That way I would be able to see the Chinese restaurant when we drove past.

It was all blacked out, no lights on at all. There was tape across the door and a sign but it was way too small to read. Just a glimpse. Then it was behind us, we were going round the mini-roundabout and along the High Street.

I got off a couple of stops before where I wanted to. Like I said, I was careful. I didn't want anyone remembering me later, linking the bus with the project. I walked towards the road, glad it wasn't raining. Most people hated these early dark evenings but I for one found them very helpful. It meant most people stayed out of the way, if they had to go out they drove rather than walked. It was still early but very few people were around, a few school kids wandering home after clubs, the odd shopper who had run out of milk.

My feet were beginning to hurt by the time I turned into the target's road. Jim had driven me past the end of the road, but we hadn't actually come up it. I was a bit surprised by how posh it was. It was a modern build but the houses were quite pretty, someone had spent time planning them. They were all arranged around a central green area. Each house was different. Some were quite large, townhouses with garages beneath them, arranged over three different storeys. Some were tall and narrow, still on three levels but I guessed only a single room at each level. Some were flats, two front doors jammed next to each other, each with its own access.

I wanted one of the smaller houses. I had studied the map, there appeared to be a footpath down the side and I was guessing that it provided access to all the back gardens. I stood still for a moment, looking around. I wasn't at all sure that the kitchen would be on the ground floor. This was a very trendy new-build; turning the houses around was something that the planners might well have done, trying to make them a bit different, so people paid extra money for something that was still tiny, a glorified rabbit hutch.

It was lucky I did stand still. While I was there, gathering my thoughts, deciding what to do, a car swept into the close and stopped right outside my target house. A woman got out and a little girl. I guessed these were my targets.

I had some leaflets in my bag, they had been left in a stack on the counter at work for customers to pick up and I'd guessed they might come in handy. Something about a special offer on hairdryers if you spent a certain amount on hair products. Not really the sort of thing one gets posted through the door but who looks at that stuff anyway? I bet you don't. An advert is an advert, it goes straight in the bin without a second glance.

Anyway, those leaflets gave me the reason for being there that I needed. I dug them out of my bag, from their corner below my treasure bottle, approached the first house and stuffed one through the letterbox. I took my time, I didn't want the targets to still be outside when I reached their house, they might remember me.

I kept an eye on the targets while I worked. She was small, short blonde hair, big hips hidden by clever tailoring on her black suit. She carried a bag, I could tell it was heavy, probably stuffed full of papers she needed to look at later, when the kid was in bed. The kid looked tired. Her mouth was turned down and she carried a book bag and lunchbox with straight arms, like they were weighing her down, stretching her limbs. I guessed she'd been stuck in one of those after school clubs for a few hours, left in a boring room with a tetchy adult until her mum was free to collect her. She probably went there every day after school, lumped together with other kids who had parents who worked, left to amuse herself while someone who really wanted to be at home with her own kids watched them to make sure they were safe.

I had delivered five leaflets by the time they went inside. I stopped then, stood on the green, well away from the fake Victorian lamp at one end, and stared at the house. Lights were spreading throughout the three storeys as they went in, shed coats and bags, put on the kettle, used the toilet. I watched, guessing what they were doing. I figured it was safe enough to move to the back; with their lights on, the outside world would appear so black, they wouldn't see me even if they looked. The woman was beginning to pull curtains across some of the windows as I approached the pathway at the side.

The path actually ran beside the next door neighbour's house, but I had guessed correctly, it joined a walkway that ran behind all the houses on that side. There were high fences, long planks of wood nailed to cross-pieces. There were lots of gaps for peering through.

Each back garden had a gate with a straight path that led right to the back door. Some people had tried to alleviate the symmetry a bit, had made their path curved, planted bushes for it to meander around. You couldn't see into their windows, there was too much stuff in the way. But the target house had left her back garden alone. The path gave a nice clear view to the back door. There was a little patio with a covered barbecue, a few tidy plants each side of the path and lawns. Not enough room to play any ball games but a patch of semi-private land if you wanted some sun.

There were no shrubs to hide me but the kitchen, or what I assumed was the kitchen, was in darkness. I pressed the latch in the gate and it snapped open. I walked down the path, not rushing but not hesitant either. If by chance someone was watching, I would appear as if I was meant to be there, nothing suspicious about how I moved.

I didn't waste any time when I got to the door. I was already wearing plastic gloves, hair was secure under a hat, shoes were clean because it was dry weather. I reached out a hand, tried the handle. It was locked. Of course it was locked. The target had only just got home from work, she would hardly be likely to go and unlock the back door would she? It was worth a try but I hadn't really expected anything else.

I used the time to peer in through the window, pressing my face against the cold glass. I could see a line of light under the door opposite. I was staring into the kitchen. It was very clean, very modern. Stretches of dark granite, white doors, ceramic-tiled floor. The sort of kitchen you buy to show friends when they come in for a drink, not the sort of room you actually cook anything in. My guess was that the target worked full time, had money but no time. She would drink though, I was fairly sure about that, a glass of wine each evening, after the kid was in bed. I scanned the floor, no pet food bowls. That was expected but still worth checking.

I moved away. Nothing I could do tonight. I went back out the gate, shutting it behind me, retraced my steps to the bus stop. It was annoying but sometimes things went like that didn't they?

The bus was ages coming, I was frozen by the time it rolled up at the stop. I went and sat at the back, over the engine, warmed up my bum a bit. I was careful to keep my bag on my lap, didn't want my treasure to get warm and start evaporating too quickly.

The target was a problem. I had no way of knowing if she worked every day or not. If she did, then during the winter that back door possibly never got left unlocked. She would open it to put out rubbish, lock it again as soon as she was back inside. People who work need systems like that, things have to be routine or they forget, they don't have time to go checking things and that makes them very organised. This was a challenge and that made it more exciting. I wasn't the sort of person to just give up you see, I was serious about this. I wouldn't take stupid risks, if I decided it was impossible I would move on, I had other possibilities. But something about that woman with her tidy clothes, her tidy life, made me want to add a little something to her life. To show that she couldn't control everything, for all her smart suit and perfect kitchen, she didn't have everything covered.

I knew about mothers like her. They lived with guilt, it was part of who they were and it usually made them aggressive towards other people, especially people like me. I saw it all the time at work. When they were working, in the office or whatever, they would be worrying about their child, about how much time they should be spending with them, especially if the kid was ill or had a school play, something that didn't fit neatly into their allocated hours. Then, when they were at home, they worried about what they should be doing for work, that report that needed reading, the conference they wanted to attend, the team building drinks they would have to miss. It made them cross, easily irritated by anyone who got in their way, slowed them up. Their lives were made up of deadlines, rushing from one place to the next. They didn't have time to be polite, to notice the little people in society. What they were doing was important and difficult. I could tell when I saw her, the way she held herself, the quick pace she used to hurry the kid to the front door. There was, I decided, a certain pleasure in my project. I liked changing the odds a little, not being the 'little person' for a bit.

The locked door was a problem. I wasn't about to start breaking in, climbing through windows or blagging my way inside. That would just be stupid. I thought the best time would be at the weekend. On a nice sunny day, she was more likely to unlock the door, to let the kid play in the garden. There would be less of a schedule at the weekend too, if she was going to be careless about locking the door it would be when she had more time, when routine was less important. Yes, I decided that the first sunny Sunday I would try another visit, see what happened. If it was still locked then I would move on to someone else, but it was worth a try.

I glanced at the time, thought I might visit Jim. It would be better to go in his car next time, the walk had taken me longer than I'd expected. I would have to change buses to get to his but that was okay. I jumped off the bus in the town centre. It was next to a supermarket so I went inside, bought some whiskey and flowers. I wasn't sure what he would think of the flowers but probably he would think it was sweet, a strangely feminine thing to do. He liked having a female in his life, I could tell. He had probably grown up thinking that having a woman, being a family, was what was expected, that being single was something of a failure. Well, I was happy to fill the role, while he was being useful.

I went straight to his flat. There was a chance that he might be in the pub but I knew he'd cut down on the alcohol a bit, since he'd been ill. If he wasn't in I would go to the pub, but I hoped he would be. He would be surprised to see me. Like I said, I like to surprise people.

He was in and he was happy to see me, I knew he would be. There was something though, a bit off, like he wasn't saying something. We did the normal chat thing, had a drink, went to bed. Then afterwards he sat there, almost mentioning but not quite. I'm good at reading people, I could tell from his eyes, his slightly forced smile, the polite way he asked about how I'd been. I moved to sit on top of him, peered into his face. Perhaps he felt I'd neglected him when he was ill, something like that. I like to know things, sort out what's going on in people's heads.

"Why are you being all polite then? What's bugging you?"

His eyes slid to the side, looked at the floor, so I knew he was lying.

"Nothing. It's great to see you, really nice. I told you that."

"Yes, I know you did. But something's up, I can tell. Why are you annoyed with me? What have I done?"

"Nothing," he paused, like he was looking for the words, wondering how to say it. "It's just that, well– "

I watched him make his decision, decide to come right out with it.

"Did you take some money when you were here last? Some is missing from that last job I did. No one else has been here and I counted it right before I put it in the drawer and now some is missing." He stopped. He was worried about how I would react; this was a big thing he was accusing me of, well, not really accusing me, not wanting to think about it really, not wanting it to be true. But it had been bugging him, playing on his mind, he needed to know.

I had two options and I considered them both fast, in a mini-second. I could get angry, take the offensive, deny everything and be hurt he was accusing me. I might even cry, let him reassure me that he'd never really thought it, he was really sorry for saying anything, he must've made a mistake when he counted it. But I wasn't completely happy with that. Jim was thick but even dumb people are careful about money, they are surprisingly canny when it comes to their hard-earned cash. He might reassure me, comfort me, be all lovey-dovey and use it as a way in to another quick bonk. But after I'd gone, it would still play on his mind, he would still wonder. It would sit there, festering away in the nether regions of his brain, ready to pop up and bite me if something else raised his suspicions.

No, it was better to put this one to rest once and for all. I chose honesty. Well, my brand of honesty.

"Oh that. Yes, didn't I say? I needed some cash and you were puking your guts out so I couldn't exactly ask you at the time. I thought it would be okay, I thought we shared stuff. Just say if that's wrong.

"It's only a loan. You don't mind do you? I'll pay you back, when this tutoring starts to pay a bit better. In fact, I've got some cash on me, I can start to pay it back right now."

I made to move, off his lap, towards my bag. He stopped me, gripped my hips in his bear claws, told me that of course that was okay, he was happy to share his stuff with me. Only I should've asked first, he needed to keep track of things.

I snuggled right back, pressing my head into his chest. I whispered that I was no good with things like that, I was so lucky I had found him, had someone to help me out occasionally. I would pay him back in a few days, I wasn't a scrounge.

He lapped it all up, felt all big and strong and protective. Which was lucky really because my purse was completely empty, I needed him to drive me back to Ma's later.

***

Two weeks later and Saturday was sunny, one of those rare bright winter days. I had agreed with Jim that if the weather was nice we would spend the day together, perhaps go for a drive. He collected me from outside the chip shop and I was there nice and early, everything I needed for my project safely stowed in my bag. I jumped into his car and pulled down the sun visor. The sun was annoying, that bright low glare that hits you right in the eyes, makes driving difficult in the mornings and when it begins to set. His visor was old, everything about that car was old. It wobbled alarmingly in my hand, threatened to fall off if I tried to change the position.

I told Jim he needed to buy a new car. He said he planned to, was saving up to buy himself a van, something better suited to moving stuff around for his job. I hoped that wouldn't be until after I had finished my project, vans are more noticeable than old cars.

We drove out of town, to a pub in the middle of nowhere. It had a large car park which was full of people escaping from the city for the day. It sat on the main road, opposite a big wood and a cluster of farm buildings. We walked towards the pub. It was quite big, covered in black Tudor beams and white plaster. I assumed it was all fake but when we went inside, I saw the ceilings sagged and the fireplaces were massive, throwing out heat from the stack of logs.

We got a table in the corner and ordered our food from the bar. When it arrived it was really not too bad, lots of chips and heat and sugar, the sort of mass produced pub food that's easy to eat and fills you up. Afterwards Jim suggested a walk in the woods. I wasn't very keen, it looked cold and muddy. I didn't want to get my shoes dirty, I was hoping to continue my project later.

Instead, we went to a little town full of antique and charity shops. We wandered around, holding hands, looking like a couple. I caught Jim sneaking glances of us in the windows we passed, smiling at our image. We looked in some of the shops, wondered who would be stupid enough to pay those prices for a load of old junk, or who had houses big enough for the gilt statues and heavy oil paintings. I suggested that Jim could buy one to go in his flat, laughed that the weight of it would probably bring the wall down. He assured me it probably cost twice what his flat did and it wasn't to his taste anyway. He spoke in a posh voice, pretending he was used to being in shops like that, looking at antiques. He was happy, I could tell. He liked being part of a couple, doing what he considered normal people did. He didn't realise that no one is normal. Not really.

After a coffee, when the sun had set and the shadows were getting longer, we went back to the car. I snuggled into my coat, smiled at him, said it had been a lovely day, really special. I reached into my bag.

I had brought some of the prawn's school work with me. Every so often she brought home what she called homework. It was usually just a printed sheet with either addition to complete or lists of words to learn. Nothing difficult, the addition was really just counting and the words were easy, three-lettered words that all had the same ending so she was really only learning one letter each time. I didn't usually give it any attention, it wasn't an activity I had time to get involved with. But today I'd decided it would be useful to borrow them. I needed something 'school like' to flash in front of Jim. He was a builder, he wasn't going to know this was little kid's work, not something a tutor would use.

"I need to drop this round to one of my students. Would you mind? It'll only take a second. I promised to get it to them by today and I didn't want to have to cancel our day out."

He looked a bit fed up, like he wanted to go straight back to the flat, not start doing errands. I told him it would only take a minute, it was important. He didn't want to argue and spoil the day, I knew it would be okay. When we got back to the suburbs, to places I recognised, I directed him to the road next to the posh cul-de-sac.

I left him in the parked car and walked round the corner. It was dark now but only just, not quite that total blackness that hides everything but still too early for the moon to really shine, so everything was dim. It suited me. I kept my hood up, moved quickly, holding my bag close. I knew the chances of that door being open were slim, the chances of the kitchen being empty even more so. But that added to the excitement. If I got in, it would prove it was meant to be, the stars were on my side. If I didn't, I would move on to a different target. I hoped it would be though, there was something I didn't like about that woman. She was a bit smug.

The cul-de-sac was empty of people. Parked cars lined the little central green and garage doors were shut. No one had pulled their curtains yet, it was too early. I could see people in their houses, like watching a lit stage at the theatre as they played out their lives. Some had fires burning in their trendy little hearths, some were watching telly already, the mindless Saturday evening diet of singing competitions and emotional dramas.

I walked along the footpath, next to the houses. Wafts of cooking smells swept across me, onions and boiled meat. I hoped my target wasn't cooking, that would be a shame.

I could see as soon as I reached the corner that the kitchen light was on, could see the glow across the garden from the end of the pathway. I felt the anger rise up, forced it down, made myself keep calm, to go and have a proper look. I rounded the corner and a dog barked. It was a couple of doors down but it was cross, didn't like me being there. It shouted and snarled, leaping at the fence, warning me to keep away. Stupid animal, there was no way it could leap the fences between us.

I stopped outside the target house, peered through the gaps in the fence. The kitchen was brightly lit, the spot lights bouncing off the shiny granite, shining into the garden, making shadows under the barbecue, causing the fence slats to make long black lines across the path. I could see the blonde woman as she moved around preparing supper. She was in carefully casual clothes, soft wool mixes that moved with her, elegant even when relaxing. She was cutting bread, filling a jug with squash from a bottle, topping it up with water from the tap on the fridge, making tea in a tiny china pot designed for one, laying plates and knives on the table, cutting cheese and ham. It was tea time for two. There was no sign of the kid.

I watched for a moment, feeling defeated while the dog swore and snarled and told me to leave. I was about to too, was about to call it a night and go back to the car. Was just about to turn away when I heard the muffled sounds of a telephone ringing inside the house. The woman wiped her hands, turned, hurried out. The kitchen was empty.

I had about half a minute, maybe even less than that. I didn't waste a second of it. I whipped open the gate, ran down the path. The door the woman had left by to answer the phone was ajar, not properly closed, probably led to the hall, but I couldn't actually see her, couldn't even hear her. Not until I had opened the back door. Yes, it was open. The sunny day had been too much of an unexpected treat to ignore; either her or the kid had spent some time in the garden, she hadn't locked up the house yet. I was inside, pulling it to, to avoid a draught, to keep out the worst of the dog noise, but not bothering to shut it, unscrewing my treasure bottle while I walked, straight across to the teapot, about four steps, poured in the treasure even as I turned away, back out the way I'd come. I took a few seconds to close the door behind me, nice and quiet, I eased it shut. Then I hurried away from the window, didn't want her spotting me when she went back into the kitchen. The dog was flinging himself against the dividing fence, longing to rip me apart, but nothing he could do. I gave him the finger as I went through the gate. If I'd had treasure to waste I would've given him some of that as well.

I didn't stop. I walked with purpose, straight back to the green. As I left the cul-de-sac I glanced back. I could still hear that bloody dog, muffled by the houses now but still furious. The lights in the target house still shone out, giving an impression of wealth and comfort and safety. Never trust outward impressions I would say.

I went back to Jim, told him that I'd said I'd be quick. We were both smiling as we drove away.

***

Other People

She did not, of course, have any idea who the father was. Nor did she seem inclined to want to find out. Margaret was slightly surprised she had told her about the baby, she would have expected her to have a quick termination and continue with her life. She wondered if perhaps university was not turning out to be quite as much fun as Joanna had hoped, if the work was harder than she had expected, and so the pregnancy gave her an excuse to leave without losing face.

Whatever the reason, Joanna wrote and told Margaret that she was pregnant and asked her what she thought she should do. The question in itself was meaningless. Or rather, it was manipulative. Joanna knew that Margaret's faith did not allow for terminations of pregnancies, that she would see such a thing as murder of a baby. Once Margaret had offered this opinion, told Joanna she should keep the baby, or place it for adoption, there was some obligation for her to help. This would entail her continuing to house Joanna, despite her having left full time education.

So Joanna had moved back into Margaret's house. Margaret insisted on discussing the situation, laying down the ground rules, making the consequences for ignoring her very plain. She decided she would provide a home for Joanna while she was pregnant but only if the girl agreed to look after herself, to go for regular health checks, to eat sensibly and to avoid all alcohol and drugs.

It had been less clear what would happen after the baby was born. Margaret felt the baby would be safer if placed for adoption, however she was slightly uneasy about enforcing this, feeling that perhaps she did not have the right to insist on the separation of a mother and her child. Joanna had been adamant she wanted to keep the baby, raise her own child. Margaret suspected this was because Joanna did not want to have to pay her way in life, to get a job, move into a flat, be independent. Joanna knew that with no baby, Margaret's willingness to tolerate her parasitic lifestyle would be limited. However, if she kept the child, Margaret would never evict a mother and baby, Joanna would have a comfortable home for as long as she required one. It was difficult for Margaret to be sure of this though. She knew Joanna was clever, could twist words to win an argument, and yet she did not know if in this case she was genuine, if in this instance the girl really did want to keep the baby. Does someone have the right to wrench a baby from its mother, to insist it is put up for adoption? Margaret had felt she did not.

Joanna obeyed Margaret's rules. Her body swelled as the baby grew, she spent her days reading or walking for hours through shopping centres, sometimes taking things that appealed to her, simply because she could. She had never stolen things for the baby, she appeared to have no interest in the life growing inside of her, it was merely a means to an end. Margaret watched her health closely, attended clinic visits with her, provided nutritious meals. When the baby was bigger and the weight of carrying it was uncomfortable, Joanna considered getting rid of it, drinking some-thing dangerous or falling from a height. But she knew this would also involve risks to her own health, so decided to tolerate the aches and pains, the loose ligaments, the aching back, the sleepless nights while her baby turned and poked and dug into her. She had never wondered about the baby, who the individual inside of her would turn out to be.

When the baby was born, Margaret was there. She watched the waxy blue body as it was expelled from inside Joanna, saw the nurses rub it dry with a towel, watched the skin turn pink and heard that first mewing cry. Joanna was tired, turned away, saying she wanted to sleep. So Margaret took the tiny bundle from the nurses. She stared down into the indigo eyes of the baby, and gave her a finger to suckle on, felt the strong suction as the baby struggled to find food.

She had fallen in love. A love as deep and strong as it was possible to feel. This baby, this miniature girl, had no one else. She had been born to a mother who was incapable of love, a family bereft of grandparents and aunts and uncles. This baby was alone, as Margaret was alone. She decided then that Joanna could stay, that she would help her to raise this child, she would watch over her safety and give her all the love that she deserved. This baby would not turn out to be a copy of her mother. Margaret was sure nurturing would compensate for nature, that she could provide enough love and stability to offset any biological traits the baby may have inherited.

They named the baby Emily. Joanna only ever called her 'the prawn'.

Chapter Nine

My Story

The phone woke me. It was early, before seven in the morning, the sky outside still black, no light creeping around the edges of curtains to tell me it was morning. It could've been midnight for all I knew, felt like midnight as I reached for the phone, fumbled with the buttons trying to work out how to turn it off, to stop that irritating buzz, like a foghorn, on and on.

When I heard his voice I woke up pretty quick, I can tell you. I was already out of bed while he was speaking, turning on the light, reaching for my clothes. I told him not to do anything stupid, not to call the police until we had talked, I would come, right now, he must wait for me. Bloody hell! What a wake up!

I pulled on the same clothes I'd left in a heap on the floor the night before, pushed my feet into boots, grabbed a coat. There was no time for even a drink of water. I locked my door, thought about leaving a note for Ma, decided there wasn't time, left.

I waited outside the chip shop for about two seconds before his car came speeding along the main road, skidding to a stop in the layby. At this rate he'd be done for speeding if nothing else, I needed to calm him down. I'd barely even got in when he thrust it towards me, pushed the paper right in my face.

"Look," he demanded, "take a look at that. Pretty good likeness isn't it!"

I stared down at the face. It was a good likeness, he was right about that. It was also a big nuisance. But not one that couldn't be handled, I just needed to calm him down a bit first.

"We can talk about this," I said, "but where can we go? Everywhere's shut at this time."

Jim knew an all-night cafe near the centre of town, one frequented by builders and winos. We went there. He was too agitated to go back to his flat, was all for haring off straight to the nick. At least I persuaded him out of that, not to go until we'd had a talk first, he owed me that much.

The cafe was almost empty. A bloke in a damp coat and a dirty scarf sat near the window, a large plastic bag by his feet. He didn't so much as look up when we went in. I smelt him as much as saw him. I went to the counter, spoke to the man with greasy black hair and a stained white shirt, ordered a couple of coffees. They were plonked on the counter, big white mugs full of steaming coffee that had slopped over the side. I carried them over to the table where Jim sat, slumped against a wall. He kept rubbing his hands through his hair and sighing.

I slid into the booth opposite him and sipped the coffee. It was hot. That was about all you could say for it. Hot and wet. But that was something, given how the morning was going so far.

"Right," I said, "let's sort this out. Let me read it properly, what are they actually saying?" I took the paper from under his elbow and smoothed it out on the table.

They weren't saying much at all, as it happens. There had been a suspicious death (no cause given) of a young mother. Police wanted to talk to a possible 'witness' (which meant suspect) who had been seen in the area. There was a brief description and then a photo-fit picture (which was actually surprisingly good.)

"The car's wrong," I said.

"Yeah, I know, but that's not the point is it?" said Jim. He picked up his mug, burnt his lip, put it down again with a scowl. "I went for a smoke, didn't I. You know I don't like to smoke in the car, so I got out, probably wandered down the road a bit, was probably leaning on this blue car when the person saw me. They must've thought it was mine." He leaned forwards. "But that's not the point. The point is it's me. They think I had something to do with this. I'm a suspect. I need to go and sort it out, before they come for me. I know how these things work, once they come for you that's it, no one ever really believes you're innocent. It'll be all over the news, someone is 'helping them with their enquiries'. Everyone knows what that means, it means they've got the tosser who did it."

He sat back, misery all over his face, even the way he sat was dejected, defeated. He'd never been in any trouble before, had been brought up to be suspicious of the police but to respect their authority, to obey their rules. This was a huge shock to him. I could probably use that to my advantage. I leaned forwards, looked him in the eye.

"Okay, look, this is going to sound bad but I have to ask, don't I. After all, we haven't known each other that long, you might not be who I think you are. But I love you and I'll stick with you whatever the answer is. Just tell me the truth okay? Did you do it?"

He sat back like I'd slapped him, stared at me with incredulous eyes.

"No, no, how could you think that? I'm not a weirdo, I wouldn't do something like that. Surely you can't think…"

"No," I said, quick to reassure him, "of course I don't. But I had to ask didn't I? I don't want to end up one of those dumb bitches you see on the news who claims they knew nothing while their partner is off being a perv. No one ever believes they didn't know, not really. I had to check, didn't I?" I gave him my best smile. "Well, that's okay then, we don't have a problem. I don't know what you're worried about, just forget it."

"What I'm worried about is this," he said, throwing the newspaper back in my face. "What I'm worried about is having my face plastered across the country as a possible psycho."

I shrugged. "That's nothing," I said. "People never recognise anyone from those pictures. The fact that it looks like you is just proof that it can't have been you."

"Yes, but it was me, wasn't it? I was there at that time, leaning against that car."

"But no one else knows that," I said. "Only I know, and I would never dob you in to the police." I sat back in my seat, took another sip of the coffee, decided it was cooler now, drank a few mouthfuls.

"Look, I don't know why you're in such a state. If anyone links you with the photo, just laugh, make a joke of it. No one is seriously going to suspect you. You can tell everyone we were out for the day, down in that little town, didn't get back until nearly midnight. I'll vouch for you if they check, say we stayed there a bit longer than we did. So, it can't be you, can it?

"Besides, you can't go to the police. You want them to catch whoever did it, don't you?"

He nodded slowly, I could tell this was not a thought that had occurred before. He'd only been worried about himself, no thought for the poor woman who'd died. Like I said before, people are just selfish. But I let it pass, continued my argument.

"So, if you go to the police, you'll become their main suspect, won't you?"

"Yeah, but it wasn't me," he said, not quite following my point. "If I turn myself in they can 'eliminate me from their enquiries', or whatever the phrase is."

"Yeah, but how long will that take? They'll probably lock you up while they do it," I told him, "and then they'll have to check everything, ask around, find out what kind of a bloke you are. They won't just take my word for it, they'll need to talk to everyone you know, probably contact your customers, your family, everyone. All that takes time. Then they'll let you go, realise they have the wrong bloke. But that will have taken a lot of time. While they're doing all that they won't be looking for the real perv will they? The bloke who actually did it will be walking free. No, much better to keep your head down, laugh it off if anyone else mentions it."

I reached across and took his hand. "You are daft to worry so much," I said.

He grinned; I could tell he was taking it all in, beginning to feel a bit better. He relaxed back into the seat, drank his coffee, wiped his mouth with the back of his hand.

"Yeah, maybe you're right," he said, "thanks". He smiled. "You're good for me you know, I wasn't thinking too clearly for a minute there."

I grinned back. "That's okay, I've got your back you know, I'll always be here for you."

I got up, I'd had enough of this.

"Come on, you can drop me off on your way back. I've just about got time to have a shower and get up properly before I need to go to work."

He held me close as we walked back to the car, his arm wrapped right round me, his chin resting on my head. We moved slowly, Siamese twins who couldn't get enough of each other. That was the good thing about being with someone a bit dim. Being in charge is usually easy.

***

Other People

Raising Emily had been a minefield involving forward planning and strategy. Neither woman trusted the other, both had their own agenda. Margaret tried to ensure the baby had as much direct contact with her mother as she could enforce. Joanna contrived to do the minimum of mothering necessary for Margaret to allow her

121

to stay. Margaret produced sufficient evidence that feeding a baby also benefited the mother, as it helped her body to return to its pre-pregnant shape. Joanna therefore agreed to feed the baby, during the day, for three months. Margaret gave Emily bottles at night. The baby slept in Margaret's room as she was afraid it would be easy for Joanna to manufacture a cot death.

When the three months finished, Margaret told Joanna she needed to have a job. She did not particularly care about being paid rent, but she felt it would be good for Joanna to have paid employment, to have a purpose, a reason each day to get out of bed. She could also contribute towards the baby's costs. Joanna then had a succession of jobs. When Joanna was at work, she was mostly efficient, charming and intelligent. If she was in a bad mood, she caused tensions amongst her work colleagues. Sometimes she simply failed to arrive for work. Most employers fired her after a few months. This never bothered Joanna, who would apply for a new position. If it was a male conducting the interviews, she was rarely turned down. Getting jobs was easier than keeping them.

As the years passed, the two women lived alongside each other fairly harmoniously. Margaret had learnt to be careful. If she wanted to keep something away from Joanna she locked it in a cupboard in her room. She tried to ensure that drugs and stolen items were never brought into the house. Her main priority was Emily, giving her a stable home, a happy upbringing. It was harder when Joanna was living there, she needed to be alert, guard the child against her mother's influence whilst also ensuring enough contact so that there was a bond there, so she felt loved by her mother. It was easier after Joanna left, after that day when every-thing changed. The day when Margaret discovered how completely she had failed.

***

You might think this was bit of a setback, that I would stop my project for a bit. But that would be letting the police witch get ahead, wouldn't it? That would be relinquishing my position at the front of the race. No, if anything, it spurred me on, made me start thinking about the next target.

I did consider not using Jim for transport, but I decided that it would be okay. I could try and encourage him to stay in the car this time, to be a bit more subtle. The police didn't actually have *his* car, they had linked him to the wrong one, so I figured his wheels were still available to me. Silly to stop using them for no reason, it was easier if I went by car. Of course, a better option would be if I drove myself. I decided that this was the way forward. I would ask Jim if I could borrow the car. I was pretty sure he would refuse, he was a bit precious about it, whined on about it being the only way he could get to his jobs, he couldn't risk anything happening to it, it wasn't insured for other drivers. Excuses like that. I would try, but he might be stubborn so I would have a back-up plan. I could easily get something from work.

I chose a house that was smaller for my next target. It was on an estate, ex-council. The estate wasn't huge, a few houses built on land behind the church, just off the High Street. It would've been easy to take the bus but I fancied a bit of comfort. The houses were terraced, mine was fourth from the end and it backed onto the church graveyard. There was a pathway at the back, for access to the gardens, and there was a block of garages at the end of each terrace. I wasn't sure if every house owned one or not, but I figured parking was unlikely to be a problem. If there were loads of cars that wasn't necessarily bad, it helped to hide mine a bit.

I ate dinner with Ma and the prawn, told her I would be going out later, was meeting a friend at the pub. The evenings were beginning to get dark a bit later by now, so there was no point in starting my project too early. That was another reason for getting on with it though. By the time the clocks moved and it was dark and late at the same time, people would start locking their doors, which would ruin everything. I didn't feel like continuing after the summer, not now I'd started. The police witch would never spot a pattern unless it all happened at about the same time. Then I could sit back, let her wallow in confusion, mark it up to an unsolved crime, stay unpromoted for a bit longer.

I met Jim about seven. He had offered to pick me up but I thought it would be better to get a bus, meet him in the pub. He would've gone there straight after work – builders don't exactly work long hours – and I knew he'd have drunk a few before I arrived. It saved me having to listen to his boring chat for a bit, got him nicely relaxed before I got there.

He was standing in a huddle of other workers when I arrived, they were laughing, holding their drinks in their fat hands, a group of men in stained clothes with dusty hair, all waiting for someone else to cough up for the next round. Not exactly an attractive bunch, but a girl does what she has to. He moved away from the group when he saw me. He'd given up trying to introduce me to his mates long ago. At first he had wanted me to meet everyone, he had this idea that because we were a couple I would want to be part of his social group too. I don't do that. I wasn't actually too keen on Jim maintaining these friendships but I couldn't be there all the time, sometimes he slipped back into chatting with them. He knew I didn't like it though. I think he assumed it was a class thing, the price he had to pay for going with a posh bird. I didn't tell him otherwise. It wouldn't have mattered how wealthy his mates were, they were in the way.

He gave me a beery kiss, asked me what I was drinking. It didn't matter really as I was going to be tipping it all away, but I told him

G and T. He seemed to think that was a classy drink. We moved to a table, I sat in the corner, where I could tip my drink onto the carpet when he wasn't looking. I didn't have long, wanted to get on with my project, I didn't want the smell or fuzz that alcohol would provide. But I wanted him nicely sozzled, as quick as possible.

I listened to his day, mind-numbing stories about electricians doing first fixes, supplies delivered late, customers haggling over prices. I managed to not yawn, to smile at him, look enthralled. Then I suggested he might be over the limit, it would be nice to go back to his place but perhaps I should drive? That sobered him up pretty fast. He was adamant, there was no sharing of his precious car, he hadn't drunk enough to not be able to drive. Annoying.

We went back to his place, I said I would cook him dinner. While he was in the loo, which always took him ages, he had issues there I think, I prepared some drinks. I had brought some decent red wine with me (untampered with, in case you're wondering, this was not a time to be using my treasure) and I poured it into dusty glasses that I found in a kitchen cupboard. I removed enough clothing to look enticing, added a couple of pills to his glass (that doesn't count as 'tampering',) and settled back on his sofa bed.

I had got the pills at work. I'd talked to the pharmacist, explained the trouble I was having sleeping, asked for something to help. She'd tried to fob me off with herbal shit, something that wouldn't make any difference to a baby. I wasn't having that, told her I'd tried them before, they made no difference. She was unhelpful about giving me anything on prescription and there was no way I could borrow anything, they were fussy about that, all kinds of security checks on what went in and out. So I went to the GP at lunch time, told them it was emergency, I was having heart pains. When I was in there I said that it was probably because I couldn't sleep, explained how I hadn't slept for weeks now. I pointed to my back for the pain, like I thought that was where you would feel them. The GP thought I was stupid but that didn't matter. I left the surgery with a prescription and the promise of an appointment at the hospital. The appointment wouldn't come for weeks, most people died waiting for those, but who cares? I had my piece of paper, collected my pills from the nerd with the white coat. They were now in Jim's drink, crushed between two teaspoons and stirred until dissolved. Which wasn't exactly what it said to do on the packet but I'd modified the dose so they needed a bit of help.

Jim looked surprised when he finally emerged from his loo. He was a beer man, I'd never seen him drink wine before. I said I'd bought it specially, I wanted to give him something nice. He was too polite to refuse. As I have told you many times, always a mistake. I watched him sort of brace himself to drink it, then take big swallows to down it quickly. I've no idea what it tasted like. I moved on to him right after he'd drunk some, didn't want him noticing that mine was untouched.

I had to wait about twenty minutes for him to get drowsy. An age. Then I said I needed the toilet, disappeared with my bag for a minute. By the time I was dressed and ready to go, he was snoring. I figured the bubbles from his beer would've helped, that and him not eating anything for hours. I found his keys in the pocket of his trousers. Car and front door, I would need both. I wasn't sure how long I had, not that it would really matter if he woke while I was gone, I'd just make some excuse and take some clothes off, he wouldn't be cross for long.

I went to where we'd left the car, jammed between a van and an old BMW down the road a bit from his front door. Parking at that flat was always a nightmare. I stalled it twice before I got it going, nearly clipped the bumper, eventually got moving.

It was odd driving again, I hadn't done it for ages. I had to sort of talk myself through everything – "mirror, signal, manoeuvre, handbrake off, clutch down, easy on the accelerator". I drove slowly, leaving big gaps between me and the other cars, lots of time to react if I had to stop at lights or junctions. I didn't hit anything and only stalled twice. When I arrived at the target road I found a space round the corner. I went for a big space, my parking wasn't up to much. I pulled out my bag, hurried to the house. I was much later than I had hoped to be, I thought that locking back doors would be starting to occur to a few people by now.

I found the path to the back gardens. It was hidden behind a gate near some homes for old people, looked like the entrance to a garden and I missed it at first, had to go back to it. The path itself was overgrown, brambles reaching out to snag my coat, the tarmac bumpy from roots pushing up. I felt the council could've maintained it better, it showed neglect. Typical really, no one cares about standards anymore. How was a kid supposed to push his bike along that without getting his eyes scratched out? I would've written and complained if I'd lived there.

I found the house easily enough. There was a low fence, I could've jumped it if the gate had been locked. There was a light on upstairs, but, the downstairs window, what I assumed was the kitchen, was black. I didn't pause, I was used to this now and speed was always better than too much caution. I went down the path, passed the little shed on my left. The door was open and a wheel poked out, as if watching the garden. I knew he'd have a bike, it was that sort of place. Lots of flat paths for kids to cycle on after school, all very safe with no fast cars, overlooked by lots of friendly neighbours. A real community.

The kitchen door was a patio one, the sort you have to slide open. I peered in, checked I was clear of dogs, then tested the handle. It was a bit stiff but not locked. When it was open I looked down at the mechanism and it looked like it was broken, maybe they never locked it. Some people were too complacent. I walked into the kitchen. There was a round table with four chairs. The remains of dinner were still there, a couple of dirty glasses, a knife, a splodge of tomato sauce. I think they had eaten sausages, there was that heavy fatty smell you get when you fry them, the kind that clings to your hair and clothes and makes you smell like a sausage yourself until you shower and change.

I was about to go to the fridge, to check for something suitable for my treasure, when the door to the hall opened.

A woman opened the door, switched on the light and stopped. She gave a little gasp, like I had made her jump, then stood there, eyes wide, a split second while she decided whether to scream or run. I smiled into that second and moved forwards with confidence.

"Oh, hello, you made me jump! I'm Angie, from number eight."

She frowned, but the screaming never happened. She just looked suspicious, running was still a possibility.

"Number eight?" she repeated. "You mean where Mrs Ardos lives?"

"Yes, that's right," I said, relieved she was helping, "I'm her niece. Sorry to appear in your kitchen like this but I did ring the front door and no one answered so I tried the back."

"No, the bell's broken." (Now that was a bit of luck!) "What do you want? Why are you in my kitchen?"

She was less worried now but still not trusting, still watchful.

"Well, aunty asked me to give you—" I started to rummage through my bag. I wasn't sure what I had that I could have given her. There was my treasure bottle of course, and Jim's keys. And some money, quite a lot of it. I pulled out a couple of twenties, held them towards her, "this money. She found it outside your house earlier. She said I shouldn't just post it through the letterbox, as it was so much, I should actually give it to you, you would be missing it. When I got to the back I saw your door was open a bit, so I thought I'd put it on the table for you. Sorry, did I give you a fright?"

The suspicion had gone but she was still looking confused, like she didn't really understand.

"I don't think it's mine," she started to say, "I haven't lost any money."

"Oh well, I'll take it back to aunty then," I said, and stuffed it back in my bag. "She can always take it to the police tomorrow, you know what old people are like."

"She's not that old," the woman was saying but I didn't care. She wasn't going to scream or call the police, it was time I left. I told her it was lovely to meet her as I walked back to the door, slid it open and went into the garden. I told her she should get the door looked at, apologised again for scaring her and left, straight up the path, through the gate, along the passage. I don't know if she watched me or not. I wasn't going to hang around to find out. Back to the car and out of there as fast as I could.

I drove back to Jim's, swearing and kicking the floor of the car. Such bad luck. I really hadn't had any options, there was nowhere I could've poured my treasure with her there watching.

When I got back to the flat, Jim was still snoring. That suited me just fine. I poured the remains of the wine down his sink, returned his keys to his pocket and left. I pulled the front door shut behind me and stomped off to the bus stop. Another wasted evening.

Chapter Ten

Other People

Emily felt as if she was living in a dream, only her pregnancy was real. She constantly felt sick, but she didn't know whether that was due to her changing body or because she carried a huge sense of dread. There was so much about her childhood she had never faced, had just left buried in her past. It was like things were connected to the child Emily, but not her, the successful young wife, the recently qualified accountant.

She spent the week behaving as if everything was normal, the same. Each morning she had risen with the alarm, showered and dressed in her suit, rushing to catch the train, hoping for a seat so she could apply her make-up in relative ease. Getting out of bed early had never been her strong point.

Even in the office, that climate controlled world of calculations, discussions and superficial conversation, her mind focussed continually on her decision. Should she keep the baby? How much of her past should she now reveal to Josh? Did she even want a baby? The last question was the hardest. Emily had always known that she would not have children, that she might give birth to another Joanna, which was best avoided. She never allowed herself to consider whether she would like to be a mother, to raise a child of her own.

Emily was good at her job. After graduating with a good degree, she joined one of the big London firms and started her accountancy training. She found she enjoyed working in the city, the smart clothes, the mix of people, the excitement of meeting deadlines. Her colleagues were all graduates, all intelligent, all ambitious. The conversation was interesting and the humour was clever. Sometimes her hours were very long, especially near a client's year end, when accounts had to be prepared and checked before the partner could sign them. In the first few months, Emily had enjoyed those periods, when they worked around the clock, a whole team of intelligent people working to meet a deadline. Later, when the novelty of long hours had worn off, never seeing the house in daylight, rarely seeing Josh, Emily found the financial compensation was sufficient. She was ambitious, she knew the path she hoped her career would take, had set herself targets for when she would be joining senior management, for when she could expect to be made a partner.

There had never been much money in her childhood. Emily's memories were vague before the age of about eight. She recalled snippets, flashes of things, like the pages of a book. They were mainly the events that had been photographed or were constantly discussed, things that were never forgotten. She did remember a few things from earlier, activities with Joanna, like being pushed daringly high on a swing or dashing across a road before it was clear. Her days at infant school were more of a blur, the faces of some friends, school outings, a couple of teachers. She recalled almost nothing about the house they had lived in, just the stars on her ceiling which had shone when the light was turned out.

Her memories of junior school were clearer. Sometimes her friends would ask why her mother was so old, or think that Margaret was her grandmother. She would simply tell them her real mother had died, and Margaret was looking after her. Occasionally someone would press for more information, children are less restricted by social norms, if they had a question, they asked. But Emily was always vague, never gave much information. The facts seemed vague in her own mind, they were more things she had been told, rather than events she actually recalled.

In her childhood, she had called Margaret "Ma," copied from Joanna. When she was older, at university, she had started to call her by her name. She wasn't really sure why, she thought of her as a mother, but she had another mother, Joanna. It was bit of a muddle. Much of her upbringing was a muddle when she tried to evaluate it, but in reality, what she had experienced, was simple. Margaret was her mother, had done everything that mother's did and loved her as much as any mother loved. The fact that she also had this other mother, the shady spectre of Joanna, did not overly trouble her. Not unless she thought about it, which she rarely did.

She had enjoyed senior school. Lots of late night discussions when friends stayed over, arguing with Margaret about how much homework she needed to do. She wanted to have ballet lessons, like all her friends, but they were too expensive. Instead she played sports for the school. She was small but strong and brave, and she quickly found a place on the hockey team. There was a certain thrill to rushing towards an opponent who was twice your size and armed with a hockey stick, to tackle the ball from them, and hurtle towards the goal. Her shins and knuckles were always bruised and she rarely wore skirts. Margaret would come to watch the games, cheering on the side-lines, shouting abuse at the referee. Emily used to pretend she didn't know her, she was much too embarrassing.

She was relatively old before she had her first boyfriend. At school she had had crushes on various boys, the first being Jeffrey.

Jeffrey had the bluest eyes you have ever seen and floppy blonde hair. He caught the same bus to school and she sat near the front, so he would notice her when he got on every morning. She would comb her hair, and apply eyeliner that she had smuggled out of the house, and then sit there, holding a pose that she had practised in the reflection of the window. She thought that if she looked sad and moody (like the heroines in the books she devoured each night by the light of a torch under the covers) then Jeffrey would feel sorry for her. He would feel compelled to ask why she was sad, and do his best to make her happy. Jeffrey was three years older than Emily. He climbed aboard the bus with his mates and shouted his way to the back seat. He remained completely unaware of her existence.

Her first relationship had been during the first year of university. His name was Edward. Margaret had been horrified, and rushed to discuss it with her. Edward was a lecturer.

Emily had been attracted to him as soon as he entered the lecture theatre. As were all the other females in the room. He was tall and athletic, and his lectures were incredibly boring. There was always a long line of girls outside his room, seeking extra tutorials. Emily was one of them. But there was something about her, her innocence perhaps, or her wicked sense of humour, that Edward noticed. They started their affair in her second term. Emily found herself completely in love. She thought of nothing but Edward, what he would like, what she could buy for him, when she could meet his family. They spent all their free time together, walking on the hills surrounding the city, staying in small hotel rooms at the weekend. When they were apart they texted each other almost constantly.

The relationship was a secret, only Margaret and Emily's closest friends from school knew. Margaret was very torn, feeling privileged that the girl should still confide in her and worried as to how to advise her without breaking that trust. She prayed a lot.

After the Easter break, Emily knew Edward was the only man she would ever love. She was sure he felt the same and began to plan their engagement, how they would tell their friends, where they would live. She began to peer into jewellery shop windows, choosing which ring she would like. Nothing else mattered, Edward was the pinnacle of her life. She decided she would leave university. She didn't have to. At the end of that term, Edward left. He wrote

Emily a short note, explaining he was moving to a new university and thanking her for their time together.

Emily was heartbroken, Margaret was relieved. The older woman had never met the lecturer, but there was something in Emily's descriptions of him that reminded her of Joanna. She wondered if the girl was attracted to a personality she recognised, or if it was a latent need for a father figure. It was a strange summer. Emily cried for a couple of weeks and spent long hours phoning her friends. Margaret made her chocolate cakes and tried to not show how happy she was.

There were a couple of brief flirtations after that, boys who caught her eye in the university bar or at clubs, friends of friends who were sent on awkward dates with her. Then, in her final year, she met Josh.

After two years, they realised they couldn't imagine a future without each other. They bought a tiny house near enough to walk to the station, and married a year later. Their life was happy and uncomplicated. They were saving up for new furniture and to extend the kitchen, which was tiny. Both worked hard all week and spent the weekends either playing sports or going out for the day. It was a comfortable life, easy, meandering along together. Until now. Now Emily was possibly about to drop a bomb on that stability. She hoped it would survive.

***

The following Saturday, Emily drove to Margaret's house. It had been a difficult week and Josh noticed her tension, even offering to forgo football that week if she wanted him to stay with her, help with housework or something. He was relieved when she had refused, and had escaped to the safety of bloke talk and exercise on the muddy pitch.

She had still not mentioned anything to Josh, she felt she needed to sort out her own feelings before she began to cope with his. She also needed to decide how much to tell him. While she was just his wife, someone who he had known and come to love, she felt her past didn't matter. She had never, as far as she could recall, ever actually lied to him. But she had certainly misled him. She had always been vague about details. He knew she was adopted and had heard from others that her biological mother was dead. She never thought it necessary to correct him. He liked Margaret, they enjoyed each other's company and he accepted that she had raised Emily from birth. He had asked why Emily chose to call her Margaret, never 'Mum' and Emily just said she always knew Margaret wasn't her real mother and that was what Margaret wanted to be called. He hadn't queried her answer. People don't, they generally accept what they are told.

Emily herself never asked any questions about her mother. When it happened, she was too young, she had picked up the tensions, known that Margaret was upset, distraught, but she had known very few facts. The television had been used to watch children's programmes, never the news. Margaret protected her, kept her away from the media, tried to make life normal. She remembered babysitters sometimes being there when she got home from school, and realised when she was older, that those must have been the times when Margaret was at the trial.

Soon afterwards they moved house, to an area where they could be anonymous, and Margaret had adopted Emily. She had taken the surname Smith. When she married Josh, who was also a Smith, she had laughed that she was just gaining more relatives but not changing her name. He had not commented on her lack of relatives, knowing only that she was adopted. He asked her once if she wanted to find her biological parents and she told him, curtly, no. He never asked again, realising this was a subject that she found painful.

But now that it affected him, now her elusive genes were to be combined with his to create a whole new human being, would he raise the question again? Would he now, for his own interests, want to know something of her history? If so, should she reveal the truth – that actually she was fully aware of who her mother was, she just chose to have no contact because she was serving time for multiple murders?

That would be a great conversation: "Do you want the good news or the bad news? The good news is that I'm pregnant, you can have the child I said we'd never have. The bad news is that actually my mother isn't dead, she's a serial killer."

She had started to look once, typed her mother's name into Google, decided to find out as many details as she could. But then she stopped, shut down the computer before anything appeared. She decided she knew enough. She knew the basic facts, that her mother killed people using a poison she had stolen during her university days. She knew people called her a psychopath, that there seemed to be no reason for her choice of victims. She knew how the police had followed her trail until they caught her, and believed she would have killed again if not caught. She knew what her mother had done. But not why.

Nor did she really understand who her mother was. She could not equate the person she heard described by others with the fun-loving, warm individual who she remembered playing with her when she was young. The person she loved. She had never asked Margaret. She felt her own feelings were too fragile. She didn't think she could cope with finding out that her mother had never loved her in return.

***

My Story

It was a Saturday morning and I had met Jim for breakfast. It was rare for us both to have time off at the weekend, so he was keen that we should meet. I didn't mind too much, I had a plan.

You see, the project had had too many setbacks lately. It was more effort than I'd hoped it would be and I felt I deserved a little treat, a bigger prize. The idea occurred to me in the shower. There I was, letting the water drip over me, trying to ignore the cold bathroom, when I had my brainwave. It was time to crank up the excitement a notch, make people really notice. My next target needed to be someone a bit more prominent, someone important, someone whose demise would really put pressure on the police witch. I decided the head teacher fitted the bill nicely.

Obviously his address wasn't on the sheet I had, that was only parents. I thought it might be difficult to find out where he lived, thought I might have to be slightly inventive. But do you know, it was easy as pie! Honestly, people are so careless, I could hardly believe my luck. I decided to look in the easy places first, so after my shower I dug out the telephone directory. Do they still have them? Maybe not in this new age of computers, but they did back then. You know, those big fat books that list everyone's name, address and telephone number. The ones that are too big to store anywhere convenient and are a right pain to get rid of when they're out of date. I only had the local one, he wasn't listed in there, but they kept a stash of them at the library, upstairs in that work room. They had ones for all the local areas. People are so helpful sometimes.

I knew his names of course, and I knew he must live not too far from the school. I figured that he wouldn't drive more than about forty minutes each morning. I ploughed through each directory in turn, going straight to the 'g' pages and searching for Gadsdon, it wasn't exactly a common name. There was just one. I scribbled down the address and left. I realised of course that it might not be the same one, I would've expected a head teacher to be ex-directory, to try and avoid fussy parents calling him at home. But perhaps he was one of those lefty teachers who thought everyone was equal and he should be the same as everyone else. Perhaps he was lonely and hoped someone would phone him. Well, he was about to get a visit.

So, here I was, eating breakfast with Jim. We were in a coffee shop, run by the baker's shop next door. It was slightly before all those ubiquitous coffee shops arrived, the ones that litter town centres today. It was busy though, full of couples taking a break from their weekly shop, teenagers who looked like they hadn't been to bed yet and a couple of mothers with noisy kids.

I picked a bacon roll from the chilled counter, Jim took two. He would get fat if he wasn't careful. We stood in line, looking for all the world like a young couple in love. Jim was happy, he loved things like this, doing normal things in public with a woman at his side. That was good, I wanted him to drive me to Mr Gadsdon's house afterwards, just for a peek, to check I had the correct address.

We handed in our rolls for heating and took our drinks over to a table at the back of the cafe but not too near the toilet and as far away from the noisy kids as we could manage. We sat opposite each other and I slid my knees forwards so they touched his, it seemed affectionate. I asked him about his week and he started to drone on about customers and builders and the cost of materials even with a trade discount. I thought about my project.

I was fairly sure the address I had would be correct, it was such an unusual name and it even had the initial A. I figured the odds were on my side. I would go there now, after breakfast and have a look. I wasn't sure what I would find but felt that the type of area, the car in the driveway, would all give me some indication of whether or not it was the right house. If it wasn't, if some elusive, unconnected, Mr Gadsdon lived there, I thought I might still include it in my project. It would still be linked by the police witch; she would clock the name and assume that someone had made a mistake but that the project was all linked to the school.

Jim was looking at me and I realised he was expecting a reply.

"Sorry, I was miles away, what did you say?"

"What do you want to do after this? Shops or flat?"

That was it with Jim, no imagination. It was Saturday so people either stayed home or went shopping. A choice of two. He was so lucky to have me, have a bit of variety in his life.

"Naw, let's do something different, I like hearing you talk," I lied. "Why don't we go for a drive? It's a nice day, we can drive for a bit, maybe have a stroll. We can go to the flat after."

Of course, if I'd had any idea of what would be waiting for us at the flat I'd have chosen differently. But I didn't. We planned our day.

I had looked up the Gadsdon address on the map. It was in a little town a short drive away. I'd been there before, years ago. There was a very old church and a few naff shops and some expensive houses. I figured being a head teacher paid well. I told Jim it was a nice place to visit, we could wander about, look at the church, stuff like that. He stared at me like I was bonkers.

"A church. You want to look in a church?"

"Not because it's a church, stupid, because it's old. Really old, has Norman arches and stuff. We don't have to go inside if you don't want to, we can just look at the outside, see what's there. It's the sort of thing that teachers need to know about, in case we need it for a project." That made me a smile a bit, it was almost true.

The mention of anything to do with teaching changed his attitude, it always did. I think he thought teachers knew everything about everything and that made me slightly better than him, educated. He was, I think, worried that one day I might notice he was a thick git and leave him for someone more interesting. So he instantly decided that an old church might be interesting after all, the sort of thing he might like to spend his day off looking at.

He wanted to go back to the flat first, use the loo and change into smarter clothes. I was worried he would change his mind, so I told him the weather forecast wasn't great, it was better to get going straight away. In hindsight, it probably wouldn't have made any difference even if we had gone back, but you never know. It might have changed everything. We didn't though. We finished our sandwiches and Jim collected the dirty crockery and took the tray to the table next to the counter. He's such an old woman sometimes, the staff are paid to do the clearing up.

When we got to the town it was busy. I knew the address I wanted was near the church, so I told Jim to head for there. The road was a one-way system, lots of cars driving badly, white vans pushing out at junctions. The streets were lined with parked cars and there was a pay and display car park near the shops. The church had its own parking, along an old wall with a big sign, saying parking was reserved for people visiting the church. I told Jim that was us and he pulled in, between a battered red car and a little sports car. I opened my door too fast and bashed the coupe next to us. Jim didn't notice and I didn't say anything, even though I noticed a dent in the shiny paint work. I hoped the driver wouldn't get back before us and make a fuss.

We took the path that wound its way into the churchyard. There were trees growing along its length and the roots had pushed up, making the path uneven. It was hard walking in stilettos and I began to wish I'd worn something better for walking in. That was Jim's fault, I had worn them to look nice, so he would enjoy being with me. I clung onto his arm and pretended I was helpless, so he could be the sensible one, help him to get over the teacher stigma.

We passed a couple of people who were walking to town, the church path led to a footpath. Jim was asking which of the church arches were Norman. I told him they all were and suggested we went back into town. I could tell he was bored, impatient to get back to the flat, and I wasn't sure how to get him to the road where Mr. Gadsdon lived, not without him getting suspicious. I needed a reason for us to go there, something that Jim would believe, and I was a bit stumped to be honest. I could start another row, walk off in a huff or something, go there on my own. But I wasn't too sure he would wait for me and I didn't know what the buses were like from here.

We wandered through the High Street, not that it was much of a High Street, more a road with a few shops and estate agents on it. That's when I had the idea.

We were just looking in the estate agent's windows, checking out the price of houses we would never be able to afford, like you do, when I saw one which was in the road I was interested in. It was a big detached thing, looked very well done up from the photos, with a massive price tag to match. I pointed it out to Jim.

"Blimey, look at that, how the other half do live!"

"Yeah," he said, sounding bored, "I sometimes get to do work in places like that. Never get to sit on the sofas though."

"Hey, let's go round it," I said. I decided that if we could look around it, it would be a good excuse to look at the road. If all the houses were the same, I might even learn some security details, the best way to get into the Gadsdon house. I leant into him, chivvying him along with the physical contact. "Let's pretend we're interested in buying it, say we want to look round. If it's empty we might have a bit of fun in there, you never know…"

He looked down at me, starting to smile. I could tell the idea appealed.

"Wouldn't we have to make an appointment or something? Come back a different day?"

"Not if we say we're only in the area for a day," I told him, not knowing but deciding it would be worth the risk. "They'll probably let us have the keys, we can go to it, have a look around, have some fun, then leave and tell them we decided not to buy it after all. Go on, it'll be a laugh. It's not like we've got anything better to do, is it? I'll give you a nice time, would be kind of exciting."

His smile was bigger now. I could tell he was planning. I held his hand and pushed open the door.

"Let me do all the talking," I said as we walked in to the agent's office, ignored the woman by the entrance, and approached the fat oak desk with the fat bald man smiling behind it.

Now, I didn't have the first idea how you were supposed to behave when you buy a house. I had never bought one, obviously. But I was enjoying the challenge and I figured a man was a man, an estate agent would be no harder to deal with than anyone else.

The fat man stood and held out his hand. I took it, shook it firmly and maintained eye contact while I told him my husband and I were interested in one of the properties in the window. He ushered us into seats and said he would need to take a few details first. I could tell by Jim's breathing he hadn't expected that, he had thought they would just give us the key. I just hoped he would keep his mouth shut, let me handle it.

I took off my coat when I sat down, letting my sweater slip slightly off one shoulder, giving the agent something to appreciate while we talked. I smiled up at him, the wide pupils dilated, so he would think I was interested, found bald men particularly attractive. He returned the smile and struggled to keep his eyes on my face.

"Gareth and I are hoping to move into the area," I said, "and we just popped down for the morning to have a quick look at what's available. We plan to have a drive around, look at a few towns in the area, decide where we want to settle. It's a company move, you see, so we need to decide quite quickly.

142

"We were very interested in that property in the window, the one in Church Close? Would it be possible to have a look? While we're here, I mean. We don't know when we'll have time to come back again and we're looking at a couple of other properties later. It was just a whim really, we hadn't considered the town before, have almost decided on one of the other houses."

I thought it would be good to let him know he needed to move quickly if he hoped to sell his stupid house, he couldn't mess us around or we would leave, we weren't desperate.

He managed to move his eyes off my body for long enough to take out a pad of paper and pen, said he needed a few details first. Jim shuffled in his seat. I patted his knee in a wifely manner, pretended he was anxious about the time.

"He wants to get on," I told the agent, leaning forwards and speaking quietly, like we were conspirators, he was on my side against a difficult spouse. "I really like the look of that house though, it would be really wonderful if you could manage to get us a quick look."

"Well," he said, sitting taller, feeling like a hero, "Usually we book viewings in advance..." ('Viewings' – I would have to remember that term) "... but we might be able to manage something, as you're short of time. The property is currently empty. Now, if I could just take some details. Do you own your own property currently and do you need to sell it?"

I managed to answer all the questions, trying to match his speech patterns so he would feel a connection, see me as his equal. He never paused or frowned so I'm assuming the answers were what he was expecting. I told him that we owned a house in Bedfordshire, but the company was moving Jim, he held a senior managerial position, and they would cover costs until we managed to sell our present home. Jim was shuffling around in his seat, red-faced and sweating. I have never seen someone look more guilty in my life. I just kept staring at the agent, hoping to absorb all his attention so he didn't notice.

Finally, when I thought all the stupid questions would never end and I was ready to just walk out, he stood up and said he would take us. That was bit of a blow, I had hoped he would just give us the key. Perhaps they don't do things like that. I acted all pleased, like this was what we had been hoping and followed him to the door. I showed him where we were parked and he told us the best route to the house and that he would see us there in ten minutes.

When we got back to the car – the dented sports car was still there – Jim nearly exploded.

"How could you do that? Tell all those lies with such a straight face? What's going to happen when he finds out?"

I kissed his cheek, staying pressed against him for a minute longer than I needed to.

"Calm down husband," I said, knowing he would like me calling him that. "We're not doing anything wrong; anyone can look at a house for sale, that's the point. We'll just have a quick nose, pretend we don't like it, and leave. Mr. Baldy won't care, it's his job to show people houses, he'll just be pleased to get out the office for an hour. Come on, it'll be fun."

I half expected him to refuse, to insist on driving us straight back to the flat. But he didn't. I guess he was interested to look at the house, was a bit nosey himself. Or perhaps he was expecting something else; I haven't given it much thought to be honest, not with what happened afterwards. But anyway, we went there.

The house happened to be right next door to the Gadsdon house. There was a gravel driveway, one of those circular ones that you can drive all the way round. We parked behind the agent and met him at the front door. He spent a bit of time fiddling with the keys and turning off the alarm. He wasn't very careful, I read the code over his shoulder as he punched in the numbers. Might be useful later. Then we followed him into the hall.

There was a white-tiled floor and arches that led to two downstairs rooms, one turned out to be the kitchen and I walked straight to the back door, gave it a good looking over.

There were patio doors leading on to a small lawn. It was on a hill and overlooked farmland, then down to a motorway. You could hear the cars, even through the thick glazing. I guess that's what brought the price down a bit. I tried to see into the garden next door but there was a high fence. Even the gate at the end looked as if it would be locked; going in via the farmland would be difficult.

The kitchen still had a cooker and fridge, but nothing else, obviously. I asked if all the houses in the road were identical. He told me they were, had been built about ten years ago and were still under some building warranty. He was droning on about what was included in the price, the age and quality of the appliances. I tried to look interested. The doors and windows looked like they would be impossible to break into quietly, I would have to hope they were unlocked when I made my visit.

We trailed around after the agent. Jim was more interested than I was, and even opened some cupboard doors and peered at the boiler. He was quite getting into his role. There was a long lounge that led through another arch to a tiny study. Then upstairs there were four bedrooms and two bathrooms. I spent some time gazing out of the window, trying to see if there was a way in to the house next door. It didn't look like it would be easy.

The master bedroom had a fantastic bathroom attached, complete with a sunken bath. I began to think it might be worth coming back later on our own just to use that bath. I could tell Jim was having similar thoughts.

The other rooms were just rooms. Clean carpets with dents where furniture had stood, gaping fireplaces, dirty patches on the walls. There was nothing interesting, you couldn't tell what sort of house it had been, who had lived there. It was also disappointingly secure. We thanked the agent, hardly bothering to answer his questions properly, and left. We would never hear from him again, I had given him a false number earlier.

Jim was chatty in the car afterwards. I think he was interested by the idea of looking at someone else's house. He toyed with the idea of going back later, on our own, wondered if we would manage to open the front door. He had noticed the alarm code too. He thought he could get that boiler working, so we'd have hot water for a bath. Then we arrived back at the flat. There was nothing obvious about the outside, nothing to warn us. We went inside as if everything was normal.

***

Other People

Emily parked her car on the driveway and went to the door. She rang the bell and turned to face the garden, lifting her face to feel the late afternoon sunshine. There was a blackbird tugging at a worm under a bush and in the distance she could hear the steady swish of the motorway. It was a peaceful scene, no one watching would have guessed the turmoil within her. She felt sick.

Emily heard the usual grinding of bolts and chains, the turning of keys, then Margaret opened the door. Dear, portly, stable Margaret. Just the sight of her calmed Emily, made her feel that it couldn't be so bad, that this latest challenge could be overcome. There was something wonderfully comforting about Margaret, about her energy and no-nonsense view of life. The dog was skipping about, excited to see Emily. She hugged Margaret and followed her into the sitting room, the dog following, bringing a slipper in case she wanted one, then slumping onto the mat when she realised she was being ignored. They sat, on gold-coloured chairs that clashed with the yellow fire rug, either side of a tiny round table. Emily watched Margaret pour tea and cut fat slices of fruit cake. She began to feel sick again and leaned back in her chair, staring at the empty fireplace, the dog on the rug, a photograph on the mantelpiece that was catching the afternoon sun and sending bright reflections in an uncomfortable glimmer into the corner of her eye. She was aware that Margaret was looking at her, asking how she was.

"I don't know. I feel a bit sick mostly," she said, then added in a rush, "I think I need to talk about Joanna."

Margaret nodded. "Yes, I thought that you might," she said.

"When did you know?" asked Emily. "When did you realise what she was?"

"Who, not what," said Margaret, correcting her, "she was a person, not a thing. The newspapers might make out she was a monster, something evil, but she wasn't. She was a person – a flawed, wicked person, but still a person. You shouldn't lose sight of that Emily, don't let her become bigger in your head than she was.

"I didn't know what she was up to, not until that day they came to the house to tell me. But I wasn't surprised, not really, I had known for years she was capable of anything; she didn't have the same restraints that most of us have. It was like she had no conscience. I hoped that she could use that ability, maybe do something great, something the rest of us weren't able to do. But she chose to go the other way. It was a terrible waste."

"Yes," said Emily, her head bowed, then quietly, so quietly that Margaret had to lean forwards in her chair to hear, she said, "I'm frightened. I'm terribly frightened I might be like her, that I might be capable of the things she did. And even if I'm not, what about this baby? What if I give birth to a monster? Something evil?" She stopped, fat tears seeping from her eyes and rolling down her nose, dripping onto the cake on her lap. All the tension from the week leaking out, now it was safe, now her defences were down. She was aware Margaret was moving, was taking her plate and putting it on the table, was putting her arms around her and holding her close. She rocked the young woman, smoothing her hair, comforting her. The dog had raised herself from the rug and swaggered over. She pushed her black nose under Margaret's arm and sniffed at Emily's face. She didn't know what was happening, but she sensed something and wanted to be a part of it. Emily reached down, fondled the silky ears.

Margaret moved back and waited while Emily blew her nose loudly and pushed the damp tissue back up her sleeve.

The dog sat at her feet. She was concerned about the girl who seemed upset, but she was also aware there was food in the area and she might be given some. She rested a heavy head on Emily's knees and stared up at her.

"Well," said Margaret, when she thought the worst of the storm was over, when Emily seemed calm again, "there are some things that we don't know. We can talk about those and make guesses but really that's all they'll be. Guesses. We never know what the future holds and I don't find that worrying about it helps.

"The other things, the parts of Joanna's life that I do know, we can talk about properly. It's way past the time that you should know a bit more, I was always uneasy with your refusal to talk about her, but I wanted you to have space. You had enough to cope with. You still do. But Emily, don't start trying to cope with things you don't have to. That would be silly. You will not know what this child will be like until it is born. No mother does. We can discuss likelihoods and probabilities, but that's all they are."

She looked across at Emily, slumped in her chair, the dog's head on her knee, her hand deep in the black fur. She remembered the day when she first brought the puppy to the house. She was a mass of wriggling black fur, a big pawed ball of excitement. Emily was equally excited, had wanted to call her Blackie or Doggy or Snowball. They named her Cassie. She had never been the most intelligent of dogs, but she was very happy, always looking for food, eager to bring gifts of discarded shoes, and tea towels left in reach of the counter edge. She was elderly now, her muzzle speckled with white, but her heart and greed were still big. Her love of people matched only by her love of food. Margaret smiled.

"And I can assure you that you are not like Joanna, not in the way you mean, anyway. Cassie is testament to that. Look at her. She is as soppy as anything, she expects to be loved and fed, she's never known anything but affection her entire life. You grew up with that dog and she couldn't be happier." Margaret stopped and shook her head. "I would never have allowed an animal in the house when Joanna lived with me," she said. "I like animals too much."

Emily looked at her. Her brow creased as she understood, as she remembered. There had never been pets in her early childhood. The closest were some caterpillars she found on a hedge and put in a jam-jar. She remembered collecting leaves for them, and Margaret helping her to make holes in the jar lid so they could breathe, telling her that she must collect fresh leaves for them to eat every day. She had been fascinated by them, spent hours watching their bodies curl and stretch as they moved on their strange sucker feet, seen the leaves gradually trimmed as they ate. She collected fresh leaves every day for the following week. On the seventh day, there was no need. The lid had been replaced with one which had no holes. It had been screwed onto the jar, too tightly for Emily to undo. All the caterpillars were dead, the glass jar misted with condensation. She never really understood what had happened, how someone could have made the mistake. Then she had forgotten about it. As she thought about it now, as an adult, she was glad that Margaret had banned animals from the house. It would have been an unnecessary risk. She wondered what else she had forgotten, what was stored in the recess of her brain, waiting to emerge. What she had buried or simply never considered to be important.

Emily watched Margaret as she reached for the teapot and poured more tea. She had watched her do that so many times. The way she removed the tea towel from the top which she used to keep the pot warm, because she had never bothered to buy a tea-cosy, the way she held the lid with her three middle fingers as she tipped the pot, always gave it a little shake when she finished pouring, in case there were drips. Margaret was her stability. She had raised Emily, guided her through her teenage insecurities, watched with pride as she built a home with Josh. Emily loved this woman. But she also loved Joanna, the woman who had never let her call her mum but who had given birth to her, the woman who was far from stable, who had let them down so badly, caused so much hurt. Was it wrong to love her too? Was she misguided, in some way evil herself, for wanting to love someone who had done such hateful things?

A thought occurred to her and she reached for her cup, took a sip, let it clatter on to the saucer. She wanted to speak, but didn't quite trust her voice, knew the emotion might rush out and swamp the words before she had managed to speak them. But she needed to know.

"Did she–" she stopped, took a breath, made herself continue. "Did she ever try to hurt me? Do you think she even loved me? Ever?" There, she had said it. The last word was a little too high, a bit soft perhaps, but she had got it out. Now she could listen, listening was easier than speaking. She sniffed noisily and took another sip of tea. There was something comforting about tea. Tea and Margaret and Cassie. With those three she should manage to get through this, obtain enough information to make her decision.

"I have to be honest," began Margaret, "and I don't know, not for sure. I know that's not what you want to hear but this won't be useful unless I am honest, even when the truth is unpleasant.

"She did take a certain pride in you, but I was never sure if that was because you were her daughter, an extension of her, almost like a possession. She wanted you to be the best in the same way someone might want to own the best car, have the latest model of phone. However, to be fair," she looked up, straight into Emily's eyes, "that is not necessarily unusual. While I was raising you, I sometimes felt other parents at the school had similar feelings about their own children. They wanted them to win prizes, be the best at maths or whatever, simply because it would reflect well on them as parents.

"She was quite competitive with you though, do you remember those money flowers you made for charity?"

Emily did. She had felt rather proud of that. Her infant school had collected money for children in India. In order to make it more interesting, the children placed the money on a large sheet of paper, the length of the school corridor. It was meant to look like a garden and all the coins were stuck to the paper in a circular pattern, like flowers. Some children had several flowers in their patch of the 'garden'. Emily had hundreds, all silver and gold. Joanna had presented her with bags of coins and told her to take them for her garden.

Margaret had been suspicious as to where the money had come from. Joanna claimed she had been to the bank and asked for bags of change. This seemed unlikely but the older woman hadn't wanted to spoil their fun, not when she had no proof that the coins were stolen from Joanna's work, when it was just a suspicion.

There was also the time when Emily was asked to take in empty cans as part of a recycling project. Joanna gave her a whole sack of drink cans to take. It was very likely they had been removed from the recycling centre at the park, but Emily was delighted. She liked to be the best. All children do.

Margaret continued, "I never liked to leave you for too long in her care, I never completely trusted her. But I never knew for sure she planned to hurt you, to hurt either of us. It was very difficult. I always thought she should be involved in bringing you up, that contact with her was good for you. But I worried that she wasn't naturally nurturing, that she might damage you somehow."

She put her cup and saucer back on the tray and brushed her skirt, as if there were crumbs on it. Moving her hands helped her to think, to order her thoughts. Really she would have liked to talk while she fiddled with something, peeled potatoes perhaps or knitted. But she thought that might look uncaring, as if she weren't giving her full attention to Emily. So she sat with empty hands, twisting her wedding ring round and round her finger, thinking.

There was one incident that stood out in her memory above all others. It was when Emily was aged five and Margaret had left her at home with Joanna while she went to the library. She was beginning to leave them together more often by this time, feeling that if anything untoward happened, then Emily was old enough to tell her about it and also that she was of an age where she would know herself if something was unusual, she was less likely to be led into something which she knew 'wasn't allowed'.

Margaret had been at the library for a couple of hours. She met a friend and they had coffee and chatted in the little cafe that joined the library. Then she had wandered round, choosing books, taking her time. She loved to read, it was her escape, more reliable than the television. She found some novels, simple romances where you knew what would happen by reading the blurb on the back, knew they would have a happy ending, be comforting, have a dark mysterious man who would reveal his love for the wild enchanting girl in the final chapter. She smiled when she found them, knew that Tom would have teased her for liking them. She had taken them to the desk to be stamped, then shoved them into the ancient carrier bag she kept screwed up in her pocket. The books were heavy and she was glad she had the car.

When she got home it was beginning to get dark. She pushed open the front door and was surprised to smell food, roast chicken and something boiled. The hallway was full of steam, no one had opened the kitchen window or turned on the extractor fan and the door to the hall was slightly ajar. She couldn't see into the kitchen, but she could hear voices. Joanna was speaking in a Russian accent, pretending to give orders. Emily was giggling, the sort of out of control giggle which told Margaret she had been laughing for a long time and was losing the ability to NOT giggle, that emotionally fragile state that only young children are capable of, when laughter and tears are sometimes intertwined. She smiled to herself, happy to hear them both having fun. Joanna must have decided to cook while she entertained Emily. She stood for a moment, enjoying the happiness that was bubbling from the kitchen. Then she dumped her heavy bag on the floor and pushed open the kitchen door.

Her heart stopped.

Emily was standing on a high stool, precariously swaying while she giggled. She was swathed in one of Margaret's aprons, a green one with tiny yellow flowers and a big pocket across the front. It reached almost to her feet and was wrapped right around her almost twice. In her hand was the electric carving knife. As the door opened, Joanna was just lifting a roast chicken from the oven and placing in front of the child, who pressed the button on the knife and set the blades in motion. The jagged steel whirred into action, the blades moving against each other as if seeking flesh to tear through and destroy, the knife jumping in the child's hand as she struggled to control it, watching it move in a wide arch, too powerful for her little arms.

"Stop!" Margaret ran across the kitchen. She swept the knife from Emily's hand and reached to unplug it from the socket, then stared in horror at Joanna.

"Whatever were you thinking?" she shouted, "Have you any idea how sharp that knife is? She could have chopped off her hand!"

"We were cooking you dinner," said Joanna, her voice slow, light, unconcerned. "The chicken needs carving, I was going to show her how to do it."

"With an electric carving knife? A five-year-old? Are you mad?"

Emily had started to cry. Margaret lifted her down from the stool and began to untie the apron. It was knotted at the back and her fingers were trembling. She gave up and instead pulled the child on to her lap and held her there, holding her tightly, breathing in the smell of her hair. She felt like crying herself. She looked up at Joanna.

Joanna turned her blank blue eyes to her. She didn't say a word, just gave a small smile and glided from the room. Margaret never knew if she had intended for Emily to be hurt or if she just didn't care if she was or not. She had not left them alone together for more than a few minutes after that.

Margaret slid the ring off her finger, then replaced it. What could she say? She wanted to be honest but how could you explain to someone that it was very possible that their mother might have killed them if they had been left alone together? She decided she couldn't. It was one of the many things that was best left buried. Especially as she wasn't completely sure, she might have misread the situation. She sighed, that was the trouble with Joanna. Once you knew what she had done, what she was capable of, it threw everything else into a different colour. But was that necessarily correct? Before the murders, before she had *known* about the murders, she had felt sure that Joanna had affection for Emily, that she enjoyed playing with her, making her laugh. Afterwards, when she had been diagnosed as a psychopath, not able to empathise or love, it made Margaret doubt what she had seen, to re-evaluate everything. But that might not be true. She might have loved her daughter at some level, she might have enjoyed her company, she might not have wished her harm. There was no way of knowing.

"Let me just talk," she said to Emily, "explain a few things as they occur to me. Let me tell you how it was and how I feel. You see, I love Joanna, I have since she was a girl and that doesn't change, whatever somebody does. I cannot deny that part of me, it is the part of me that admires her. She has done some terrible things, some wicked things, but I do not believe she is evil. That is for newspapers and fairy tales. Real people are more complicated than that." She stopped. There was so much she wanted to explain, to help Emily to understand. It was just very difficult to put it all into words. But she must try, for the sake of both Emily and this new baby, she must try.

"I don't believe anyone is totally evil or totally good," she began, "even people in history who we think of as evil, I expect they had their good points, things they did well. An evil dictator might be a caring father, a cruel king might write beautiful poetry. The bad need not obliterate the good. Sometimes we lose sight of that, we like to put people into a box and label their whole personality.

"The same is true for those people who we say are good, of course. People may have done great things but been terrible parents, they might be saints but never have cared for their own parents when they were old. Again, we don't like to think about that, we want our heroes to be perfect, we feel let down if we find they have faults."

Cassie lifted her head. She decided she was unlikely to be offered any cake after all and trotted back to the mat, turning in circles before flopping heavily down. She gave Emily a long look, then lowered her head and closed her eyes, her ears alert in case a walk should be offered.

Margaret shuffled in her chair, adjusted the cushion behind her back, swallowed.

"Emily, I think it's time that I was blunt." She smiled, actually she was always blunt. It was a skill that she had acquired while living with Joanna. If she was polite, left things half said, then Joanna would claim that it hadn't been obvious, Margaret hadn't *actually said* something and she hadn't understood. She was good at twisting things, tying you up in mental knots so you were left feeling unsure whether you had actually said something or not.

"I think you have to do two things," she continued, "you need to face who Joanna really was and decided whether you can forgive her. You also need to think about the implications for the baby. It would be good to be realistic, to know what you might be dealing with and to be prepared. However, as I said before, you should not try to solve everything now, to cross bridges before you get to them.

"You also need to tell Josh – I assume he still doesn't know about Joanna?"

Emily looked down, shook her head. She knew Margaret had never liked the deception and was glad she chose not to revisit the lecture that she often gave. She just tutted, a succinct expression of disapproval.

"I don't know how you can expect me to forgive her," she said, looking up at Margaret. "Have you?"

"Yes, actually," she said, "but I'm not saying it was easy. For me, that's what God is about, that's why I believe what I do". She watched Emily's eyes shutter, the normal response to any religious conversation. She sighed, decided she needed to continue.

"Emily, when I started to attend church it was, quite frankly, because I wasn't coping. Joanna was too difficult for me, the problem was too big. And I was proud, which was a big mistake. I didn't want to go back to Social Services, I didn't want to admit that I was barely coping, that this girl had problems that were beyond me, that I didn't know what to do.

"Joanna, as you know, would never come with me, she called it my 'cult', liked to tease me about it. To be honest, I was glad she didn't want to come. People think churches are full of saintly people, all praising God, all very secure in their faith. But actually they're not, they're full of weak people, people like me. Churches are a place for people to go who *haven't* got it sorted, who know they need help and support. That was me, I needed support.

"I was very aware though that some of those people were just the kind of personality that Joanna liked to manipulate. She was so clever, so gifted at being whoever she wanted to be. She might easily have learned the right words to say, to appear contrite and sincere, and then to start to influence others, to make them dance to her own particular tune. No, I was glad she never wanted to come."

"Nor did I!" said Emily, remembering the arguments, the times she had announced on a Sunday she wanted to stay in bed or go out with friends, her anger at Margaret's insistence she should accompany her to church, that until she reached the age of sixteen – where that age came from she had no idea – until she was sixteen she must attend church every Sunday.

"I know," said Margaret, "but as you are about to find out, parenting is all about doing what you think is best for your child, not about doing what your child wants. I thought it was good for you, to hear people talk about good things, a positive way of living, an ethical view. I also hoped you might recognise God, of course, but even if you didn't, I decided that being with people who were trying to be good would be a good balance to living with someone who always seemed to be trying to be bad!"

Now it was Emily who smiled. She had hated those hour-long services, found them boring and irrelevant. But if she was honest, she did value the relationships she made with the people there. There was something genuine about them. As Margaret said, they were all trying to be good, which was a change to how most people lived their lives. She reached again for her cake. It was soggy from her tears in one corner. She felt calmer now, the conversation was more philosophical, less personal. She wondered if that was why Margaret had chosen this subject to start with. She broke off the damp patch and took a bite. Margaret was still talking about forgiveness.

"It took me a while to understand what forgiveness meant," she said, "in fact, it wasn't until I heard someone who had been abused as a child talking about forgiveness that I fully understood. Forgiveness is *not* saying that something doesn't matter. It's *not* pretending that what someone has done is unimportant, not bad. No, to truly forgive you must recognise they have done wrong, that their actions were hurtful and damaging. But then, instead of holding on to the anger, the resentment, the wanting to hurt them back, you let those feelings go. Forgiving someone doesn't absolve them, it doesn't mean they shouldn't be punished. Forgiving them doesn't actually affect the person at all, which is why it doesn't even matter if they are sorry or not. Forgiveness is about you, about your attitudes. If we are going to discuss Joanna openly, if you are going to look at who she was, then it is important you try to forgive her for that. Holding on to hurts only damages you, it doesn't change anything for her at all."

"But how can you?" asked Emily, "After all you gave her, the home, the money, the care, how can forgive her for being so bad? She ruined our lives too you know. Sometimes I feel like she might as well have poisoned us along with the other victims. We are just as much her victims as they are, it's just we have to continue living with it. I will ALWAYS be her daughter, the daughter of a murderer. Do you have any idea how that feels?"

Emily paused. When she spoke again, her voice was louder, her emotions barely in check. "Do you know what it's like to continually question yourself, to evaluate every action? If I laugh when someone falls over on ice, is that a normal response or is it uncaring, the daughter of a psychopath? When I'm angry, is that how everyone feels or might it spill over into cruelty? When I told lies as a child to avoid a punishment, is that how every child behaves or is it because I have no moral compass? Do you have any idea how that feels? To never be able to trust yourself, to always wonder what destructive genes are whizzing around inside of you, waiting to turn you into a monster. Do you? Do you have any idea?" She was shouting now, her cake forgotten, her anger bubbling out in hot angry words.

Margaret let her finish. Then she sat, quietly assimilating what she had heard, trying to hear the words not the anger, trying to answer the questions. She wanted to help this young woman heal, she loved her too much to argue back. She knew the anger wasn't aimed at her, that it was healthy for some of it to start to come out, to be expressed.

"No Emily, I don't. Only someone who has been in your position can truly understand. But I can guess. I can guess how much self-doubt you must have to live with and I wish I could reassure you.

"You have described Joanna as a psychopath, and I think you might be right. But do you know what that actually means? Have you read anything about it?"

Emily shook her head. To her psychopath meant killer, it was a term used in films and it fitted her mother perfectly. Someone who coolly planned to murder strangers, someone who cared nothing at all for other people, who enjoyed inflicting pain.

"Well, I have done a little research," said Margaret, "I didn't understand all of it to be honest, but I wanted to try and understand Joanna, to know if it was my fault."

She stopped, emotion rising up. This was very hard to discuss, to be honest and to listen to Emily's fears and voice her own. This discussion should have happened years ago, it might have been easier then, less like picking off a scab that had hardened, to expose a wound.

Margaret had so much self-doubt, a nagging feeling that if she had done more, alerted the right people, not been too proud to ask for help, then perhaps she could have diverted what happened. She could have saved lives. She talked about forgiving Joanna. That was the easy bit, so much harder to forgive herself, to know she had made mistakes, face up to them and allow herself to be forgiven. Knowing God forgave her helped, but she wasn't sure if she would ever manage to completely forgive herself, even though she knew she must try.

She had received good teaching – first she must accept God forgave her for all the things she had done wrong; even the things concerning Joanna, even those mistakes which might have prevented someone stopping Joanna, before she became so destructive. She knew she could be forgiven, knew that Jesus had paid the price for it to be possible by dying, and that one terrible price was enough. One price, paid for all times, enough to cover everyone. Even enough to cover her own failings. When she was feeling rational, sensible, she knew this. But sometimes she felt like an accessory to Joanna's crimes, as if she too were guilty of murder. Then the guilt came flooding back, twisting in her mind and churning in her stomach, because perhaps she could have stopped her. Perhaps.

Next she must forgive herself. Forgiving others *must* include herself. She felt it was almost impossible. She coughed and cleared her throat. Her voice had a tremor as she continued, trying to order her thoughts, to make the discussion less personal for a moment so she could explain properly.

"It is relatively recently that psychologists actually defined what it means to be a psychopath. I got terribly confused when I was reading, sometimes people said 'psychopath', sometimes they used the term 'sociopath'. It was hard to understand the difference. I think, but I might be wrong, that a 'psychopath' is a genetic condition, they are born with a brain that doesn't work like most other peoples' and a 'sociopath' is created – they have suffered abuse or neglect and been made anti-social.

"No, wait, hear me out," she said as she saw Emily about to interrupt, knew that she wanted to tell her this was why she didn't want the baby. But Margaret wanted to explain first, for her to understand before they discussed options.

"When Joanna was first convicted, everyone automatically called her a psychopath – that was the name that anyone who killed people was called. Later, psychologists changed the label, they said she was a sociopath. Fairly recently, someone devised a checklist of traits which applied to psychopaths, many of them apply to Joanna. It was all very muddled, I'm not sure that even the psychologists themselves always knew what they were talking about. They were called in to give evidence at the original trial and were consulted whenever parole was mentioned. But the terms seemed to be almost interchangeable depending on who was using them. It didn't seem a very exact science.

"Now that they can do MRIs, can see inside the head, they are able to know if someone is a psychopath or not. Something in the front bit of the brain doesn't respond to things like most brains do. But Joanna has never, as far as I know, had an MRI. She has certainly

161

never told me about one in her letters, and I can't think why she would have; unless they happened to be doing research in her prison, they would have no need to spend all that money.

"So, we cannot know for sure if she is a psychopath or not. I know that she had had problems before she came to me. I don't know if that's because she caused problems wherever she went or if, when she was young, her biological parents harmed her in some way. Social Services were less open in those days, the foster parents weren't always given all the details, it was felt it was better for a child to have a 'fresh start', to not arrive with a lot of labels that would colour how they were viewed.

"So Emily, it is entirely possible that her problems were caused by people, that she is not a psychopath, there is no mental disorder for you to inherit. You were loved from the moment you were born, I can guarantee that. I was very careful to keep you safe. There is no reason for you to worry that you will be like Joanna."

"Except," corrected Emily, "she *might* be a psychopath. She might have passed on to me a whole lot of weird genes; my brain might be like hers. Or if mine isn't, my child's might be."

"Yes," said Margaret, "that is true". She paused. She wanted to get this right.

"So, let's assume the worst-case scenario, let's assume that Joanna is a psychopath, that her disorder can be inherited, that she comes from a long line of murderers and anti-social individuals. That you have a mixed bag of genes silently waiting inside of you.

"Firstly, you have never displayed any of the traits of a psychopath. I have watched you your whole life, I would know. I have cared for several damaged children during my life, you never seemed anything other than a normal child. Again, from what I have read, psychopathy tends to start to appear very early on, even in young children. They don't connect with people, they don't have the same emotional responses, they don't care about how other people feel, they have no sense of conscience. The very fact that you are worrying about this, that you don't want to be the same as Joanna, tells me that you are not a psychopath. A psychopath wouldn't care."

"And my baby?" said Emily, placing her hands on her belly, "Or my grandchildren? Do I have the right to risk carrying on a line of genes that at any time might dominate, might create another malformed individual? Isn't it better to stop the line here? If I don't reproduce, then my gene pool ends with me. Do I have the right to inflict possible Joannas on future society?

"It would be okay," she whispered, "I'm used to the idea now. I know Josh wants kids, but I told him from the beginning that I didn't, I don't feel like I'm letting him down, not really. There's more at stake here than just what we want, isn't there?"

"Emily, no one knows what their child will be," said Margaret, "everyone who gives birth is taking a risk. But we are all born with our own set of problems, I do believe that. No one is born perfect, we all have to make the best of what we are.

"Some people have a natural inclination to gossip. They have to learn to control that, to only say what is helpful. They don't need to have their tongues cut out though."

"This is a lot bigger than gossiping!" said Emily, feeling cross now, as if Margaret wasn't listening, was just trying to persuade her to her own viewpoint, which was clearly skewed towards her religious beliefs.

"I know that," said Margaret, sharply. She was trying her best here. "I know what we are discussing is big, dangerous, frightening. My point is that we all make choices. I don't believe the direction of your life is determined by your genes. They will make some choices harder for you, you might have things that you struggle with, but ultimately, how we live is our decision.

"I do not believe that we can say Joanna takes no blame for her actions, that her brain was different to ours and so she couldn't help what she did. That is rubbish! Joanna may have had an inability to empathise, been unable to naturally feel guilt when she did something wrong, to not care about other's feelings. But that does not excuse her. She did not have to kill people. That was her choice. It may have been easier for her than it would be for you and me, but she still made that choice on her own. She wasn't forced by another person and she wasn't forced to by her genetic make-up. We all make choices. We all choose how we live. We all have faults. That is why I believe what I do about God, because I believe that he helps me to live better. Not better than other people, but better than I could live on my own, without his help. I have my own faults, my own genetic imperfections. God sees beyond that."

"I do not know how you can believe in God after everything that's happened," said Emily. "I could never trust a God who was cruel enough to allow the terrible things that I see in the world, so much suffering and evil." As soon as she was sixteen, when church became optional, she had stopped attending. If there was a God, an all-powerful God, how could he have allowed someone like Joanna to be born?

Margaret did not rush to answer. She didn't want this to become a discussion about theology. She had nice pat answers, learned from books, she could defend her God if she wanted to. But that wouldn't help Emily, that wasn't what she needed to hear right now. And Margaret had learned long ago that it wasn't necessary to defend God, he was big enough to do that himself, could cope with people not believing in him. Her role was to explain what God meant to her but nothing more, she could never change anyone's mind by arguing. She would try to leave God out of the discussion for a bit, that might be more helpful, make Emily hear what she was trying so hard to say.

"I'm not talking about that," she said, "I just want to make the point that we are all born with something, whether it's a mental imperfection or a physical one. It can make things harder for us, but it doesn't excuse our behaviour, our choices. I believe we can decide which way our lives go, we are not stuck with where we are born. We can face our weaknesses, we don't have to accept the route they lead us.

"I even believe that some of the traits of psychopathy can be a strength, if used properly."

"What? Like killing people? If you're James Bond perhaps!"

"No Emily, there is more to it than that. I think it is up to us how we use what we are born with. So, for example, a psychopath has no empathy, they are not affected at all by how other people feel. They are not autistic; they understand if a person is happy or sad, they can even manipulate those feelings, but they do not 'catch' them, they don't share the feelings. So if a toddler laughs, most people will smile, it makes them happy too. Not a psychopath, they will feel nothing. That can be a terrible weakness. But not always. Do we want a general in the army to be distraught every time one of his soldiers is killed, or do we want him to make logical, dispassionate decisions? Do we want a brain surgeon to go to pieces when a patient dies, or do we want him to calmly explain to the grieving parents what has happened to their child? And to then go on to operate on another patient. You see, that trait can be either a weakness or a strength.

"Sometimes not being influenced by how those around us feel is a great strength. Perhaps that is what has enabled people to be heroes or great politicians. The ability to go against the tide of public opinion, to make difficult decisions that would upset most people."

"And the others? The desire to hurt people? The need to manipulate people around them?"

"No, I am not saying that some things don't need to be squashed, controlled. I'm just saying that some aspects of psychopathy might be strengths if used correctly. Which is where choice comes into the equation. We all make choices about how we will live. We are not machines, pre-programmed, unable to control our actions.

"If your baby is born with the genes for psychopathy, there are some things, like lying, being impetuous, being callous, that they will need to control. There are other traits that might lead them to become a great politician, a brilliant actress, someone who adds value to their world.

"But can you see, this is true for anyone? Every parent fears their child might be born with a defect, they might be disabled in some way. We want to give birth to perfect babies. But no one does. I am not belittling psychopathy, it is at least as much a handicap as having a physical defect. But that is not a reason to not be born, not in my mind.

"Raising a child with psychopathic traits will be very hard. You will suffer, you will need help. But Emily, you are a strong woman, and so am I. We will cope with what we have to."

She stopped. She was suddenly horribly aware of what she had said, the implication of her words. Emily could now point out that actually, in exactly this position, she, Margaret, had not coped so well. She had allowed a psychopathic child to grow into a serial killer. But was that her fault? Could she have done something different, have stopped it happening? She didn't know. She would never know. She still felt sick inside when she thought about it. It was a burden she was learning, gradually, to put down; there was nothing she could do now to change the past. She could accept the things she had done wrong, as every parent should accept the things they have done wrong, but torturing herself about the rest, the unknown, would help no one.

Emily said nothing. If she realised the link, she was too kind to say it. She merely asked if Margaret was still in touch with Joanna, if she ever visited her.

"No, not now. I did at first, of course, when we lived nearer. It was always a difficult day, I never knew what mood Joanna would be in, whether what she was telling me was true."

Margaret paused, remembering those visits.

She had been diligent at first, booking her next visit while she was there, using her full allocation of visiting time. As Joanna grew used to the prison system, settled in and started to behave as expected, she earned herself enhanced status, her visiting times increased to twice a week, each for three hours. That was a big time commitment, one that Margaret found to be a drain, especially as Joanna seemed to gain nothing from the visit.

Margaret hated the whole experience, the rub down by staff, walking past the sniffer dogs, going through the metal detectors. Everything designed to keep the prisoners secure but it also made the visitor feel like a suspect, not trusted. Margaret wasn't used to being seen as a suspect. Trying to not use the toilet while there, wondering who had been there before you.

It was a hassle too. Having to remember to take coins for the vending machines and the locker to keep her handbag in during the visit, sitting on chairs that were fixed to the floor at an unnatural distance from the tables. You felt awkward, uncomfortable. Wondering what mood Joanna would be in, whether she would want to have coffee, would chat about her week, tell her stories, be amusing. Or whether, as sometimes happened, she would appear, sit for a matter of seconds and then stand, say she had nothing to say, was going back to her room. Leaving Margaret sitting there on her own, the other people looking at her, wondering what she had said to upset Joanna. She would travel back home, knowing she had used up most of the day in travelling, security, waiting, just for Joanna to show her power by refusing to be visited. No, it was not time well spent.

"Then, as I learned more about her disorder, when the

psychologists assessed her against their checklist and told me that she had enough psychopathic traits to be classified as a psychopath, I read some articles about it. I realised that my visiting made very little difference to Joanna. As I found it upsetting, I decided to stop going.

"Joanna didn't seem to need emotional support, she just wanted people to control and manipulate. I found the visits very difficult. Prisons aren't friendly places. I felt shabby going there and all the other visitors would see who I was talking to, Joanna is still well known. I would feel watched, assessed. It made me feel dirty, violated somehow. So one day, I asked myself why I was going, was it out of duty or was it some kind of guilt that forced me there; trying to make up for whatever I had failed to do when I was raising her. I realised it served no purpose, I couldn't erase the past, my visits weren't helping Joanna, they were just a torment for me. I decided Joanna had tormented me enough. I stopped going as regularly. I haven't been for ages now, though I will at some point, just to see her. I have never stopped caring, I have simply learned to put up some barriers, to protect myself."

She smiled. "I use my age as an excuse. I tell myself the journey would be too much for me at my age. Which is rubbish of course, but that's what I tell myself.

"I still write though. I send her letters, emails mostly, telling her about my life. Not very interesting ones I'm afraid. She doesn't reply very often, only if she wants something."

"Do you tell her about me?" asked Emily. She wondered why she had never asked this before, it seemed very important now.

"A little. Nothing very specific, nothing personal, only things that other people would know. Like that you are married, have a job, things like that. I would never tell her your address or even which town you live in. That's up to you if you want her to know those things. I used to send her photographs, when you were little, those ones that the school used to take. I would always include one of the little ones in with my letter. I felt she had the right to see you. She is still your mother."

"No, she isn't, not really. You are. You know that you are."

Margaret nodded, acknowledging the truth of the statement. Emily was the child that Tom could never give her and she had willingly moved into the space left by Joanna's disinterest.

"Am I like her at all? Not the killing, I know I don't do that! But the other things."

Margaret smiled, happy to remember the other parts of Joanna, the noncontroversial aspects, the things that she admired. She looked at Emily now, curled in the chair, skinny, straight hair. She could be twelve years old.

"Well, you look very like her of course. Though your father must have had brown eyes because Joanna's are blue. You have some of her energy." She paused, considering, then added, "There are a few things that are similar. She was your mother after all, it would be odd if there weren't. But that doesn't make you a potential killer Emily.

"So yes, you look like her. You are brave like she was, I don't really remember you being frightened of much when you were growing up.

"But you don't lie like she used to. I could never trust her. Even when she wasn't lying she would twist the truth and she had a huge ability to exaggerate. Especially about her own abilities. You have always been very open, even when you were a teenager and found me irritating, you never really lied."

No, Emily could only remember one big lie in her life. She had been at infant school. The children were all given reading books, they read each one in turn, progressing through the colour bands. Then, when they had read all the 'core' books, the ones that were kept in the cupboard at the end of the hall, they became a 'free reader'. The free readers were allowed to choose books from the shelves in the corridor, there was no order to what they read, they could pick any that appealed to them. Emily had been a fluent reader, she could read even before she started school. But she read slowly. She was advancing through the core books very slowly and she was desperate to finish them, to be a 'free reader'. Then, one day, her teacher left unexpectedly and a new teacher arrived to take the class. When it was Emily's turn to read, the teacher couldn't find her card, the piece of yellow cardboard that recorded all the books that Emily had read. The child grasped the opportunity presented and told the teacher that she belonged to that special band of 'free readers'. The teacher believed her and, from then on, Emily had chosen books from the corridor. But the guilt felt by the child was huge! She had lain in bed at night, wondering if she should confess, torn between not wanting to return to those dreaded 'core books' and wanting the lie to be finished. She never told anyone, but it had stopped her from lying in the future, that queasy feeling of guilt was too strongly embedded in her mind. She was aware that Margaret was still talking.

"You are funny like her though, you share her sense of humour and the ability to tell a good story. It's sort of ironic that Joanna pretended that she was a teacher, she would actually have made a very good one. People listened when she spoke, she was such a good presenter. Even in court, during her trial, no one spoke or whispered when she gave evidence. There was something about her that captivated you, made you listen, made you want to watch her."

Emily remembered her mother's eyes. It was not always a comfortable memory, but it was one seared into her mind. You could never guess her mood from her eyes. She remembered going into her mother's room, finding her sprawled on the bed, reading. The bed seemed very high to Emily. Her mother would turn and look at her, those blank blue eyes, was she about to smile and offer to read aloud or to swear at her to leave the room? Emily would never know until Joanna spoke. Those eyes still made her shiver when she thought about them. She picked at her thumb nail while she thought about it, picking at the skin that was dry along the edge.

She remembered a few times when Joanna had scared her. Joanna loved to jump out unexpectedly, to make her jump. Sometimes when she had been asleep, tucked up in her bed, Joanna would suddenly appear, leap onto her and make her cry out, then hurry away before Margaret could come and see what was happening. Her stories would sometimes be scary too, horror stories whispered at night time that kept the young girl awake at night, listening for monsters, or for the dead man who lived under her bed to start moving, to slowly come and get her and take her away. Not the kind of stories that one finds in a children's book, but told with vivid realism just before she went to sleep. Emily shivered, wondering why she had never told Margaret.

"I think your brain is better than hers," continued Margaret, "so perhaps that is from your father too. I always assumed he was another student. Joanna was bright but she wasn't as clever as she liked people to think. I think that she struggled a bit when she got to university, found the course too difficult. You have always done well academically.

"You share her sense of fun. Do you remember how she would make us laugh? Sometimes when I was driving and she was telling a funny story, I would have to stop the car, she made me laugh so much!" She smiled now, remembering those days.

She recalled an afternoon when they had gone out for burgers. It must have been a birthday or something, they rarely went out to eat, even fast food was a treat. They drove to the restaurant, the three of them, which hardly ever happened. Margaret parked the car while Joanna and Emily went into the restaurant, to save a place in the line. Emily was excited, skipping beside Joanna, and Joanna laughed and raced her to the door. The door had been heavy, too heavy for the child to push open on her own, a long red bar for the handle.

They went inside and waited in the line of customers, staring at the menu board, smelling the food, waiting to be served. Margaret joined them and they discussed what they would eat. Joanna said she would order it, they could go and wait at a table.

Then, when she reached the front of the line, Joanna gave their order using a very high pitched squeaky voice, like a cartoon mouse. She kept her face completely solemn, gave the correct order, but all in the strange voice. The girl serving hadn't known whether or not she was pretending, clearly had trouble not laughing but knew that would be terribly rude if this customer suffered from a vocal handicap. Emily and Margaret were in floods of laughter, they could see everyone nearby was listening to Joanna, not sure whether or not they should laugh. It was one of those funny moments that binds a family together. Margaret reminded her of the story again, it was one that she liked to tell. It had kept the memory of the occasion alive in Emily's mind. Memories like those confused her.

"I feel guilty for thinking about things like that," said Emily, "it feels wrong when she caused so much suffering. I think–" she paused, unsure if she wanted to put it into words. "I think that I still love her, but that I shouldn't. She was such a bad person. But the bits I remember make me smile, I thought she was great, I wanted to please her, be like her. She was more like a big sister than a mother, but she was a big sister who I wanted to copy. Now I feel guilty for ever thinking like that."

"Emily, you were a child. And as I said before, she wasn't a monster, she was just a bad person. A very bad person. But there were good things too. It's okay for us to remember the good as well as recognise the bad.

"But we should also bear in mind how Joanna herself viewed those events. I don't know if her memories make her smile too, but I am fairly sure that the things that she did to make us laugh – and she *did* make us laugh, she was very funny – were for her own benefit. I don't think that she wanted us to laugh so we would be happy, that would give her no satisfaction. I think she wanted us to laugh because it was a form of power over us, another way to control us. Even controlling our emotions, deciding when we would be happy or cross was like a game to her. I could never rely on her behaving well, even if it was a special occasion, a birthday, a holiday, if I was ill. It was always on Joanna's own terms. If she decided she wanted us to laugh, she would make us laugh. But it was for her own amusement, not ours."

Emily nodded, beginning to understand. There was a certain freedom in that. It released her from any kind of duty towards Joanna, she didn't owe her anything, and she wondered if deep down, in her subconscious, she had felt that she did. She perhaps felt that having happy memories of someone meant that you shouldn't then abandon them.

Margaret began to collect the plates. She gestured to the cake but Joanna shook her head, she didn't want more. She picked a crumb from her plate and threw it towards the dog. It fell short, was too light to be thrown far. Cassie noticed though. She heaved herself to her feet and lumbered over, sniffing loudly until she found the speck of food. Then she continued over to Emily, wagging her tail, letting her know that more would be acceptable. Emily stroked her head and pushed the wet nose away. Margaret stood, picked up the tray, then paused, holding it as a thought occurred to her.

"I sometimes wonder if the good side took over in the end, if she wanted to be caught, to stop what she was doing."

"Has she ever said that?"

"No, she never discusses what she did." Margaret said, "She

mainly just asks me to send money for cigarettes. I have to post a cheque, payable to the prison governor. It feels very odd. They put it into an account for her and there's a little shop, she calls it the canteen, where she can spend it. To buy toiletries, things like that.

"But the way that she was caught, she was so careless. I wondered if she had had enough, if deep down she wanted someone to stop her because she knew that she couldn't stop herself. She was so careful when she started and made such big mistakes by the end.

"I'll just clear away these things, then I'll tell you about it. About how she was caught, how it all ended."

Chapter Eleven

Other People

Emily stared at her. She had never heard this before, had only a vague idea of what happened. She knew the police had found enough evidence to convict Joanna, but little else. She rose to help Margaret but was waved down again.

Margaret took the tray into the kitchen and emptied it into the sink. She would wash up later. She thought that if she was going to explain what had happened, to finish her story, she needed to be busy with something. It was still painful for her to think about, there were too many conflicting emotions, even now. Sometimes she wished Joanna had just run away, left the country or something, had never been caught. There had been something rather wonderful about her as well as something terrible. Her freedom from all restraints, her focus. But she knew this was wrong of her, she should be glad that justice had been done. She collected her knitting bag from the table under the window and went back to the sitting room.

Cassie had given up on her quest for food and was now back on the rug. She looked up, tail wagging when Margaret entered, hoping for a walk, saw the knitting bag and lowered her head.

Margaret sat, pulled out a fat ball of green wool and a pair of metal needles. She glanced at the pattern and began to cast on stitches. Emily curled her legs up into the chair and moved a cushion to where she could hug it while she listened, as if she needed some protection from what she was about to hear.

"As I said, Joanna began to get careless. I think she also didn't really consider what the police would discover through the autopsies. They could of course, look at the contents of the stomach. The poison worked very quickly, so they could easily determine what the victims had eaten that had been poisoned. I think that Joanna knew the food might not be eaten for a while, so she knew there was no way to prove which day it had been added to the food. But *where* it was administered was easy for them.

"The police soon realised there was a link to the school. For a while they thought it might be a teacher or another parent. They let the staff and pupils know they might be at risk, warned them to be alert. They even sent detectives to a couple of big events at the school, thinking they might be likely targets. They never found anything of course, Joanna never returned to the school after that first visit. It did, however make the parents very aware. That's how they got the photo-fit of that poor boy. Someone remembered seeing him near one of the houses."

Margaret paused and counted her stitches. She checked her pattern, then continued.

"I think the police had their first major breakthrough when that woman found Joanna in her kitchen. She was a parent at the school, so she had received all the warnings. As soon as Joanna left, she phoned her neighbour, the one who Joanna claimed to be related to. Of course, she quickly learnt the neighbour didn't have a niece, had no idea who Joanna was, so the woman phoned the police. They went straight to her house and took a statement. They then guessed this was how Joanna had administered the poison, entering through the kitchens. They were able to go back to the other houses and check for fingerprints. They didn't find any, but they were lucky. At some point, Joanna must have pressed her face against some glass and for some reason it had been sheltered, the mark was preserved. It all added to the evidence against her.

"The woman was able to give a detailed description of course,

Joanna hadn't been in any sort of disguise. The police did one of those drawings, the ones that usually don't resemble the person at all. They took it to the school, asked the staff if it looked like any of the parents or ex-pupils. That's where they got lucky again, one of the teachers realised it was the person who had looked around the school a few months previously, when they were interviewing for a new teacher. She had a good eye, was bit of an artist herself, so she was able to help the police make a much more accurate drawing. All the staff were able to confirm the likeness, they all recognised Joanna.

"Of course, the school had no contact details for the mystery woman, even the telephone she used turned out to be stolen. But the police knew they had what they needed to catch her. She was so distinctive, you see."

Margaret stopped and looked at the young woman curled next to her. She saw the same snub nose, the same big eyes and clear skin, the straight hair and the childish body. They really were very alike.

"The police released her picture to the media. The response was pretty immediate. Surprisingly, Joanna herself never saw it. Or at least, she claimed she never did. As I said, I wondered if she wanted a way out, if she half wanted them to catch her.

"That young man she was using, Jim, he saw it. But he refused to believe it was Joanna, he said that he couldn't see the likeness, though it was plain as day to everyone else. Even some of his work colleagues saw it, showed him the photo when they saw him in the pub. He just got angry with them, told them they were jealous, just being nasty. I don't know if he started to wonder though, if in private he was beginning to suspect and might have asked her about it if he'd had more time. But they were arrested a few days after the picture was released, so we'll never know. It went against him of course, people wondered why he hadn't turned her in, if he was innocent.

It seemed to matter to him that she was a teacher, I remember that coming out at the trial. For some reason he thought someone educated, a different class to him, couldn't possibly be responsible for the things they were accusing her of. And of course, he loved her, he hoped they would make a life together. He said at one point he'd always thought she was too good for him, too good to be true, and it turned out that he was right. Such bitterness. It was so sad. I worried he took too much on himself, he behaved almost as if he thought it was his fault somehow, that he deserved for her to be bad. I do hope someone put him right, helped him to see that she used all of us, none of us were to blame for what she did."

Margaret looked up from her knitting, met Emily's eye.

"Not even us. You must always be sure of that. I may have made mistakes in raising her, but you did nothing. What Joanna did, she did because she wanted to. I don't believe either of us could have stopped her.

"Anyway, the police soon had her name. A few people had contacted them, past employers, people from the pub she used to go to."

"Did you?" asked Emily.

Margaret put her knitting on her lap again and frowned.

"No, actually, I hadn't seen the photograph. I was often too busy in those days, I didn't really keep up with the news. But sometimes I ask myself what I would have done if I had seen it. I think I would have known immediately that it was her, and when I read the reports I would have known that she was responsible, was capable of being responsible. But would I have phoned the police? I like to think that I would have."

She paused, then added, "But if I'm really truthful, I don't know. When you raise a child you become very protective of them. And Joanna was such a muddled little thing when she arrived, I'm sure she had suffered when she was young, before they gave her to me. She was like a wild animal really, you knew you would never tame her, you just hoped to live alongside her. But turning her in to the police would have been hard for me. I'm grateful that I didn't have to. Once they had her name, she was easy to find, she had rubbed up against the police her whole life, her name was on their files. The police came to me."

"Yes, I sort of remember that day," said Emily, "not that I knew what was happening".

"No, you were very young," agreed Margaret, "and I did my best to keep you out of it. They arrived at the house with warrants all prepared, they wanted to search the house. I played with you in your room, do you remember?"

Emily shook her head.

"We stayed in there for hours, had a picnic tea on the floor. I didn't bring you out until most of the police had gone, just one officer was still there.

"It felt very strange, knowing they had searched the house, gone through all our things. Joanna's door was locked, she always kept it locked. I gave them permission to open it. I'm glad you don't remember, you were upset about that door, seeing it broken.

"The police did interview you, but they were very gentle, I think you just thought it was some kind of a game."

"Did the police arrest her at the house?"

"No, she never came home."

***

My Story

I think I should just jump in here a second. Like I said before, that house was never home to me. It was the place where Ma let me live, her warped idea of being a do-gooder or something. Though she's right, my project was abruptly halted that day.

We got back to the flat laughing, Jim explaining how he could get the boiler working in that house, me thinking it might not be such a bad idea. Perhaps we could go back later, when it was properly dark, take some wine, have a laugh. We managed to find a parking space and walked back to the flat, passed all the parked cars that were always there, not paying any attention. Of course, I know now they weren't the same ones at all, that at least some of them belonged to the filth, but we didn't notice. No one would have.

Jim opened the door and we both stepped inside, still laughing, I remember that. Then they appeared. Pounced really. A Ninja attack but with polite English voices, explaining we were under arrest, walking forwards with handcuffs, clipping them on.

Someone was talking, telling us our rights, that we were being arrested on suspicion of murder, that we had the right to remain silent, all the words you know by heart from watching rubbish police dramas on telly. It felt like a police drama to be honest. Jim was shouting, yelling at them to let him go, he hadn't done nothing, they couldn't just barge into his flat like that, it was private property. He got one arm free, tried to take a swing at one. That didn't help, course it didn't.

I was thinking fast, could almost hear the thoughts rushing through my head. I felt alive, ready for the challenge, looking for a way out of this. I didn't resist at all, just let them cuff me, gave them my 'sweet but confused' look, asked them what it was all about. I had a quick glance around, not for more than a second. I was looking for the police witch, wanted her to see I wasn't bothered, all this was nothing to do with me. She wasn't there though. It didn't matter. I had enough of an audience even without her. I was asking them what was the matter, what had Jim done that was so bad? I managed to twist my face towards him as they led him out, watched him bucking as he tried to resist, using all his strength to throw them off course. Stupid really, but he never had been the clever one.

"What did you do?" I shouted to him, "What have you got me into?"

He stared back at me. I saw all the anger and confusion burning out his eyes, opened his mouth to say something, then he was gone, practically shoved down the stairs and into the street. We were bustled into separate cars and taken to the nick - not the local one, the one where the murder squad was based. I was pleased about that, pleased they recognised this was something important, not some silly local thing.

I talked all the way to the police station. I would say "chatted" except the plods in the car never really answered, just kept telling me I'd get my chance to ask questions when we got there. I was very calm of course, things like that don't bother me. I see them as a challenge, I don't go to pieces like most people. I talked a lot about Jim, about how you never really knew someone did you, and whatever he'd done, it was nothing to do with me. Then I gave them a running commentary on the places we were passing, the pub for tired builders, the hairdressers if you wanted a blue rinse, the shop on the corner where you could buy anything all night long but you needed to check your change. It was all rubbish, all meant to use up the air, stop me saying anything I might regret. I could tell they were listening, beginning to warm towards me. One of them even laughed at one point, a sudden snort of laughter then looked quickly out the window, like it hadn't been him, not wanting to look unprofessional.

When we arrived at the nick we went straight through to the custody Sargent. I had to stand there, waiting, while the arresting officer explained I was to be detained for questioning, that I might pose a risk to others. He was right about that, not that I showed it. He was quite nice looking, I watched him, gave him the eye a bit.

He noticed, I could tell, stood a bit taller, had a slight smile while he spoke. Men are all the same, as I've told you before. They like to be admired, even by someone being arrested on suspicion of murder.

We had bit of a disagreement then. They wanted my clothes, I suppose to test them for traces of poison or something, like I was an amateur, would've been careless. I was a bit narked to be honest, but I also did not want to wear some hideous prison outfit. You never know what kind of person might have worn it before, plus I knew it wouldn't fit right. I argued for a bit, told them it wasn't necessary, there was nothing to find, were they all perverts, liked to examine women's clothes did they? It didn't make any difference. I knew it wouldn't, but no point in making this easy for them. I could see they were starting to get annoyed, thought I was a hassle. I didn't want them to start getting all official on me, so I changed track, turned all flirty again. I told them I was a size 8, did they have anything in my size, something to show off my cleavage? Of course, they all then had a quick glance, to see if it was worth displaying, which it was. They were men.

It didn't go quite so well when I was in the cell, being given a tracky to change into. The woman looked like the back end of a bus, what you'd expect from a WPC really. I tried to connect with her, confided that I fancied the plod who had made the arrest, asked what it was like working there, smiled a lot. I might as well have not bothered. Was like being processed by a machine. Someone came and took swabs, treated me as if I were one of the specimens in the lab. I made a fuss, told them I knew my rights. Made no difference. They're cold those people, inhuman, you can't get through to them.

I made a joke about it later, in the interview room. They'd offered me a solicitor, said it would be free. But I didn't want that. If they're free they're not worth having, that's my view. And I didn't want someone speaking for me, telling me to be quiet when I wanted to have my say. I figured I was at least as clever as any lawyer. I led the interview from the start, walked in with hips swaying, head held high, boobs to the fore. There was a woman and a bloke, so I ignored her, smiled at him and settled into the chair. Treated it like a big joke. Obviously I had been duped by my evil boyfriend, nasty old Jim had been up to something and I was in the dark. I would help them as much as I could, but really, I didn't know anything, and as soon as they could sort it out and we could all go home, the better. It was a shame for them to be wasting their time like this, when there were real criminals out there, walking free.

The interview changed track after a while, I think the woman was fed up with it being a friendly chat. She started banging questions at me, showing me photos, asking who I knew, where I was on certain dates. I played the dizzy blonde. Shame I wasn't wearing my wig. My memory for dates was awful, yes, I did remember Jim taking me to those places, I didn't know why though, I assumed he had some pay to collect for work he'd done. That's what he told me anyway. I didn't recognise anyone in the photos. Not even the photofit of me. I took a long time over that, said I thought I might have seen her somewhere, wasn't sure where..... Well, I was hardly going to tell them it was me and congratulate them for the awful likeness was I?

After a while they took me back to the cell. I wasn't sure I preferred it actually, it was very boring. I refused their kind offer of a phone call. I didn't think it concerned anyone else, no point in involving Ma, she'd be no use at all. I even decided to not mention the prawn, I couldn't see how I could use being a mother to my advantage, decided it wasn't a strong enough reason for them to release me, so I kept quiet. Maybe I could use it later, say they had violated my rights or something. So there I sat. For hours. Used the time to think about what I would say next time, tried out a few ideas ready for another interview, wondered what I could request that would cause them some bother.

I was ready for another interview by the time they came for me again. I thought I might try the 'weak and exhausted' routine, go for sympathy rather than empathy. But they didn't want to interview me. I was taken out the cell, made to stand in front of the custody sergeant again and charged. Simple as that. Hardly a fair process.

***

Other People

Margaret looked across at Emily. She was managing to listen, holding in any thoughts and not too emotional. She decided to continue, to finish the story. She began with Jim.

"I did feel sorry for that poor man, he was thoroughly duped by Joanna. I know he felt stupid, afterwards, when everyone was accusing him of being involved, and then refusing to believe that he hadn't known what she was doing. It ruined his life as soundly as it ruined ours. People remember things like that. He felt so foolish, I could see it in his eyes at the court when he was giving evidence. It sounded so silly, you see, all the lies that he had believed. He didn't even know Joanna's real name or where we lived. I really think that he loved her too. Even when it was obvious to everyone else that she was guilty, he was still trying to defend her, to say she had been set up. Such a shame. It could have been so different if she had made different choices."

She stopped again, remembering. Jim had worn his best clothes to the trial, they didn't fit very well. A crumpled shirt and tie and a dark suit bought for funerals that had hung unworn in his wardrobe for years. She had noticed his face puffy from lack of sleep, his eyes had a haunted look, as if he still couldn't quite believe the truth, like he was waiting, hoping, to wake up and find it wasn't real.

Margaret approached him at one point, tried to reassure him, to explain that she too had been deceived by Joanna. But he hadn't wanted to listen. He pushed past her, told her that her family had done enough damage, he wanted nothing more to do with them. She didn't know what happened to him after that, whether he had moved, built a new life for himself. She hoped so. He was a good person, you could see that just by the things he had said, the things he had been hoping for when he joined up with Joanna.

"The police searched his flat but they didn't find anything. The only evidence they found was at our house, in her room. They found lists of addresses and of course the poison."

"What was it? Arsenic?"

"No, it was some complicated name, I'd never heard of it before. She had stolen it years before, when she was at that little university in the north. I don't think they had even missed it, they were at the trial of course, had to justify their procedures. I expect someone lost their job over it, which is right really, they should have been more careful.

"It was a tiny university though, it was run more like a school in many ways. I had hoped it would suit Joanna, there would be less opportunity to be wild. I went with her before she applied, had a tour and listened to a talk, met some of the lecturers. They seemed to focus on the course, getting the students through the work, taking care of them. It was all organised into colleges, a bit like Oxford and Cambridge, though it was tiny, as I said. It felt more like a senior school, with the students put into houses. There wasn't too much emphasis on social things, the student bar, the nightlife. I thought it was a good idea for her to go, that she would be safe there."

She shook her head, "I made so many mistakes. I sometimes

185

forgot that it was others who needed protecting from Joanna, not the other way round. Especially then, when she was younger. It changed a bit when you were born, I think I became more aware of how dangerous she might turn out to be. When I had you to protect, Joanna seemed more a threat, less a victim.

"I hate thinking about that poison being in the house for all those years." She shivered, thinking of what might have happened, glad in some ways that Joanna had insisted on the locked door. At least no one had found it inadvertently, at least Emily had been safe. But was that selfish? Perhaps if Emily had stumbled on it, others would have been saved. Perhaps losing Emily would have been a fair price to pay for not noticing what was happening, for not realising what Joanna was capable of.

She took out her pattern and checked her stitches, counting rows, pushing the thought away.

"I wonder if I will ever stop being haunted by guilt," she said. "However much I rationalise it, however many times I tell myself there was no way I could have known, that Joanna was bad from the start, I still have that little feeling gnawing away at my stomach.

"I continually question myself, asking if I could have done things differently. Perhaps if I had asked for help from professionals when she was a teenager. Or maybe I ignored her too much after you were born. She was so difficult to be with at times, it was easier to live independently, to share the same space but not have too much interaction. Was I partly to blame? It tortures me sometimes. And other times I am peaceful, I know that there was nothing I could have done to change who she chose to be."

Margaret sighed and shook her head. Such a muddle of feelings, so many unknowns. But wasn't parenthood always like that? Didn't every parent wonder if they could have behaved differently and avoided their child having that illness, that anxiety, that fault?

"Joanna never came home after that of course, they kept her

locked away. I think the case against her was very strong, they had the witness, they had found the poison in her room. For a while they considered the possibility that I might have been involved or Jim, especially Jim. But eventually they realised we knew nothing, even if perhaps we should have done.

"I never saw Jim again, after she was sentenced. I don't think he keeps in touch with her."

Trials were strange like that. A whole mix of people brought together from various corners for a few intense weeks, weeks that often changed the course of their lives. There was no escaping the questions, sometimes intimate parts of your life were examined, everyone in the courtroom heard, you just prayed the journalists would pick something else for their reports, that your life would stay out of the newspapers. Then nothing, no contact, no information. Everyone went back to their lives. It wasn't as if they were all going to start exchanging contact details, and yet there was something strange about sharing such an intense experience and then going their separate ways.

"Did they ever think she was insane?" asked Emily. "Surely no one who was sane would do the things that she did."

"Apparently not. I don't know how anyone manages to be legally insane actually. You have to be able to prove that you didn't realise what you were doing was wrong at the time that you were doing it. Joanna knew very well that it was wrong, against the law, even if she felt no guilt. The fact that she took precautions to cover her tracks, wore gloves so there were no fingerprints, things like that. It showed it was all premeditated, all planned."

"Will she ever be released?"

Margaret shook her head behind her knitting, "No, that seems very unlikely. From what I understand they feel she will always be a risk to society, what she did was too cold, too calculating. She had no reason to kill those people, they were strangers."

She glanced up.

"You have never wanted to visit her, have you? Do you think that you might now, now that you are going to have a child?"

"Well, I still haven't decided if I am going to have this child. But no, I really don't. My feelings are very muddled, but from what you say, visiting Joanna would make me more muddled, not less. If she knew I was confused about my feelings she might try and use that, to manipulate me again. Like you said, we don't owe Joanna anything, she gave to us because she wanted to control us, not because she loved us. In a funny sort of way, that sets me free. You see, it means I don't owe her anything back, I feel no obligation to her. You were my mother really, I always felt that. If I cried, needed help, I would never have run to Joanna, always to you. I don't feel I missed being mothered."

The two women looked at each other and smiled. They didn't need to discuss their feelings for each other, it was all in that smile, understood, accepted, final.

Chapter Twelve

Other People

When Emily left Margaret's house, she felt happier, more at peace with her past and her feelings towards Joanna. But she was no nearer making a decision about her own baby. As she left, Margaret pressed a book into her hand, told her to read it when she was at home. Emily opened it there, standing on the doorstep. It was a book of photographs, each one showing the development of a baby as it grew inside the womb, week by week. It told her when the baby had fingerprints, at what age it could hear, when it began to swallow.

Emily was cross, had told Margaret that this was not a fair gift, that she was trying to manipulate her decision. It was tantamount to emotional blackmail. Margaret informed her that when a baby's life was at stake, she felt it bypassed the need to 'play fair'. She said she was not trying to force Emily's decision, she was merely equipping her with all the facts, letting her know exactly what she would be destroying if she decided to terminate this pregnancy.

Margaret was a determined woman. She was also prepared to live by her convictions, her beliefs weren't simply theories. Which is why, when Joanna was pregnant, Margaret had encouraged her to return home, knowing she would be forfeiting her own freedom if she were to stop Joanna aborting her child. For Margaret, abortion was taking the life of an unborn child. She had not managed to stop Joanna killing others, but she would do her best to stop Emily - because if she was honest, she wasn't sure if it was different. She didn't point this out, had merely given Emily the book and justified her action. She knew it would anger Emily, a small price to pay, for the unborn baby's right to be acknowledged.

Emily arrived home before Josh. She let herself in, glad for the solitude. He had probably gone to the pub after the game, she would have another hour before he arrived home smelling of beer and shower gel.

She threw her keys onto the shelf by the door and went up to their room. Lying on the bed, propped up with a stack of pillows, she reached for her laptop and rested it on her knees. She would do some research, tackle this problem scientifically. Following her feelings was getting her nowhere.

She went first to sites that explained psychopathy. She learnt what it meant, from a scientific point of view, to be a psychopath. It was an uncomfortable reading experience, she recognised Joanna in much of the description. She found she was chewing her cheek as she read and flinched as her teeth drew blood. Some of the research papers were contradictory or vague but there was sufficient information to build up a picture. She was especially interested in the correlation between psychopathy and serial killers. There were thought to be many more psychopaths than criminals.

Emily stared across at the window, her brow creased. Was Margaret right? Was being a psychopath not necessarily evil? Was it possible to parent a psychopathic child so they learned good behaviour, so their disorder became a strength? Was she strong enough to undertake such a thing, was she prepared to take the risk? Did she even want to?

Emily knew that if her mother had not been Joanna, if she had been a normal child with a normal parent, then she would have welcomed this pregnancy. It was too early in her time with Josh, much sooner than they would have planned to have children, but that would not have stopped her having the baby. She would have had to rearrange her life, put her career on hold while they sorted out child care, but her and Josh would make good parents, she would enjoy it. She thought about Josh. If she decided that keeping the baby was a possibility, he should not be a silent partner. She should allow him to help make the decision.

As if on cue, the phone rang, making her jump. It was Josh. He'd finished celebrating with his team mates, thought that he might call in on his parents before he came home. Did she mind?

She said she didn't, even though she did. She closed her phone and frowned. She wanted him to come home, felt irritated. She knew his mother preferred that, to have her boy to herself again for a couple of hours, and usually Emily was happy enough to not accompany him. She had nothing against Josh's parents, they seemed nice enough people. There was the occasional tension when his mother tried to direct her cleaning methods or suggest that Josh should help less in the kitchen, but mostly their relationship was harmonious, if not close.

She glanced at the clock and decided she would go out, sitting at her computer wasn't helping her to sort out anything. Emily disliked decisions like these. She was happier with number problems, wished she could allocate a number to each option and formulate the solution. Real life issues were always tricky.

She found her boots where she had left them by the front door and grabbed a coat. It wasn't cold but she planned to drive to the park, walk a bit, see if it cleared her mind. The roads were slow, full of elderly people returning from their weekly shop and parents ferrying their children home from weekend clubs.

Emily drove to the park and left her car in the small square carpark at the side. It was adjacent to the children's play area and she strolled across, drawn by the shouts of children on the swings.

There were two families there, two sets of two children with both parents. One father roamed the grass area beyond the low wooden fence, watching a golden retriever as it sniffed the ground.

Emily thought how much easier having a dog would be to having a child. You knew where you were with a dog. Then she thought of the nasty little brown thing that had snapped at her when she last in the town and changed her mind. Maybe raising anything was a risk, gambling with genes that you couldn't fight against. Biological roulette.

The children were chasing each other over the roundabout and under the swings. They shouted as they ran, one trying to catch the others, who laughed every time he made a grab for them and missed. The mothers sat together on the bench, chatting, ignoring their offspring. The other father was bored, trying to persuade one of the boys to go on a swing, offering to push him. Emily watched. There was no way of knowing what these children would grow up to be, who would succeed in life, be independent, useful to society, and who would be a drain, causing hurt and misery. No guarantees, she thought again, no parent could be sure of what they would get, what kind of child they would be required to nurture and guide.

She turned away and headed for the park, striding across the grass. Did she want a child? If she was prepared to face the risks, to believe that her and Josh could guide a child towards good choices, to develop strengths and control weaknesses, did she even want a child? She enjoyed her job, but she could see it wasn't enough to fulfil her forever. Her and Josh had talked about travelling, seeing the world. But was that to fill the space which children would naturally take, a sort of consolation prize? Was raising happy healthy children what she was designed to do, or was it merely the image that the world liked to create, despite its claims of emancipation?

She slowed, suddenly tired. It had been a long afternoon. The images of the babies in the book that Margaret had forced upon her, were clear in her mind. They were little people, floating in their own world. It was strange to think one was developing inside her now. She began to walk back to the carpark.

When she reached the car she sat for a while. She felt cross, nothing had been solved. She still did not know what to do. But one idea was becoming clearer. She needed to tell Josh. She could no longer deny him the right to participate in this decision. Which actually, was the end of the discussion because she knew what he would say. Josh would want this baby. Josh, with his blue eyes that were so different to her mother's, eyes that were filled with emotion, Josh with his ideals and passions and morals and huge expressions of love. Josh would want this baby. There was no doubt in her mind at all. He would be shocked when she told him about Joanna, anyone would be. He might even be angry with her for not telling him sooner, he might shout and swear, as he often did when angry. But never for long. Then he would come to her, find where she had hidden, while he bashed cupboard doors or stomped to the shed. He would come to her and put his arms around her, whisper that he was sorry, that he loved Emily. He would tell her that his love was strong enough for their present and their future, that it could obliterate her past, that she should have trusted him sooner. He would want this baby. He would help her to care for it, he would love and nurture it as he loved and cared for Emily. There was no doubt in her mind. The decision to include Josh was really a decision to keep the baby. You could not separate the two.

She turned the key, listening to the engine. She would buy some wine on the way home. Then she paused, thumped the steering wheel. She was pregnant, pregnant women aren't supposed to drink. As she drove home she began to wonder what else she would have to give up.

***

Josh did not shout or swear. She told him during dinner. They sat, either side of the little table in the corner of their lounge and she told him, between mouthfuls of limp cabbage and dry chicken, she explained about her past. She started with Joanna first, it seemed fairer than letting him get all excited about the baby and then throwing the horrible truth into the mix afterwards.

So she told him. She explained that her mother was alive, in prison, serving time for multiple murders, a certified psychopath. She explained that Margaret had adopted her and they had moved away, started their lives again as two anonymous people, that she grew up telling people her mother was dead because that was easier and allowed her a certain freedom, to be released from her mother's legacy.

Josh had watched her while she spoke, those eyes framed by lashes that were too long for a man, 'girl eyes' Emily always thought. He didn't interrupt her, allowed her to speak. Then he had gone to her side of the table, pushed her plate of congealed dinner to one side and sat on the table, in front of her, put his arms around her shoulders, held her close.

"Poor, poor, you," he whispered into her hair. "No wonder you didn't want people to know, I can see that, I do understand." He moved back a little and stared into her eyes, his own very blue, very intense. "I wish you had felt able to tell me sooner, could've trusted me a bit better. But I think I understand."

He stood, walked away from the table, brushed his hands through his hair, leaving it standing in spiky tufts on top of his head. He stared towards the window, his eyes unseeing.

"Wow, Emily, this is big." He exhaled loudly, the air hissing through his teeth as his mind tried to understand this, to absorb this massive piece of information that his wife was now, finally, handing to him. It felt like mental indigestion. He wondered if he would prefer to not know, that she had kept the secret forever, decided that no, it was better he knew. He realised what it had cost her, to carry the knowledge and not share it. And now to decide to tell him, to risk allowing the facts to leak to another individual, to allow him to see her as a complete person, with her past, her childhood, trailing behind her.

A thought occurred to him and he frowned.

"Why now? What made you tell me now? Has she asked to see you or something?" He turned, facing her again.

The light was behind him, the evening sun low in the sky, dazzling her as she looked at him. He was a blank silhouette, a hulk of familiar form with no details. She couldn't read his face, couldn't even see it, all was shadow. Only his voice gave her clues, strained, intense but calm. She knew he was struggling to understand, wanted to protect her, was on her side. She swallowed, took a sip of water that was slightly warm from having sat for too long on the table.

"I'm pregnant."

There was no way to soften it. It was not an occasion for romantic music and candles, little messages in gift bags, emotional scenes that could be posted on Facebook. It was a fact, stark and scary.

"I am pregnant and I don't know what to do."

He came at once, hurrying across the space between them. He hugged her, almost lifted her from her seat.

"But Em, that's wonderful! Wow. That's big but good, so good. I'm so pleased, so happy. Hey, I managed it, I'm not firing blanks after all!"

He was excited, enthusiastic, boisterous, all in a flash. She could see that he hadn't linked the two. Hadn't considered why she was telling him both things at once. He pulled back, noticing her tension, not understanding.

"What's the matter? What am I missing here? This is good isn't it? I mean, I know it's not what you wanted, not what we planned. But surely you don't mind that much? Now that it's happened, surely you can accept it? Change your plans?"

He moved back round the table, sat on his chair. There was something boy-like, young, about his confusion. His eyes were worried now, knowing he was missing something but unable to find it. He knew she had been adamant about not having children but he hadn't considered that she might not want to keep one should it appear.

Emily watched him. She saw his eyes change, the confusion begin to harden, his mouth set into a thin line. She knew at once what he was thinking, could almost see the thoughts as they followed each other through his mind. First that bubble of happiness, then confusion as he realised she wasn't celebrating, now anger as he thought that she was putting her career before their child, that she was determined to continue with her life plan at the expense of what he wanted. She lifted her glass again, drank more not cold water, giving herself time.

"I know we agreed to not have kids Em," he said, "but surely now you're pregnant, we can change that decision. I was willing to stick with your plan, to let you have your way. But not now. This changes all that. You surely cannot be thinking of..." He paused, unwilling to say it, to actually put into words the horror that was forming in his mind. "Surely you aren't thinking of killing our baby."

He stumbled over the last words, his face flushed. Emily thought he might cry. She needed to explain, to say the link that he had missed but she didn't know how. She didn't know how to crush him so completely, but nor could she leave him there. She started to move cutlery, to put forks and knives together, to scrape the food onto a single plate.

"Leave that!" he was angry now, seeing her with new eyes, furious she would deny him this thing that seemed to have dropped from Heaven.

When she spoke he had to lean forwards to hear, the words came through a mist of hair and tears.

"You are forgetting what I just told you. About my mother. The baby–" she stopped, not sure if she could say it, picked up the plates again, moved the cutlery from one side to the next, stood, cleared her throat. "The baby might, might be, the same."

There, she had said it. It was out. Everything linked, her whole past present and future in a long twisted line of warped genetic potential.

"Oh. Oh, I see." He stayed in his seat, watched her leave, carry the plates into their tiny kitchen.

She lowered them into the sink, leaned against the stretch of work surface that ran from one side of her kitchen to the other. It was barely a kitchen, more of a large cupboard with units where she cooked. She waited. There was no sound from the other room. She wanted his arms around her, felt empty. She wanted him to come to her, to comfort her, to tell her it would be alright.

But he didn't. There was a rustle of clothing, footsteps in the hall, the slam of the front door. She was alone.

Emily left the plates in the sink, not even bothering to scrape the food into the bin or run water into the saucepans that stood on the stove. They were abandoned, as she was abandoned. She had not expected him to leave. To shout perhaps or bang the furniture. To be angry and frustrated. But not to leave, for her to be left so totally alone.

She heard his car leave the little patch of parking that they shared with their neighbours, the engine growing fainter as he drove out the cul-de-sac, to goodness knows where. She wondered how long he would be, how long before he deigned to share his views and feelings with her. The anger was beginning to take over now, the emptiness replaced with a hot hard stone.

How dare he just leave? She had done her best, tried to be honest with him, let him know about her past, what it meant. This was something they must face together, a shared problem. Now he was shutting himself away, allowing himself the luxury of time and space while she was left alone, not knowing, waiting.

She stamped her way up the stairs, went into the bathroom, slammed the door. She wanted to break something, shout at someone, scream.

Instead she took out her cotton wool from the mirrored unit above the sink, began to remove her makeup. She smeared remover across her eyes, wiped it with the cotton wool, twisted her hair into an elastic band. She turned on the water and washed her face, rinsing away the last traces of black from her lashes. Then she stepped to the shower, turned it on, removed her clothes, stepped back into the flow. The water scalded her skin. It calmed her, forced her to focus on the present.

She was dry and sitting up in bed when Josh returned. She heard the car, then the key scraping in the door, his footsteps as he came up the stairs. He stood in the doorway, silent, just looking at her. She lowered the book she was pretending to read. His eyes were red and his hair looked as if it had been back combed. He looked broken, young, vulnerable. She was angry, started to form words that would smack him, let him know that this wasn't just about him, how dare he walk out on her, behave like a child.

"Sorry."

Just that word. That's all he said. Her anger melted as swiftly as it had grown. He meant it, she could see. He was sorry. He knew he should have stayed, knew that leaving was wrong, irresponsible, selfish. But it was all he had been capable of. Now he was sorry.

She dropped the book onto the floor, held out her arms. He came to her, buried his head in her, squeezed her close.

"I'm sorry. I had to go. To think," his words were muffled, coming from deep inside of him. "I love you Em," he said, "really love you. This is horrible, really horrible. But it might not be. We might be able to do this, the baby might be alright."

He drew back and looked at her for a long minute.

"Please Em, please can we try? Please can we keep this baby? It's our baby, ours. Not your mother's or some mutant. It's our baby. Let's give it a chance. Please Em."

She looked back at him. She loved this man. There was no decision, not any more. She had known there wouldn't be. This baby would be born. It would have its chance.

***

My Story

So now you have it. The full story. All the things I had to cope with, Ma and her cult, the weakness of the prawn. They're in the past now, never really give them a thought these days.

You thought my bit was finished? This is MY story, surely you wouldn't expect someone else to have the last word?

You might be wondering how I am getting on in here. Well, it's not as bad as you might think. There are lots of people to lead, to have some fun with, toying with their lives. I have a whole group of them, my girlies I call them. They all give me much more respect than Ma ever did. All sorts of losers just waiting for a little guidance. There is loads of potential for fun in here, it's like a science lab. You can set all the elements for a little conflict, a fight perhaps, then sit back and watch the players in action. The anger being vented, the suspicions being voiced, the staff struggling to control situations. Ah yes, it is not necessary to be bored, the games can continue, even when the doors are locked.

Living is basic but not so terrible. I get my own room of course, even if the showers aren't exactly en suite. Of course, I'm lucky I'm female, I get to wear my own clothes, not like the men who have to wear whatever's assigned to them. Sharing underwear has never

199

appealed. I'm category A, which has a certain ring to it, don't you think? I like to think it's A for effort. Who would want to be classed as a B? So not my style.

I can even leave my Houseblock – Houseblock Two – if I decide to visit The Bridge. We can learn stuff in there. Nothing interesting of course, nothing designed for a person with a brain, but it might be useful at some point. I've been learning about hair and beauty, 'Vocational Qualifications' they call it. Fancy name for a piece of paper that says I can cut hair and paint nails.

Of course, the project has never been finished, not conclusively. Not yet anyway. There is always a chance I might continue when I get out of here.

Are you surprised at that, that one day I will walk out of here? Perhaps you should spend a little less time reading novels, and a little more time researching the prison system in your country. You do rely on it to keep you safe after all, safe from people like me. Most people walk out of here eventually. Some of my girlies are frantically trying to arrange that now, but they're going about it all wrong of course. They are putting their faith in the legal system, spending hours reading law books, looking for loopholes big enough to squeeze out of. Some of them are more knowledgeable than their lawyers.

I have gone a different route, one I feel will be more profitable. You see, they allow us lots of access to books in here. No internet of course, but we have an abundance of time and a well-stocked library. One can become an expert in all kinds of things. There are lots of books on psychology, explanations of every kind of neurological illness, every mental disorder known to man. We can study them at leisure. There are also a couple of qualified psychologists doing time here. I made an effort to get to know them, got them to trust me. I spend time gleaning information from them, learning their skills. Much more profitable than hairdressing, much more useful.

Every so often some wet-nosed kid straight from college comes and administers tests, surreptitiously, as though we don't know that we are being assessed. It doesn't take a genius to know which answers to give, the timeframes required to show you are making progress, that you understand and are sorry for your crimes, a changed person, won't ever do it again miss. I'm doing very well, I can read it in their eyes.

Oh yes, it shouldn't be long now before I'm walking out of here, back into your world. Not that you will recognise me. I will be that friendly middle-aged lady on the bus, the one with the funny sense of humour who's so friendly, always stops for a chat. I will be the leader of the institute, the chief librarian, the shopkeeper who cares. Perhaps I will be the hairdresser who comes to your home, so much more convenient than having to go to a salon, cheaper too. And you'll get an excellent hair cut for the price, great value with some witty conversation thrown in for free. Everyone loves to talk to their hairdresser, who do you trust more?

You will meet me but you won't know me. And perhaps one day I will resume my project, it did have its exciting moments when all said and done. Perhaps I will pay you a visit one day. You will leave a door unlocked for me, won't you?

***

Other People

She would be seventy-five next week. Not that she would be celebrating. Birthdays always seemed a bit odd to her anyway, now she was older. Birthdays were for the young, those with their whole lives spread before them like an unopened gift. When you were old, what was there to celebrate? It would be an 'I'm not dead yet' party. She always thought that when she saw photographs in the newspaper: Michael and Dorothy celebrate their one hundredth birthday. No, she wouldn't be doing that. She had little to celebrate anyway.

The taxi pulled into the drop-off bay and she reached for her bag. The driver was twitchy, checking his mirrors, worrying in case they were blocking the road for an emergency. Well they weren't, this was where he was supposed to drop her and she wouldn't be hurried, not today.

He was telling her the price and pointing at his meter, the little red numbers confirming what he'd said. As if he wasn't sure if she would understand, needed to see the amount as well as hear it. Silly man, she was old, not foreign. She held out a note and waited for the change, watched as he counted it into her hand, then passed him back one of the pound coins for his tip. Not that he deserved one, he had driven much too fast, but she considered it polite. You always tipped taxi drivers and hairdressers. That was how the world worked.

She struggled with the door, managed to get it open and heaved herself out. He didn't get out, didn't help her. He just sat there, checking his mirrors, his hand on the key so he could start the engine as soon as her door was shut. She watched him leave, wanting to go back with him, to not face this. Perhaps if she wasn't there, it wouldn't be real. But it was. She took a breath, told herself to not be stupid, then walked towards the revolving door of the hospital.

She ignored all the signs, she knew where to go, had done this almost every day for the last few weeks. She hardly even noticed the other people now, the woman with the scarf wound around her head to hide her baldness, the man on crutches, swinging his good leg like some gymnast, the anxious woman with the crying child who was searching the hospital map to find where to go. She passed them all, not hurrying, not pausing. Past the information desk in the foyer, past the coffee shop littered with dirty cups and exhausted people, past the steps down to radiology. It was hot and she unwound her scarf as she walked, pulled off her gloves and threw them into her bag, on top of her knitting.

She veered off when she reached the little shop, went in to buy a magazine. She ignored the rows of get-well-soon cards, it was too late for that. She went straight to the magazine rack, scanned the shelves, looking for something interesting. Cross looking girls smothered in make-up stared back at her, the writing across their faces shouting about getting a promotion, avoiding STDs, and marriage advice from a divorced royal. She selected one with recipes and pictures of blossom, went to pay at the desk covered in disposable razors, chocolate bars and pens. The woman in front of her had bought a card, was struggling with the cellophane wrapper so she could write in it before she visited whoever it was that she had come to see.

She took her change and stuffed the magazine into her bag, next to the gloves. Then she made her way to the stairs. She always avoided the lifts, had never liked them. She knew that when she arrived, breathing hard and slightly dizzy, Jim would tell her she was silly. He would say that at her age she shouldn't be doing stairs, that it was time she started trusting lifts, no one ever got trapped in them, she had watched too many films.

She climbed the stairs, stopping at the first floor to catch her breath. They were grey, with a grey rail for her to cling on to which she was sure was covered with germs. All the fixtures in the hospital were grey or cream, whoever designed it disliked colours. Illness was drab.

She reached the second floor and walked to the ward, nodding to the nurse at the desk as she went past.

"Hello, Mrs Carrington," she said, looking up briefly from her notes as the elderly lady passed.

"How is he?" she asked.

"The same, really," said the nurse, not wanting to say. It wasn't her job to say, it was for the doctor. "We're keeping him comfortable," she added, "but he's very drowsy today. I'm not sure if he'll wake up for you. If you need anything, come and ask at the desk."

She thanked the nurse. They were all very kind in here. They all looked about ten years old.

The nurse nodded and smiled, paused for a moment as if she wanted to say something or to pat her shoulder, give her some kind of comfort. Then she looked down, continued with her work.

Rosemary continued. Past the beds with their curtains pushed back. Some patients were in bed, connected to tubes, trying to read or do the crossword. Some were sitting on those high backed blue chairs that look more comfortable than they are. They had got dressed for the day, were trying to feel normal, like a person not just a patient. They were failing – they would feel like a patient until the day they went home. If they went home.

She trudged on, to the end of the ward, to the little alcove at the side. The curtains were open, so the staff could see him, watch him when they passed. He wouldn't be watching anyone. She stood for a moment and looked at him.

Jim lay, propped up by pillows, his head at an angle and his eyes shut. His skin was yellow from the jaundice and one arm, the one that lay as if forgotten on the cover, was bruised. He looked smaller, smaller even than her, his body, which had once been so big, so strong, had wasted to nothing. He looked like an old man. The thought came to her that his face looked like an almond, it was a similar colour and had lines all over it. He was her son. She had grown him. How proud she had been when he grew as a teenager, taller than her, then even taller than that good for nothing playboy she had married. Jim was big, and as he started his job, doing manual labour, he grew strong. She had been so proud of her boy, her big strong son.

Now she was watching him waste away, powerless to stop it. It wasn't natural, went against the order of nature. You shouldn't watch your child die.

Rosemary folded her coat and placed it on the end of the bed, then settled into the chair next to the bed and pulled out her magazine. She opened it but continued to watch Jim, to watch his chest going up and down, the only sign that he was still breathing. It was that girl's fault of course, all those years ago, that Joanna; she had destroyed Jim, wrecked his life as surely as she had killed those other people. Memories of those years flooded back, sitting here in this unnatural place.

Rosemary had never actually met Joanna, had just heard about her from Jim, usually when he was phoning with excuses about not visiting. She had hardly seen him during those months when he was with Joanna but she could tell he was happy. There was an enthusiasm in his voice, as if he had at last found his place in the world, knew what he wanted. Then the arrest, that awful call from the police station, her life turning upside down. She hadn't gone to the trial, Jim told her the media were swarming over everyone, someone might link her to him, start asking questions. So she stayed at home, watched it on the news, read her son's life being picked over by the newspapers. It made for half an article in a Sunday magazine, a few lines on one front page, barely a mention in the news on telly. That was what they reduced her son to, a bit of background interest.

He gave up on women and turned to whiskey, said it was safer. She didn't realise how bad it was until that Christmas, a few years ago, when he came home, she could smell it on him, even in the mornings, when he eventually staggered out of bed. He would pass her on the landing and she would smell that sharp odour of alcohol seeping from his pores and know he had drunk himself to sleep again. She had tried to talk to him, even got Steven, his brother, to have a word. Not that it made any difference. He was angry with the whole world and that included them, he wouldn't listen, wouldn't change. He was a middle-aged man and he would make his own decisions, he didn't need his family interfering.

For a while she hardly saw him. She would phone occasionally but he rarely picked up and when he did she could tell he was drunk, slurring his words and talking nonsense. Then he rang her, asked if he could move back home for a bit. He wasn't even fifty but he seemed to have given up on the world, certainly on himself.

Steven had gone to collect him, to help him move his stuff. He told her the flat was terrible, hadn't been cleaned in months, stank of rotting food and sour pipes. Jim wasn't working, of course, had been given up on by anyone who had used him when he was well. They weren't even sure if he'd bothered to sign on, if he was collecting the social. There was no money at the flat, nothing of value. Nothing that you might expect a middle-aged man to own, a man who should have been in his prime, perhaps taking on someone younger, an apprentice, to help with the work, building up a decent business.

One of his mates kept in touch. Just one. He came down a couple of times, sat in Rosemary's kitchen and drank her tea, then went to sit with Jim for a while, try to talk about the game on Saturday or what was happening back in his old life. That friend told her how they watched Jim going downhill, had tried to save him. The drinking started almost straight after the initial arrest, he struggled to even be sober for the trial. Then he continued drinking after work, the same as the others initially, they all liked to unwind after the day, have a few pints and to chat about the job before going home. After a few years though, when the others began to marry, raise children, Jim stayed on his own. He had a few one night stands, but nothing serious, nothing that was likely to give her grandchildren. It was like he'd lost the ability to trust, he was suspicious of women, wondered why they wanted to be with him.

A few years ago it got worse. He began to slack off with his work, finishing earlier and earlier each day and drinking on after the pubs had emptied, way into the night. He lost his car license first, which meant he couldn't drive to jobs. For a while his mates had collected him, tried to keep him working. But he was turning up late or drunk, making mistakes that cost them all money, slowing the job right down. So they'd stopped using him, they'd had to. They couldn't afford to carry him, even though he was a mate, they had their own work to take care of.

Rosemary turned a page on her magazine, her mouth pursed. She did understand about his mates, of course she did. When it comes down to it, you only have family really, no one else really cares. Not enough to get you out of the gutter anyhow.

So now, here she was, watching him die. He wouldn't stop drinking, even when they'd told him he had cirrhosis, that he wouldn't last another five years unless he gave it up completely. If she was honest, she didn't think he wanted to last another five years, he just wanted it to be over.

It wasn't just the girl, though she could tell that he loved her, had wanted to marry her. Rosemary didn't know why, perhaps she was fun. She was certainly pretty, you could see that even from the newspaper, much better looking than his usual girlfriends. But no, it wasn't just that she'd betrayed him, led him up the path. He could've coped with that, a bit of a binge perhaps, a lot of swearing, but eventually he'd have recovered, picked himself up.

No, thought Rosemary, it was more than that. It was partly what she'd done, all those families wrecked and Jim hadn't stopped it. He had even helped her. There was some guilt in that, he tortured himself with it, she could see it in his eyes. Mothers never lose the ability to read their children. Not that he knew what Joanna was doing of course, Rosemary was quite sure of that. But other people weren't so sure, they all wondered, thought he must've known something. A few people even wondered if he was in on it, but had been too clever to get caught. He carried the guilt and suspicion around with him like a collar, for nearly two decades.

His photograph had been in all the newspapers at the time, and there had been films of him, hurrying to and from the court, with some poncey reporter telling everyone who he was, how closely linked to 'the accused' he was. You never forgot that, and you assumed no one else did either. He thought people would recognise him, even years later, wherever he went. Whatever he did, he felt people were watching him, assessing, accusing. Or laughing at him, which was worse. He'd felt such an idiot and it was so public. Imagine how that feels, thought Rosemary, the whole world, everyone who you know, laughing at how stupid you've been. No wonder he turned to drink, needed his senses numbed. It was the only way he knew to stop his mind going over and over everything. By the time his brain had settled down, his body was too used to the alcohol, refused to let him cut down, kept him addicted. She tried to send him to the doctor, or one of those self-help groups. But he told her he was alright, to leave him alone. She wondered if he felt the need to punish himself, if he saw this as a kind of penance.

Rosemary looked down at the magazine on her lap, realised she was turning pages but not looking at them. She went back to the beginning and tried to concentrate on the words, tried to be interested in making a window seat with matching curtain ties.

Jim made a noise and she glanced up, hoping he might be awake. He wasn't, nothing had changed and she wondered if she had imagined it. It shouldn't be long now, the doctor had told her that. They had taken her off into a little room on Monday, to speak to a doctor. At least, she assumed he was a doctor, Mr. Somebody-or-other, she didn't catch his name. She asked to speak to a doctor and he smiled and said he was the consultant hepatologist, which she supposed meant that he was a doctor of some kind. He was very young, but patient, and his eyes were kind even though they were very tired.

He had sat there, Mr Whoever, in a little room, behind a desk, with a laptop open in front of him and files of paper stacked beside it. He told her about Jim's disease. He didn't call him a drunk, although that was what he was, that's what Rosemary's father would've called him – always Brahms and Liszt. No, he explained very slowly, as if to a child, that the alcohol in Jim's system had caused fat deposits in his liver.

When Jim didn't stop drinking, this led to alcoholic hepatitis, which was why he looked yellow. This had then become cirrhosis, which was a last warning really, the red light that should have stopped Jim from drinking. But it hadn't, which was why Rosemary wondered if he'd done it on purpose. He'd known, you see, known that if he didn't stop drinking they wouldn't offer him a liver transplant, even if all the other odds were in his favour. They were all steps along the way. Now, the doctor had told her, Jim was at the final step. The cirrhosis had caused encephalopathy, which she knew meant something in the brain had gone wrong.

Bodies were like that, she thought, staring at her son, they were all connected. She had thought the same thing when her mother died. You start with something in one place, like Jim with his liver, but it wasn't that that killed you, it was something else, something linked that you didn't realise was linked. So it wouldn't be his liver that finished him off, it would be his brain.

Rosemary put down her magazine and stood by the bed. She reached out a hand and stroked his forehead, wishing she could stroke away everything that was wrong. But she couldn't. It hadn't really started with the liver even, thought Rosemary, it had started with that girl, all those years ago. All connected.

She felt very alone, as she stood there, waiting for her son to die. She had phoned Steven and he was on his way, would be there as soon as he could. But if she was honest, she wasn't sure if she wanted him. Jim was her son, she had borne him, raised him, guided him, released him into the world. Now she was waiting for him to leave her again. There was nothing that Steven could say to make it better, she was losing her son. She wished she believed in a God she could shout at or had a lucky charm that she could rub, but she didn't. It was just her, in this strange alcove, surrounded by orange curtains, with a blue chair. She sat again on the chair and closed her eyes, waiting for Joanna's last victim to die.

***

Emily opened her eyes to another blue chair, in another hospital. Her curtains were blue but she didn't notice, her whole attention was taken by Josh, who was sitting in the chair and the bundle he was holding, which was their child. Their daughter. She had been born an hour earlier, an emergency operation because her heart rate was falling. It was too early, three whole weeks too early, but the baby was safe, the doctors assured her of that.

Emily had been taken to the hospital yesterday, after her weekly check-up had worried the midwife. They had attached her to monitors and Josh had rushed there as soon as he'd heard. After a night of worry, a night when Emily realised how much she wanted this baby to survive, how she would give up everything just to save her, the doctor decided they would operate. Emily was whisked away for a caesarean section and Josh paced the corridors.

When she woke up, Emily had been told by the midwife that she had a daughter but she hadn't seen her until they wheeled her bed back to the ward. There was Josh, in the blue chair, holding a tiny someone wrapped in a white hospital blanket. He smiled when he saw she was awake and came to kiss her. She reached for her baby and he placed her in Emily's arms. The baby was awake, her mouth opening and closing, searching for food. The midwife came, showed Emily how to attach the baby, and she felt the prickle as the baby suckled. She looked down, ignoring the discomfort, searching her child's face. The baby opened her eyes and stared at Emily. A long, intense, unblinking stare. Her eyes were very blue.

Also by Anne E. Thompson

Hidden Faces
Counting Stars
Invisible Jayne
Clara Oakes

See anneethompson.com for details

Joanna never again mentioned her sister, it was as if she had never
existed. You can read her story in Anne E. Thompson's compelling
new thriller....

CLARA OAKES

Read on for an extract....

Clara Oakes

My new Gucci sneakers were definitely out of place. They looked very white as I walked towards the flats, the embroidered bee emblem shining royally as it caught the sun. They were excellent shoes. They looked great, were a joy to wear and shouted to the world that I had money and knew how to dress. Of course, not everyone would be listening. Not everyone would recognise quality for what it was. Like Sam. I doubted he would know a Gucci shoe if it rose up and hit him on the nose.

It was two weeks ago that I had decided to visit Sam Whittaker. I knew he was known as a wise old man, but it wasn't his wisdom I was after. No, what I needed was a bit of renewed credibility, someone who could inspire a little trust in me. I knew I had 'burnt my bridges' as Martha would have said, what I was hoping was that Sam might build me a few new ones.

I didn't bother to phone before I went. He was old, I figured his life would be mainly empty, centred around church activities and outings to the shops. It was Wednesday afternoon, the shops in the village would be closed and the oldies group met Tuesday mornings. I parked in the little layby next to the flats and walked up the stairs to the second floor, I didn't fancy the foul smelling lift. Mind you, most old people's flats smell like toilets, so I wasn't going to be taking deep breaths while I was there.

The steps were concrete, probably as smelly as the lift, the harsh tang of disinfectant mingling with something worse, assaulting the nose. Not that it bothered me, smells rarely did. But I noticed. Made me wish I wasn't there. Added to my unhappiness, my discomfort

1

at the necessity of the whole thing. I wasn't used to needing people, asking for help.

My hand hurt too. I had hidden it inside my pocket, a sort of attempt to keep it clean, stop it getting infected. It was too painful to bandage, even the thought of something touching it made me feel slightly queasy. I could feel it rubbing against the lining of my pocket, raw, the nerves exposed and screaming. My feet stomped up the steps, loud, angry, resentful. I wanted choices and I knew I didn't have any. Not any more. No choices, just one slim chance and it depended on the decision of an old man who should have died decades ago.

I knocked on the front door - three loud knocks so he would hear me - there didn't seem to be a bell. I heard the bang of a door inside, heavy steps as he walked down the hall, the scrape of the chain being put in the slot. The door opened all of three inches. I smiled down at Sam, my best, 'please trust me, looking slightly contrite' smile. He frowned up at me, surprised but not necessarily antagonistic. Perhaps I did have a chance.

"Hello Mr Whittaker," I said, loud enough that he would hear me, old people are usually deaf, "It's Clara Oakes, I hope you don't mind me popping in. I was hoping you could give me some advice."

"Oh yes?" he said. He didn't move, didn't open the door and invite me in. That was a bit unexpected. Perhaps he had more sense than I'd assumed. Never mind, I could do this, I could persuade him that I was harmless and humble and needed his help. The help bit was true anyway.

"You see, I've made some," I paused.

I didn't know how much he knew and I didn't want to make things worse by admitting to things that weren't public knowledge. On the other hand, if I didn't appear sorry for things that he knew about, it would go against me. I needed this old man to trust me, to speak for me. "I've made some big mistakes. I've hurt a few

2

people. But I'm sorry, I realise I was wrong and I want to change. Can you help me? Will you give me some advice? Tell me what I should do?"

I did not, of course, expect that I would be listening to his advice. It was the me talking bit that was important. But I thought if I appealed to his 'wise old man' image, he was more likely to let me in, to listen to my side of things. Everyone likes to be flattered, as long as you don't overdo it.

He stared at me for a full minute, those watery blue eyes with milky whites and damp lashes looked right through me. I waited. I was at the point of leaving, turning away, when he made his decision and nodded. He shut the door so he could unhook the chain, opened it wide enough for me to enter.

"Alright, come on in. I'll hear what you have to say. Don't take me for a fool though, I'm old but I'm not stupid. I know people like you. Go on," he gestured with his head, that I should go first, "second door on the left. You can sit in there."

He followed me down the narrow hall, past his greasy kitchen, old fat smells mingling with damp carpet and dust. I led the way, interested that he had positioned himself so he could watch me. Perhaps he was right, perhaps he wasn't a fool. That was okay though. Most of my story was true, and I really did need his help.

The carpet was thin, stained in places. I turned in through the doorway he'd indicated. It was a sitting room, small, too much furniture and too much heat. I did a quick scan of the room, from habit as much as anything. A quick evaluation of anything with value. There were some old frames on a sideboard that might be worth something, the photographs inside faded now, one a sepia print of a young woman, one a wedding photograph. The rest was rubbish, would go straight into a tip when the old man finally died. Unless there was something worth having in the sideboard itself of course, but I doubted it. Perhaps a medal from a long forgotten war. Maybe some kind of heirloom. Sam Whittaker had never been rich, anyone could see that. I've no idea why he was held in such high esteem really. But sometimes people are weird, a bit twisted in their priorities.

I took a seat on a hard chair next to the electric fire. I considered asking if I could turn it down a bit, maybe open a window, let in some air. Decided to keep things simple. I would tell my story, hope for the best.

I wondered if he would offer me some tea. Not that I fancied any, not from that kitchen. Probably catch something, nothing in that flat looked like it was cleaned very regularly. But he didn't. He just lowered his stiff bones into the chair opposite, leant his stick against the chair arm and looked at me. He didn't speak, didn't make it easy. He just waited. Watching me all the time with those faded eyes. I had no idea what he was thinking. I struggled out of my jacket and shoved it behind me, buying myself a bit of time, trying to get my thoughts properly sorted. Then I began to speak.

I must've talked for over an hour. Sam got up at one point, raised his hand so I paused, then heaved himself to his feet, told me to wait, left the room. I sat there, listening to his heavy footsteps as he went down the hall, into his bathroom. I waited, stared at the sideboard, the yellow patterned curtains at the window, the faux fur rug lying in front of the electric fire. I heard the flush, his heavy steps as he came back, lowered himself into his seat, nodded for me to continue. It was a bit rude really, treating me like he was deigning to listen to my story, like he was better than me. But I swallowed it down, took it all in my stride. It's always important to keep the final aim in mind, and I knew I had to take whatever he threw at me, had to appear humble and patient. Otherwise he wouldn't believe me.

By the time I had finished talking, my throat felt sore and I might even have accepted a drink, had he offered one. But he didn't. He let me finish and then he sat there, for what felt like ages. Thinking I suppose, deciding what he was going to say. I wasn't sure what I'd do if he decided not to help me, not to persuade the others that I had changed, was someone they should continue to accept. There wasn't anything else I could say, I had told him everything. Well, not about my hand, that was just embarrassing, not something you want other people to know about. But I had told him everything else, the whole unbelievable story, which I hoped, because it was true, he would actually believe.

So I sat there, waiting. I could hear the clock ticking away the seconds, some kids swearing outside, a door bang in another flat, Sam's breathing, slow and wheezy. Then he cleared his throat, a great rattle of rearranged globs of phlegm, helped along by a thump on his chest with his gnarled fist. He nodded. I took that as a good sign, meant he was accepting what I'd told him.

"Alright, I believe you. Reckon some people need a sledge hammer and that's what you seem to have got. No real options left for you young lady. You're right, you do have to change.

"I don't know why he would bother with you actually. Perhaps you can do something the rest of us can't, I don't know. Not really my place to say why. But I can tell you one thing, your place isn't here anymore."

I started to protest at that. The whole point of coming was so that he would speak on my behalf, make it possible for me to stay. I had not sat in his pokey stinky flat for the fun of it, nor for any sort of need for penance. I wanted him to help me. I began to wonder if I had wasted my time. He raised a hand, indicating I should settle down, let him finish.

"No, just listen. You came for advice, now listen to it." (Actually, I hadn't, I'd come so he would help me, but he didn't know that. I listened. Wish I hadn't now.) "You have something to do. I don't know what it is, maybe you do, maybe you'll find out later. But it

5

isn't here. You need to move away, leave the folk here in peace."

He looked up at me, those ancient eyes staring into mine. Not unkindly, perhaps even with sympathy.

"Do you know where you should go?"

I hadn't known, not until he said that. But as soon as he did, as soon as he asked the question, it was obvious. Everything fell into place and I found I actually wanted to go. It was even quite exciting, and I like exciting, bit of a risk.

I was going to India.

Matt R. Allen • William B. Gartner
Editors

Family Entrepreneurship

Insights from Leading Experts on Successful Multi-Generational Entrepreneurial Families

palgrave
macmillan

Editors
Matt R. Allen
Babson College
Babson Park, MA, USA

William B. Gartner
Babson College
Babson Park, MA, USA

ISBN 978-3-030-66845-7   ISBN 978-3-030-66846-4   (eBook)
https://doi.org/10.1007/978-3-030-66846-4

This Palgrave Macmillan imprint is published by the registered company Springer Nature Switzerland AG.
The registered company address is: Gewerbestrasse 11, 6330 Cham, Switzerland

For my wife Heather and my three beautiful children. I believe there is at least a little entrepreneurship in every family. It explains, in part, how a family is always much more than the sum of its members. Mine is most certainly the best excuse that I can offer for anything useful I have ever done.

Matt R. Allen

For all of the prior generations who sought a better future, my family of diverse talents and dreams, and to my wife, Saunie, for her wisdom and courage in our adventure together.

William B. Gartner